ALTERNATE ACADEMY

Book 1

Melissa Woods

ALTERNATE ACADEMY BOOK I
Copyright ©2023 Melissa Woods
All rights reserved.

ISBN: **978-1-63422-538-0** (ebook)
978-1-63422-544-1 (Print)
Cover Design by: Gem Promotions
Developmental Edits by: Susan Harris
Proof by: Ashley Brilinski
Typography by: Gem Promotions

For Dad. As always, the first book in the series is dedicated to you. If not for your humour, love, and encouragement, I would never have got this far. Thank you.

CHAPTER ONE

Oops

Drip, drip, drip.

Nova stood in silence, blood dripping from her finger-tips onto the tiled floor of the previously pristine kitchen, wondering how exactly she was going to explain this to Barbara. Barbara was her stepdad's wife, and had never really liked Nova. Now that Nova had made the woman's husband explode right in the middle of the kitchen, she doubted that this opinion was going to improve.

Drip, drip, drip.

The splatters on the floor looked like splotches of paint, or tiny flowers. Almost pretty. Small pools were gathering at Nova's feet. What would happen when it dried? Would she be stuck to the floor like a statue? Rust-coloured, and smelling like an old wound?

Nova could feel blood on her eyelashes too. She had closed her eyes when he exploded, like she knew it was about to happen, which was impossible really. How could anyone predict something like that?

Drip, drip, drip.

The blood was cool now. How much time had passed? How long had she been standing there? Nova glanced up at the wall, at the space where the clock had always been. It was gone. Nova blinked, glancing around slowly, as if every movement of her head required a huge amount of effort. She spotted the clock, over by the kitchen door. The glass front had smashed. Hit by a flying limb, perhaps? There were bits of Gary everywhere. I guess it made sense that at least some of the kitchen would've taken a hit from the resulting carnage. Now that she was paying attention, she noticed that all of the mugs on the counter had smashed. Likewise, the framed photo of Gary and Barbara from their holiday in Mexico. The microwave door was hanging off its hinges, and there was an enormous dent in the fridge.

Nova observed all these things with a strange calmness. She was covered in blood, standing in the middle of a scene of total destruction, yet somehow, felt like she wasn't there at all. It was as if this was all a movie, and she was waiting for the credits to roll.

A tinkle of music broke the silence that had settled over the house. Nova recognised the sound. The ice cream van was making its way up her street. That meant it was almost four.

Barbara will be home soon.

The realisation brought Nova back to reality with a sickening thud. She shook her head to try and organise her mess of thoughts, ignoring the raindrops of blood she sent flying. What was she going to tell Barbara? The truth sounded ridiculous; that she and Gary had been in the middle of an argument, and she'd gotten so mad that it felt like her whole body was on fire. That years of rage had bubbled and churned from somewhere deep within her, until suddenly they burst out from every pore of her skin. That she had closed her eyes and screamed, and when she opened them, Gary was gone.

Except he wasn't gone. He was still there, littered around the room in a thousand tiny pieces.

Even though Barbara had always thought Nova was odd, it was doubtful she'd believe she had blown Gary up with her mind. More likely, she'd think Nova had gone crazy with a knife. Or had YouTubed "how to make an explosive device" and decided to experiment on her stepfather. Now that Gary was gone, and with only the marriage tying Nova to her, Barbara wouldn't think twice about have her insane stepdaughter dragged away to spend the rest of her life locked in a cell.

I could lie.

That was another option. Nova could pretend she hadn't been at home. Barbara would assume someone else had come in and killed Gary. Or that it had been some kind of terrible accident, like a gas leak maybe?

Sure. The kind of gas leak that causes a person to explode from the inside out and is confined to a single room in the house.

Nova leaned to the right to look out of the kitchen door and down the hallway. Sure enough, not a single object was out of place. The pictures on the walls remained unshattered, the drinking glass on the table by the door, upright and unbroken. The only clue as to the carnage inside the kitchen, was the lone toe that had somehow made its way to the welcome mat. That would be the first thing Barbara would find when she walked through the door.

Welcome home! Here's your husband's toe.

For some reason, Nova let out a burst of laughter at the thought. It sounded harsh and out of place in the silent house. She took a breath. There was only one option left: run.

It wasn't like she hadn't thought about it before; life with Gary and Barbara had always felt comparable to having her teeth extracted one by one. She'd never had the nerve to follow through, though. First, she had nowhere to go. They'd only just moved to this area of London; she had no friends at her new school, and no one she felt like she could trust. Her only real family, her mother, had been dead for 11 years. She had no idea where, or even *who* her real dad was.

Second, Nova didn't have any money. Gary had used up everything her mother had left her, which meant even if she got far enough away to avoid being caught, she had no way to live on her own. Where would she sleep? How would she eat? She shuddered at the thought of what other girls did just to survive on the streets. She couldn't do that.

Nova shook her head. She'd find a way to make it work. Somehow. Right now, running was the only choice. Barbara would be home soon, and if Nova had to choose between being locked away, or sleeping in a doorway, she would choose the doorway.

She raced upstairs to her tiny bedroom, and began tossing things into a backpack. She didn't have much: a couple of pairs of jeans, a few t-shirts, some books. She didn't have a phone or a laptop. No jewellery or make-up, or things that most other 16-year-olds would grab before leaving home forever. She bit back the anger she felt about that; about how she had less possessions to her name than Barbara's beloved cat, Lucifer. Now wasn't the time to be bitter, and if she was honest, blowing up the woman's husband was probably punishment enough.

Nova peeled off her stained clothes, stuffing them into a bin bag, and quickly changed into clean ones. She pulled her hood up over her hair, forcing her dark curls inside. They were being even more unruly than usual, as if Gary's blood had somehow imbued them with the power to resist. She wished she had time to wash her hair. What if someone saw the blood and asked questions? But there was no time.

There was a rustling from behind her, and Nova spun around to see Lucifer sniffing around the bin bag.

"Get out of there." She waved her hand, directing him out of the room. The last thing she needed was the damn cat dragging a bloodied sock through the house and giving her away before she'd even had the chance to get out of London.

Nova moved to her bedside table and picked up the framed photo of her and her mum. It was the only picture she had. There must have been more once, there had to be. But after her mum had died Gary had moved her and Barbara from house to house over the years, and once she got old enough to ask where the rest of the pictures were, they had already been lost for a long time.

Carefully, she slid the photograph from the frame and tucked it into the front pocket of her backpack.

Taking one last look around the small, sad space that had briefly been her bedroom, Nova slung her backpack over her shoulder, picked up the bin bag, and headed out. As she hurried down the stairs, she tried to figure out where she could dump the bloodstained clothes. Ideally, it would be somewhere they wouldn't be discovered for a while. If the police found them, they would start looking for her, and she needed to give herself as much of a head start as possible. Maybe she could chuck the bag into the Thames on her way to the station? Though if anyone saw her, they would surely ask questions.

Something caught her eye as she reached the front door. The welcome mat, the one that said 'Live, Laugh, Love' – Barbara must've had that slogan scattered around the house in at least 20 places – was now missing a toe. Nova glanced around, eyes scanning the carpet. Gary's toe had disappeared. Had Lucifer taken it? Was eating a toe bad for a cat? Should she leave a note about that?

"Going somewhere?"

Nova spun around. There was a woman standing in the kitchen, at the end of the hallway, right in the place where what was left of Gary had been.

Except all the bits of her stepfather were no longer there.

Through the open doorway, Nova could see the room looked exactly as it had before the explosion. Spotless white walls, black and white tiled floor, shining marble counter-tops, and a distinct lack of the bits of human flesh which had littered the room only a few minutes ago.

She took a few steps closer, craning her neck to see more of the space. How was this possible? What happened to all the blood? All the mess? All the...Gary?

The woman – in her late 30's or early 40's – had shoulder-length, poker-straight copper hair. She was smiling. Her teeth were so white they almost didn't look real. They perfectly matched her pressed white skirt and blazer. With her neat clothes, and without a single hair out of place, the stranger looked as though she'd never so much as seen a crease in her life.

Her voice was soft and friendly. "Hello Nova. My name is Elizabeth Perrin."

Nova swallowed. "H-how do you know my name?"

"I knew your mother."

Mother. That word was banned in this house. No one spoke about Nova's mum. Not Gary, and especially not Barbara. The photos were gone, clothes and keepsakes had long been sold. Other than the picture safely tucked into Nova's backpack, there was no evidence her mum had ever existed. She had effectively been erased from their life.

Nova felt her heart race even faster. "You knew my...How?"

Elizabeth smiled again. "I'd be happy to talk about it, but we should probably leave now. Barbara will be home soon, and I'm sure she will have questions about where your stepfather has gone."

Nova took another step closer, arriving at the door to the kitchen, and looked inside.

"Where *has* he gone?" she asked. Everything was pristine, just as it had been when she arrived home from school. Or, at least, *nearly*. There was no blood, no remains, and the floor was shiny and clean. The things that had been broken, however – the mugs, clock, and smashed picture – were also gone. The fridge still had a dent, and though the microwave door had been pushed closed, it didn't look quite right.

"He's gone away," Elizabeth said. "Don't worry, no one will find him. Shall we go?"

She took a step closer, and Nova stumbled back. "I don't know you."

Elizabeth stopped and nodded. "You're right. I'm a stranger, and you have no reason to trust me. If you want to stay here with your stepmother, I understand." She gave a final smile, walking past Nova to the front door. She opened it, then paused. When she spoke, she didn't turn around. "If you come with me, I promise I'll tell you everything you want to know about your mother, and everything you *need* to know about what you are. What you *really* are."

Nova shifted from one foot to the other, and found herself asking: "Where would we go?"

"Somewhere safe. Far away from here." Elizabeth stepped outside into the sunshine.

CHAPTER TWO

The Journey

Nova went with Elizabeth. It wasn't like she had many other options, and how could she possibly resist the offer of finding out what she was? If this woman said she had answers, Nova needed to hear them.

She also had a not-so-small feeling that Elizabeth, whoever she was, was like her. Not necessarily that she was in the habit of making people explode, only that she was *different* in some way. There was no other explanation for her being able to get rid of everything in that kitchen so quickly.

A black car was parked outside the house. Elizabeth got into the passenger seat, and Nova climbed into the back, tossing her backpack in first.

"Ready to go, Miss Perrin?" asked the man in the driver's seat.

"Yes, thank you," Elizabeth replied.

The engine came to life, and the car pulled away. Nova watched through the rear window as Barbara's blue Ford arrived. Her stepmother parked on the driveway and got out, carrying a large bag of cat litter, and wearing the scowl Nova suspected she reserved for times when she was expecting to come into contact with her stepdaughter.

The black car turned off the street, and Barbara was gone.

That's the last time I'll ever see her.

Nova knew she should feel guilty. Barbara would never know what happened to her husband, or why his step-daughter had suddenly disappeared. Most likely, she would blame Nova for the pair of them being gone. She blamed her for most things.

Though, on this occasion, she would be right.

And although she had technically ruined Barbara's life, Nova didn't really feel that sorry for her. Barbara had done everything in her power to make her stepdaughter's life hell from the moment she had moved in two years ago. Whether it was forcing her to cook meals that she wasn't allowed to eat, hiding her belongings because she thought it was *"weird that a girl spent so much time reading books and not out with boys"*, or locking her out of the house overnight 'by accident'. Barbara had made it clear that she'd much rather have a life without Nova in it.

And as for Gary? How did Nova feel about what had happened to the man who had raised her for the past 11 years? She wasn't sure yet. It frightened her that amongst the chaotic mess of emotions swirling within her, the biggest felt almost like relief. Relief that he was finally gone.

It didn't take long to arrive at the London Bridge station. Elizabeth walked briskly, in heels so thin Nova couldn't even imagine attempting to stand up in them, let alone power walk. In fact, Nova found herself struggling to keep up, even though she herself was wearing her comfy old trainers. At one point it seemed like Elizabeth was going to take her hand to hurry her along, then thought better of it.

They rushed through the station, and boarded the train only seconds before it pulled away. They found an empty carriage, and took two seats facing each other, with a table between them.

Elizabeth made a quick phone call, while Nova looked out of the window. As the city disappeared behind her, she tried to picture where she might be going. Elizabeth had said it was safe, but a cell was technically 'safe'. Nova had come along without any real idea of what she was walking into. Elizabeth clearly knew stuff about her, about what she could do. What did that mean for Nova's future, though? Would she be locked away? Experimented on? Would she ever come back to her old home?

She hoped the answer to all those questions was: no.

It began to rain, lightly at first, but soon heavy droplets hammered against the glass. Nova traced the path of one with her finger. She remembered a game she used to play with her mother in the car when it was raining; choosing a droplet and seeing which one would reach the end of the window first. They'd name their raindrop, and cheer it on as it raced the others. The memory made her happy and sad all at once.

She realised that Elizabeth had finished her phone call, and was watching her silently.

"What?" Nova asked, sitting up straight in her seat.

Elizabeth smiled. "I half expected you to be peppering me with hundreds of questions. You're very quiet."

"I guess killing someone kind of takes it out of you,"

Nova joked, and then immediately regretted it. She hadn't said the k-word aloud until now. Though she had meant to sound indifferent, it caught in her throat.

Elizabeth's smile became sympathetic. "It was an accident."

"Tell that to him. I think I saw a bit of his ear near the toaster."

Elizabeth reached across the table, giving Nova's hand a gentle squeeze. "You didn't mean to do it. I know that."

"Maybe. But I'm not sorry I did." The words were out of Nova's mouth before she could stop them. What kind of monster was she if she didn't regret killing a person? "I didn't mean that," she said, quickly.

Elizabeth's expression didn't change. "It's okay if you meant it. Let's keep that part between us for now, though."

Nova drew her eyes back to the window as she retracted her hand from Elizabeth's grasp. "Where are we going?"

"Somewhere you will be safe. There are others there, people like you. They know how it feels to be different."

"*Different*," Nova repeated. That word didn't feel strong enough for a person who could blow a grown man into a thousand gory pieces.

"*Special*," Elizabeth added.

Nova tucked a stray curl back under her hood. "What *am* I?"

Elizabeth scanned the empty carriage, checking the coast was clear. "You're what we call an Alternate; a human born with exceptional abilities. You're not the only one. In fact, there are many, many more just like you."

"Are they all at this place we're going to?" Nova asked.

"No. Most are living normal lives, as you were. Some

are unaware of their abilities, some choose to hide them, and then there are others who use them carefully. Alternates work hard to keep what they are secret."

Nova thought about this. "Why?"

"Because not all humans are accepting of those who are different. Especially if they can label them *dangerous*."

"Can all Alternates do what I can do?"

Elizabeth shook her head. "There are many different abilities that they might be gifted with."

Nova put her palms flat on the table in front of her. They were still spattered with blood. "This doesn't feel like a gift."

Elizabeth waved her own hand over Nova's, and the blood vanished.

"They usually don't at first. You get used to it."

Nova met her eye. "You're an Alternate too."

"Yes."

"That's how you...why the kitchen was..." Nova searched for the right words. "You make things go away?"

Elizabeth smiled. "To put it simply, yes."

"How?"

"Can you explain how you do what you can do?" Elizabeth asked. "If I want something gone, I can make it go."

"What if you want it back?"

Elizabeth paused. "That part I'm still working on."

"Can you make *anything* disappear?" Nova asked.

"The bigger the object, the more energy it requires."

"What's the biggest thing you've ever got rid of?"

Elizabeth thought for a moment. "A two-story house."

"Why?"

Elizabeth lowered her voice playfully. "It was in my way."

"Have you ever made people disappear?"

A shadow crossed Elizabeth's face. "Yes."

"Why?"

"Because my life was in danger. It's not an action I would ever want to repeat." She leaned closer to the table. "I know how it feels to be scared, Nova. And I know how it feels to do things you never thought you would ever have to do. You don't need to be ashamed of what you are, or even fear it. We can help you."

Nova bit her lip. "This place we're going, what's it like?"

"It's a school. The teachers are there to look after you. Some will help you learn to manage your ability, while others will simply continue your regular education. It's a place for you to be yourself, without fear."

Nova's stomach felt like it was filled with stones. "What if I hurt someone else?"

"Many of the children at our school have gifts that could be dangerous," Elizabeth began. "Our job is to teach them how to control their abilities, and how to use them safely. Everyone has the potential to hurt others. It's the choices we make that matter. We *will* help you, Nova, I promise."

It was all so much to take in. A school for freaks like her? A place where everyone had the kind of weird magical powers she'd only ever read about in books or seen on TV? Was this really happening? Nova half-expected to wake up any minute in her tiny room. Barbara would be yelling at her for not vacuuming well enough, the damn cat would be peeing on her bed, and Gary would be in one single, non-bloodied piece.

But it wasn't a dream. The train was still moving, the rain was still hammering on the windows, and Elizabeth was still right there, waiting for the next question.

"How did you know where to find me?" Nova finally asked.

"Every time an Alternate uses their ability, it requires energy. When that energy is released, it creates ripples. The smaller the energy required, the smaller the ripple. What you did today, however, was-"

"Big," Nova interrupted.

Elizabeth nodded. "It released a lot more energy, enough to reach us. We had been looking for you for years, but never in the right places."

"We moved recently. Gary's job is...wait, you were looking for me?"

"Yes. It was your mother's wish to have you attend our school, as she had, and I'm so grateful we can finally do what she wanted."

"My mum was an Alternate too?" The words sounded ridiculous the second they left Nova's mouth.

"Yes."

"What could she do?" Nova could hear the desperation in her voice; the hunger to learn anything about her mother. She remembered so little about her.

Elizabeth looked as though she was about to answer, then cocked her head to one side. "Nova, you look exhausted. Why don't you sleep for a while? I'll wake you when we arrive at the station."

"I'm fine," Nova insisted, though her eyelids felt heavy,

and the gentle rocking of the train, paired with the hum of the wheels on the tracks, and the patter of rain, was almost too soothing to fight.

Elizabeth wasn't buying it. "What you did today will have taken its toll on you. You've been able to keep going on adrenaline, and now you need to rest. I promise, we have all the time in the world to talk. Sleep now."

Nova didn't argue, but though she fell asleep less than a minute after closing her eyes, her rest was unsettled. She dreamt of shadows and screams, and the overwhelming feeling of being trapped. There were whispers behind her back, cold fingers reaching for her neck, tightening their grip.

And there was a voice. Sorrowful. "*I'm sorry.*"

Nova startled awake.

Elizabeth looked over. "Are you alright?"

Nova felt beads of sweat on her forehead. What was that about? She tried to remember the dream, but as quickly as it had slipped into her mind, the pieces were drifting away like sand through her fingers.

"I'm fine," she croaked. "Just a bad dream."

They were interrupted by a squeak as the train came to a halt. The sky outside the windows was dark. Nova had to have been asleep for hours. Though Elizabeth was still regarding her with a concerned expression, there was no time to discuss it, they had arrived at their destination.

Wherever the hell that was.

CHAPTER THREE

Friends With Eight Legs

Elizabeth took the backpack, and Nova followed her off the train and through a tiny station. There was a ticket office – which appeared to be closed – and a couple of benches, and that was it. The night was cold, and Nova hugged her arms across her body to keep warm.

"Where are we?" she asked.

"A long way from London," Elizabeth answered.

Nova followed her through the lone ticket barrier, where another black car was waiting. The driver wore a uniform that kind of reminded her of a prison guard; black trousers and a white button-up shirt with a black tie. He was youngish, and briefly smiled at Nova as she got into the car.

"Good journey?" he asked Elizabeth, once they were inside.

"Yes, thank you. Let's go."

They drove for hours, through several small towns, then through even smaller villages, and then along winding tree-lined roads. The streetlights disappeared, and the world outside the car windows turned inky black. They were in the middle of nowhere. There were no buildings, just the road and the trees. The moon was barely more than a sliver, and, not for the first time since leaving the house, Nova began to wonder what she'd gotten herself into. She had no idea where she was, no guarantee of who Elizabeth was, and no real clue what to expect.

Eventually, the car began to slow, as the headlights illuminated a large pair of iron gates up ahead. There were tall stone walls on either side, with a small security booth built into the one on the left. There was a faded sign set into the wall to the right.

"*Tidemarsh Prison for the criminally insane*," Nova read aloud.

Elizabeth explained: "Our Headmistress, Ms. Juniper, bought the facility many years ago." She waved to a man who had come out of the booth. There was a gun in the holster at his waist. "We keep the sign up to discourage passers-by from getting too close. It's very effective." She turned her attention to the guard now, who was waiting with a clipboard. "Nova Harris," she said to him.

He nodded, and Nova drew her eyes away from the gun as he returned to the booth. The gates opened slowly with a rattle and a creak, and the car headed inside. The road surface changed, and the car bumped and jolted onwards, following a long, narrow driveway, lined with trees on both sides.

Elizabeth continued. "The grounds of Tidemarsh are roughly 200 acres, and surrounded by a 10-foot stone wall, topped with barbed wire. The forest adds another layer of protection from prying eyes. No one can see us, and no one is getting in."

"Or out," Nova muttered.

Elizabeth laughed. It was a light, tinkly sound. "I can assure you, none of the children here are being kept against their will."

She sounded sincere, yet Nova couldn't settle the growing unease in the pit of her stomach. A 10-foot wall topped with barbed wire? Armed guards at the gate? Surrounded by trees so no one could see what was going on inside? It all sounded a hell of a lot like the kind of place where someone could do all sorts of awful things to weird kids like her without consequences.

And what if there weren't any other kids? What if this whole thing was a lie, and she was being taken to a lab where she would get poked and prodded and tested on for the rest of her life? What if, when they reached the end of the driveway, the only thing waiting was a bed with restraints and doctors in white coats? What if this 'school' was actually just a cage? What if it was a hole in the ground filled with sharks?

Okay, it's probably not that.

Cursing her ridiculous imagination, Nova took a breath and tried to calm her nerves. When they reached the end of the driveway, the school...prison...whatever it was, came into view. There were three large red-bricked buildings set around a spacious, well-lit courtyard. In the middle of the courtyard was a fountain, surrounded by benches, well-kept trees, and several raised flower beds.

Not so terrible yet, I guess.

Nova and Elizabeth climbed out of the car, and the

driver pulled away, leaving them on their own. The air was cool, and blew strands of Nova's curls across her face. She pulled her hood down, it was hardly doing the job of keeping her hair contained anyway.

She and Elizabeth walked across the courtyard to the building on the left. Most of the windows were dark.

"Tidemarsh is made up of three main buildings," Elizabeth explained, and pointed to the one they had stopped outside. "This one was previously prisoner housing, and is now student living quarters, split into several dormitories." She noticed Nova's expression, and quickly added: "It was converted years ago. Don't worry, you're not sleeping in a cell." She winked, and then pointed to the building on their right, which was the one in the middle of the three, facing the driveway and the forest. It was also the largest.

"That used to be patient treatment, and is now the main school building, which contains the gymnasium, most of the classrooms, and teacher offices and accommodation."

The last building was directly across from the dormitories. "And that one over there has several more classrooms, as well as the swimming pool, and Greenhouse, which many of the students enjoy tending to." She smiled. "Welcome to Tidemarsh, Nova."

They stepped through the large wooden doors into the dorm building. The walls were painted a warm cream, and there were several comfy-looking sofas in a sitting area to the right. In the main entrance hall, there was a large checking-in desk with the words 'Booking Area' carved into the dark wood; an echo of what the place had once been. A man and a woman sat at the desk and gave a friendly wave.

"Mr. and Mrs Driver.," Elizabeth said to Nova, as they

passed by. "They stay up all night to ensure the children are safe and comfortable. If you ever need an adult after lights out, just come here."

They continued on towards a large staircase in the centre of the room.

"There are a little over 200 students at Tidemarsh," Elizabeth explained, as she and Nova headed upstairs. "They range in age from 18, down to 11 years old. That's usually when a child's abilities become strong enough for us to detect, though they begin manifesting much earlier. Parents usually try to keep what their children can do hidden, in an attempt to protect them. Alternates often have non-altered children, and equally, most of the children here come from parents who are 'normal'. As you can imagine, most of those people have absolutely no clue what to do when their child begins levitating or turning household objects into water." She smiled. "But – of course – we do get students who have a parent who is an Alternate themselves, which is a real treat."

They reached the second floor, and Elizabeth led Nova along the corridor to the left. They passed several closed doors, each with a different letter stamped onto the wood.

"Academic classes are age-appropriate," Elizabeth continued, "However, all classes pertaining to your unique abilities are sorted according to several factors."

"What factors?" Nova asked.

"Type of ability, whether it could be classified as dangerous – which affects how many students are in a class and how many teachers are required – and whether or not the student is confident using it."

"I never want to use mine again." Nova shuddered at the memory of being showered with Gary's blood.

They headed through a door at the end of the hall, which led to another staircase, though this one was smaller, and creaked loudly as they climbed it.

"Unfortunately, I doubt you will have much say in that," Elizabeth said, sympathetically. "Our abilities manifest according to our emotions. If you want to stop using yours, you must first learn to master it, and to recognise your triggers."

They reached the top of the building, and stopped outside the first door, marked with the letter M.

"This will be your dorm," Elizabeth said.

They went inside. There was enough moonlight coming through the window for Nova to see that the room was long and narrow, with a sloping roof on the left side. There were five beds on either side of the room, all of which were occupied, except for the one on Nova's right, closest to the door.

Elizabeth spoke quietly. "I'll leave the girls to help you settle in, once they've finished pretending to be asleep. We'll talk again tomorrow." She gave Nova's shoulder a gentle squeeze, then the door clicked, and she was gone.

Seconds later, the room was bathed in light, as every resident flicked on the lamp on her bedside table. The girls jumped out of their beds and rushed over. They were all wearing long, dark blue night-gowns in varying stages of shabbiness. Nova was blasted with a hundred questions at once.

"What's your name?"

"Where are you from?"

"What can you do?"

"Are you from the-"

"Don't be ridiculous, she's not from there. She's new."

"Are you the one who caused that fire downtown? It was all over the news. Jules said it had to be one of our kind."

"She doesn't look like she sets fires."

"My dessert says it's something with plants. She looks like a plant girl."

"You're on."

"Alright, everyone give her some room." A girl who hadn't spoken yet, pushed some of the others aside to get closer. She was around Nova's age, had dark brown, cat-like eyes, and long chestnut hair with thick bangs. Her lips were full, and she had the kind of cheekbones Nova had only seen in magazines. In fact, her beauty might've been the most striking thing about this girl, had it not been for the tarantula perched on her shoulder.

That's a spider.

On her shoulder.

There's a spider on her shoulder.

The girl addressed the crowd surrounding Nova. "You'll have time to interrogate her in the morning. For now, sod off."

There were a few disappointed looks, but the others trudged back to their beds. Nova's rescuer smiled, which softened her sharp-angled face considerably.

"What's your name?" she asked.

"Nova. Nova Harris"

The girl grinned. "Hello Nova Harris, I'm Kate Stone."

Nova's cheeks burned, but Kate quirked her head.

"Come on, I'll show you where you're sleeping." She headed away from the only empty bed, towards the very back of the room. Nova followed, though made sure she kept as much distance between herself and the spider as possible. Tarantulas didn't jump, did they?

As they passed the other girls, Nova noticed one who hadn't come over in the initial foray. She had thick, honey-coloured hair, and was laying with her head at the foot of the bed, with her long legs resting on the wall as she read a magazine. Or pretended to, at least. Nova got the distinct impression this girl was making a point of looking totally uninterested in the new arrival.

Nova and Kate reached the back of the room, and Kate turned to the bed on their right. It was occupied by a girl who couldn't have been older than 13. She was braiding her red hair, and eyed Kate quizzically when they arrived.

"What?" she asked.

"Get up," Kate said. "This is Nova's bed now."

The girl's eyes widened. "Oh, come on, Kate..."

Nova's stomach twisted. The last thing she wanted to do on her first night was make enemies. "It's fine, she doesn't have to-"

Kate ignored her protests. "Time to move, Laura."

"I'm not going."

Kate narrowed her gaze. "It's funny, it's almost as if you think I *won't* put spiders in your bed."

Laura stiffened, eyes flicking to the tarantula on Kate's shoulder. "You wouldn't."

"I guess we'll have to see."

After a tense few seconds, Laura got up. "Fine."

Nova kept her gaze on the floor during the agonizingly

awkward five minutes while the girl carried her belongings over to the other side of the room. When it was finally done, Kate immediately lost her sharp edges again, and smiled.

"Welcome home."

Nova sat down on the bed. "You didn't have to do that."

"You don't want to be down there by the door. You'll wake up every time one of the others gets up to go to the toilet. And trust me, that happens a lot." Kate nodded to Nova's backpack. "Let me help you unpack." She reached inside, pulling out a couple of books, and placing them on a small shelf next to the window. Nova took out her clothes and put them in the tiny wardrobe, and placed the photo of her mum in the drawer of the bedside table. Kate reached back into the bag, coming out empty. She furrowed her brow. "Is that it?"

"Yeah."

Kate sounded surprised. "Where's your *stuff*? Your make-up, phone, hair ties, your..." she searched for the word.

Nova didn't know what to say. "I don't have any of that."

Kate paused, then gave an awkward smile. "Well, I guess you're done unpacking then. It's not like it's worth having a phone anyway, there's no signal anywhere in this place."

Nova glanced over to the other side of the room, where the girl they had evicted was setting up her new belongings. "Will she hate me now?"

"*Laura*?" Kate gave a snort. "Trust me, of all the girls here, she's the last one you need to worry about." She sat down on the bed opposite Nova's. There was a jar full of spiders on the nightstand, and what looked like a millipede on her pillow. Kate took the tarantula off her shoulder, and stroked it as though this was a completely normal and non-horrifying thing to do.

She laughed at Nova's expression. "You don't like spiders?"

"I'm not *afraid* of them, not really...but I'm not sure I'd be holding one that close to my face."

"This is Colin," Kate said. "Don't worry about him, he's a pussy cat." She paused. "Well, not really. Actually, he's an incredibly dangerous spider, but you know what I mean."

"You're allowed to keep him here?" Nova asked.

"Absolutely. You can keep anything if they don't know about it." Kate winked, placing the tarantula in the drawer of her bedside table. "Trust me, Colin is *nowhere near* the most dangerous thing hidden in this dorm."

Nova's eyes widened. "I'm not sure that's reassuring."

Kate laughed. "It's easier if you don't think about it too much. Anyway, you should get some sleep. You look exhausted."

Nova was. Despite her nap on the train, and being wired from everything that had happened that day, at that point in time she felt about ready to drop.

"Here," Kate said, tossing over a night-gown. "You can borrow this for tonight. You'll get your own tomorrow."

"Thanks." Nova changed, and then slipped under the sheets. Though the bed looked old, and creaked like it was being tortured, it was surprisingly comfortable.

All around the room, the girls began turning off the last

few remaining lamps, and soon it was dark again. Voices became quieter, and drifted away as the others fell asleep. Nova rolled onto her side, eyes on the window. She could see the woods, though it was too dark to make out much in detail.

She had no idea where she was, or what the next day had in store. She was also mildly alarmed about the idea of there being more dangerous things in the room than the tarantula. But for now, at least, she was safe. The other girls seemed nice enough, and she was potentially going to find out more about what the hell she was tomorrow. That was good; it would be handy to know whether she was at risk of blowing any more people to pieces any time soon. Maybe everything was about to start getting better?

When Nova fell asleep, she dreamt of a long corridor. She walked and walked, but couldn't reach the door at the end. The air was cold, and she was surrounded by the sounds of dripping water, scraping metal, and crying.

I'm trapped.

She broke into a run, struggling to stay upright on the slick stone floor. The cries from the shadows got louder, and now someone was screaming.

Doors slammed shut on either side of her. She kept running, running as fast as she could, but she wasn't getting anywhere. The door was still so far away. She fell, and desperately tried to stumble back to her feet. When she brought her hands up to her face they were covered in blood.

Someone grabbed her shoulders, and she was dragged backwards into the darkness.

CHAPTER FOUR

Slugs And Snails And Painted Nails

Nova jolted awake. A bell was ringing, and for a second she had no idea where she was. The bed was different, and the wooden beams above her head didn't belong in her tiny room. She shook away the remains of her dream and focused on the space around her.

It all came rushing back. The school, the kids, Elizabeth, the blood, the explosion.

Gary.

"Morning." Kate stood beside her bed, holding a wash bag. She was without her eight-legged friend today. "How did you sleep?"

Other than the nightmare, and waking up to the memory that I accidentally killed my stepdad yesterday?

"Fine. Thanks."

Kate quirked her head towards the door. "Come on, I'll show you where the bathroom is." Her eyes flicked to Nova's hair. "I've got a spare towel if you want to shower."

Nova's chest tightened. She'd forgotten about the blood in her hair. Thanks to arriving after dark, the others didn't seem to have noticed it last night, but it wouldn't take them long to see it now. What would they think of her then? Would they ask even more questions than they'd bombarded her with upon her arrival? Or would they all suddenly back off, and want nothing more to do with her anymore? Maybe they'd start acting as though she was contagious, like the kids at her school used to.

Nova wasn't sure which was worse.

But Kate didn't recoil, nor did she ask any questions, she simply walked with Nova out of the room, down the stairs, and along the hallway to a huge bathroom.

There were at least 30 girls inside. Most must have come from other dorm rooms within the building. There was a long row of sinks in the centre of the room, and showers over by the back wall, separated by tiled walls between each one, and curtained at the front.

Nova wasn't sure how comfortable she was being naked and surrounded by so many other people. If these girls were anything like the ones at her last school, they'd find it hilarious to hide her clothes or rip the curtain open in front of everyone.

Unfortunately, the blood in her hair wasn't going anywhere on its own, so she mustered up her courage and headed to an empty stall, hanging her towel and nightgown on the hook just outside. She showered quickly, scrubbing the flakes from her hair and skin. It was rather disconcerting, watching the water run red, while surrounded by the sounds of laughter and cheerful chatter, as the girls around her began their day. None of them knew what she had done, that there was a killer only a few feet away from where they stood, washing away the evidence.

When the last flecks of blood had gurgled down the drain, Nova turned off the water. She was relieved to find her towel and nightgown exactly where she'd left them. Perhaps the girls here were nicer than the ones back home.

Not home, she corrected herself. *This is home now.*

She wrapped herself in the towel, before joining Kate at the sinks. She had showered too, and had her hair wrapped up at the top of her head.

"It's kind of crazy in here in the mornings," Kate said, lathering something sweet-smelling from her shower bag onto her face. "It's the only time we all use the bathroom at once. The rest of the day and the evenings are better."

"Is this the only bathroom?" Nova asked.

"Two for the girls, and two for the boys. There are more girls' dorms on this floor, and another at the top next to us. The boys are on this level, with a couple of rooms on the ground floor too. They pack us in pretty tight." She handed Nova a small bottle. "Use this on your face, it smells amazing."

"Thanks."

Despite Kate's abrupt relocation of Laura, and the rather alarming number of spiders she seemed to enjoy keeping around, Nova was starting to like her. She got the feeling Kate was the kind of person who said exactly what was on her mind and didn't really care about what others thought of her. Nova could only imagine what that felt like; not to be constantly worried about what everyone else was thinking.

"I forgot to pack my toothbrush," Nova groaned, as the realization hit.

"I can help with that," said a girl at the sink to her left.

She was short, pencil-thin, and had a shock of purple hair. She smiled, and her braces glinted in the bathroom light. Nova recognised her from their dorm. She had been one of the ones asking questions last night.

Kate sounded doubtful. "Are you sure, Beth? Last time-"

"Absolutely," the girl replied. "I know how to do it now." She took Nova's hands and positioned them, palms up, in front of her. Then she took a deep breath, and ran her own hands over the top. Nova felt something drop into her palm. It was a pink toothbrush!

"That's..." she searched for the words. "I can't believe you just did that."

"No problem," Beth said with a smile. She grabbed her stuff and headed back to the door. Her place was immediately taken by another girl.

Kate leaned a little closer to Nova. "Make sure you use that really fast."

"Why? Will it disappear?"

"Something like that."

After they'd finished in the bathroom, Kate and Nova headed back to the dorm. There was a pile of clothes folded on Nova's bed: two night-gowns, and three sets of school uniforms. The uniform consisted of a white blouse, a black cardigan, a black knee length skirt, long white socks, and black shoes. Nova got dressed. Everything seemed to fit well enough. She ran her thumb over the school crest, stitched on the front left side of the cardigan. It was made up of four segments, each containing a different symbol. Nova didn't understand what they were meant to be.

Kate came to stand beside her as Nova looked in the

mirror on the inside of her wardrobe door. She pointed to the crest. "It's the four types of ability."

Nova cocked her head. "What do you mean?"

Kate pointed to the first quadrant, a picture of an eye. "This represents Mental abilities." She pointed to the next symbol: it looked a bit like an hour glass with a diamond inside. "Then you have Transformative." The next symbol in the quadrant, directly under the eye, was a circle with a line which came off from the bottom, and then broke into other lines. "That one represents Physical abilities," Kate said. The last quadrant contained a picture of a sun rising or setting over the water. "And Elemental. It's probably easier to explain it all when we get to breakfast."

"Why?" Nova asked.

"You'll see."

Though the two girls wore the same uniform, Nova saw that Kate had made some alterations to hers. The skirt was significantly shorter, the blouse was tied at the back (hidden by her cardigan) to make it tighter, and her shoes were completely different, with a heel and pointed toe.

As Nova glanced around the room, she noticed that several girls had similar alterations. The tall blonde had a skirt so short it was practically a belt, and she eyed Nova up and down with a smirk. Nova's stomach sank.

It's my first day at a school for monsters, and I'm still the odd one out.

Breakfast was in the gymnasium, situated in the building across the courtyard. Students collected their food from a counter at the back, and then sat at any of the 30 rectangular tables spread around the room. It was pretty much like any school cafeteria, except for the random unexplainable events happening all over the place.

"Okay," Kate said, as the girls entered the room. "Let me give you a crash course in the four types of abilities that an Alternate could have."

At the nearest table, a piece of toast in a boy's hand spontaneously burst into flames and disintegrated into charcoal in seconds. He pushed his plate away angrily.

"Elemental abilities," Kate explained, "Are any kind of ability that allows the Alternate to control the elements. Wind, water, fire, earth, pretty self-explanatory. Those kids can shoot fire or form lightning bolts in their hands. Impressive when it works, kind of awful when it goes wrong."

She pointed to another table, where three girls sat next to a fully grown tiger as if it was the most natural thing in the world. A few feet above them, several birds were flying in circles. One of them landed and immediately turned into a girl with frizzy red hair. She grabbed a piece of bacon, stuck it in her mouth, and then transformed back into a bird and flew away, clutching the bacon in her beak.

There are kids who can turn into animals here.

"Transformative abilities are the next kind," Kate said. "They're pretty cool, though of course the ones who can do it always show off. Another easy one to explain; if you can turn into an animal, or change your appearance in any way, you're a transforming Alternate." She pointed to another table, where a group of boys were encouraging the salt and pepper pots – which had sprouted arms and legs – to fight each other. "That counts too," she added. "Being able to transform other objects is transformative. Though that gift is rarer."

As Nova followed Kate to join the line for food, she saw a boy the size of a teaspoon yelling at his friends, because they had trapped him under a drinking glass. They were laughing, and piling more and more things on top of the glass, while he pounded his fists against the sides. A few tables over from that, a girl was holding out her hand while her friends painted her nails, which were twice the length of her fingers, and pointed at the ends like claws. One of her friends shot out her tongue, which was at least two feet long, to eat off another girl's plate.

The girl with long nails gasped. "Nina, that's really rude."

A boy appeared as if from nowhere, planted a kiss on the cheek of the girl with long nails, and then shot away, running so fast Nova lost sight of him in less than a second.

"That's a physical ability," Kate explained, following Nova's gaze. "Kids who are fast or strong, or have mutations like horns or claws."

The girls moved forward in the line. "It's a lot to take in, right?" Kate asked.

"Yeah," was all Nova could say.

"You get used to it; I promise. Sometimes the types of ability cross over, it's not always black and white. Don't worry, no one is expecting you to remember any of this." Kate smiled reassuringly, and took another step forward as the line moved again. "Oh bugger!" She lifted her foot out of the puddle she'd walked into, shaking it vigorously and sending droplets of water flying in all directions. She tapped the shoulder of the boy in front of her.

"Harvey? Seriously?"

The boy, tall and blond, turned around. "What?"

"You soaked my shoe!"

He shrugged. "Maybe you should look where you're going." He stepped forward, leaving puddles of water wherever he went, even though his clothes seemed to be dry. When he reached for his tray, Nova saw droplets trickle from his fingertips and down onto his food.

"He needs to learn to control that," Kate muttered, sidestepping the next puddle, and reaching for her tray.

"Elemental, right?" Nova asked.

Kate smiled. "You got it."

Once they'd collected their food, the girls found an empty table. Breakfast looked pretty decent: toast, scrambled eggs, bacon. There was also some unidentified green stuff that Nova knew she wasn't going to attempt. Green stuff or not, back home all she had was the flavourless bran cereal Barbara bought. This was already a step up.

"Last night you told me Laura wasn't the one I needed to worry about," Nova began, as she and Kate took their seats. "Who *do* I need to be scared of?"

"I wouldn't say you need to be *scared* of anyone. Especially not now that you have me watching your back," Kate added with a smile. "It's just that some of these girls are demons from the underworld, and their powers don't exactly encourage them to rein it in."

Nova's eyes widened, and Kate laughed.

"I mean, they're not *literally* demons. Sorry, I forgot that anything probably seems possible to you right now. What I mean was that not everyone here is as wonderful and charming as I am."

"So, who should I watch out for?" Nova pressed.

Kate thought for a moment, then gestured to a girl a few tables over. It was the blonde with the skirt-belt from their dorm. She was surrounded by people, who all seemed to be hanging on her every word.

"That's Madeline," Kate said. "She likes to think she's the Queen bee around here. You don't need to be afraid of her, but it'd make your life a lot easier if you kept under her radar."

Nova watched as a girl appeared at Madeline's side, carrying a tray of breakfast. She put it down in front of her without a word, and scuttled away. "What can she do?" Nova asked.

"It's more what she can make *you* do. She has what Elizabeth calls 'Power of Persuasion'." Kate rolled her eyes as she said it. "It means she can tell you to do stuff, and it feels like a really good idea, so you do it. Stuff like that – mind control, telekinesis – is called a Mental ability." Kate frowned. "The number of times she's made girls stick their finger up their nose in the middle of class, or lick the floor of the bathroom is unreal."

Nova winced at the thought. "Has she ever done it to you?"

Kate let out a single laugh. "She wouldn't dare."

"Why?" Nova remembered what Kate had said to Laura the night before. "Because you'll put spiders in her bed? What type of ability do you have?"

Kate glanced around, and then put down her toast. "Come on, I'll show you."

CHAPTER FIVE

A Demonstration

Kate and Nova headed out of the main building and across the courtyard, towards the building that housed the pool. They had to stop on their way, though, because two kids were having a fight. Not that it was anything like the kind of fights Nova had seen at her last school. Those had usually involved fists or feet. In this altercation, one boy was throwing what appeared to be tiny tornadoes in the direction of another, who was holding up a heavy-looking bench as a shield, as though it didn't weigh anything at all. A crowd had gathered and were cheering the guys on. As Nova got closer, she saw that both boys were smiling.

"That all you got?" the one holding the bench called out over the roaring winds.

"Just getting warmed up," laughed the other, forming a larger tornado – the size of a small dog – between his hands, and launching it in the direction of his opponent.

The cheers and laughter from the crowd got louder.

"Send him spinning!" someone suggested.

"Throw the bench at him!"

"Knock him on his arse!"

Then the laughter stopped when someone yelled: "Farley's coming!"

Immediately everyone dispersed, as a woman in her 60s wearing a blue tracksuit and a furious expression sprinted across the grounds in the direction of the commotion.

"I see you, Seth!" she yelled, in a thick Scottish accent. "Put that bench down at once, Robert! I'm writing you up, right now!"

Kate pulled Nova by the arm over to the pool building. Once inside, they headed along the main hallway to a door at the end of the wall on the right. When Kate opened it, Nova felt her mouth drop open.

"*This* is the greenhouse?" she asked.

It was a million miles away from what Nova would ever have pictured when she thought of a 'greenhouse'. It was so large, and so dense with plant life, that it was impossible to see where the walls were. Nova had never visited a jungle, but she imagined it would be something like this. There were trees, shrubs, vines, and flowers of a hundred different colours. The air was warm, and thick with the rich aroma of life and soil. The ground was soft, a mixture of moss and dirt, as if the floor of the building had sunk into the earth.

The ceiling was made of glass, broken in several places where the plants had fought their way out. In fact, Nova had never been anywhere before where it was so obvious that the flora was in charge.

Kate motioned for her to follow. "It wasn't always like this. From what I've heard, it started out with a few plants scattered around in pots, or these." She rapped her fingers against a raised, tiled planter. Nova spotted several others, each exploding with foliage.

Kate continued. "None of the teachers ever came in to take care of it, and over the years it got out of control. There are a few kids with abilities to do with plants, and once they got involved it got *really* out of control."

"Do the staff mind?"

"Why would they? Most of them want an easy life, and letting the students help a few flowers grow bigger than they're meant to doesn't hurt anyone. At least, it hasn't yet." Kate smiled wickedly.

Nova stopped to touch an enormous apple tree, when two eyes appeared from nowhere in the middle of the trunk. She jumped back, exhaling sharply.

"Kate, this tree has eyes!"

Kate laughed. "Not quite."

Nova looked again. A shape formed around the eyes, and she saw they belonged to a girl, who was camouflaged perfectly into the bark. Though camouflaged didn't feel like a strong enough word, because when the girl stepped away her skin was rippled and cracked, exactly like the tree. She giggled, and her skin smoothed, revealing a pale face smattered with freckles. She hurried off, still laughing as her clothes slowly returned to the original school uniform colours.

"In this place, things aren't always what they seem," Kate said.

Nova glanced back to the spot on the tree where the girl had been. "Yeah, you can say that again." She thought for a moment. "That's a transformative ability, right?"

"Yes."

"What kind is yours?" Nova asked.

"Mental."

Nova's eyes widened. "Can you read minds?"

"Unfortunately not. I'm just really smart and perceptive." Kate grinned. "Come on, sit over there." She gestured to a small patch of dirt in the middle of a circle of trees. When Nova sat down, Kate stepped in front of her, quirking an eyebrow.

"You're not easily scared, right?"

"I guess we're about to find out," Nova said, attempting to sound more confident than she was. What was Kate planning to do? Turn into a giant spider? Turn Nova into one? No, that wouldn't be a mental ability. Whatever it was, though, Kate's question suggested it was going to be unpleasant.

Seconds passed, though, and nothing happened.

"Are you going to do it?" Nova asked, flicking a wandering ant off her arm.

"I *am* doing it."

"I don't understand." She brushed two more ants from her other arm. There were four more on her leg, and as she displaced them, she saw a beetle crawling across her shoe.

What am I, covered in honey or something?

Two spiders dropped from the tree branch a few feet above Nova, hanging from fine webs, and began spinning in slow circles a few inches from her face. There was something cold poking against her hand – currently flat on the dirt – and she raised it to find a worm slithering out of the ground. When its body was halfway out of the soil, it stood upright like a snake being charmed.

Slowly, Nova drew her eyes over to Kate. "A-are you doing this?"

In answer to her question, at least 200 ants popped out of the ground, moving together in perfect synchronization, to form the word 'Yes'.

Nova closed her eyes. "This might be starting to freak me out."

"What is?" Kate asked.

When Nova opened her eyes again, every single insect that had been performing in front of her, only seconds before, had vanished.

Kate held out her hand, "I thought a demonstration might be more...vivid."

Nova let Kate help her to her feet. "You can say that again."

"Are you okay?"

"Yeah, it's just not exactly something you see every day." Nova thought about that for a second. "Actually, I guess here, it probably is."

"Sort of," Kate said. "There are others who can do similar things to me, but I'm pretty sure right now I'm the only bug girl."

"Can you control other things?" Nova asked. She was fascinated by what Kate could do, and already had at least a hundred questions lined up.

Kate shook her head. "Only insects. Or basically, tiny beasts: molluscs, arachnids, that kind of thing. If it's small and wriggly I can probably get it to do stuff." She tilted her head. "What about you? What's your thing?"

Nova opened her mouth, then closed it again. Where could she even begin? She liked Kate. She got the feeling they might even be becoming friends, which would be pretty incredible, because Nova hadn't had a real friend in years. How could she risk blowing it by telling Kate what she could do? She doubted that even this girl – who didn't seem the type to get spooked by anything – would want to buddy up with someone who had the potential to accidentally murder her at any time.

But what would happen if she refused to answer? Kate had seen the blood in her hair; she had to have her suspicions already. Would not telling be just as bad?

A bell rang out somewhere behind them.

"Saved by the bell," Kate said. "Look, I can see you're not exactly desperate to show off your ability yet. I get it, trust me. Not everyone here likes what they can do. But our powers are what make us special, and I bet in time you'll realise that whatever yours is, it's pretty cool."

Nova shuddered. She wasn't so sure about that.

CHAPTER
SIX

Answers And Questions

It turned out that whether you could control insects, squirt water from your hands, or blow people apart with your mind, science class was still pretty much the same. Nova's teacher was a man in his 40s called Mr. Bellamy. He dressed as though he'd styled himself on every teacher he'd ever seen in an American teen movie; from his wire-rimmed glasses, to the patches on the elbows of his moth-eaten jacket. His brown hair was overdue a cut, constantly flopping down over his eyes when he bent down to get something from his desk, and his tie had teeny test-tubes on it.

Nova liked him immediately.

He smiled warmly when she scuttled in behind Kate. "You must be Nova."

"Yes."

"We're so happy to have you here." It sounded like genuine enthusiasm. This was a switch from the teachers at Nova's last school, who – since she joined a couple of months before – had struggled to remember her name at best, and at worst had watched her with a kind of wary unease. As if they thought she was about to do something weird at any given moment.

She supposed in the grand scheme of things they hadn't exactly been wrong.

"Please take a seat." Mr. Bellamy gestured to a table at the back of the class, where Kate was already heading.

There were 15 kids in the lab, all around the same age as Nova. Madeline was sitting at a table near the front, along with two more girls from Nova's dorm. She didn't recognise any of the others.

There was only one other person at their table at the back, a boy with curly brown hair and bright green eyes, who gave Nova a friendly nod as she sat down.

Mr. Bellamy took his spot in front of the blackboard. "Alrighty then," he said, searching for a piece of chalk amongst the many fragments at the base of the board. He finally found the largest one, which was still smaller than his thumb, and began to write. The board had been written on and wiped almost clean so many times it was dark grey instead of black. The ghosts of old equations lingered behind his new ones. There was also a dent in the lower left corner. In fact, as Nova looked around, she couldn't help but think the whole classroom had seen better days. One of the overhead lights flickered every few minutes, as if every moment of lighting the room was a struggle, and the posters on the walls were peeling and faded. Several seemed to have been strategically placed over large cracks. It hadn't exactly been effective, as the cracks were beginning to creep out from the sides.

Nova waited for Mr. Bellamy to start writing, and then leaned closer to Kate. "This place is kind of-"

"Old?" Kate interrupted. "Tell me about it. I'm pretty sure Ms. Juniper had to pay for everything herself when she set the school up."

"That's the Headmistress, right?"

"Yeah. Anyway, Tidemarsh doesn't get government funding, because we're freak-kids in a secret school. We haven't exactly got state-of-the-art equipment."

"Or books," said the curly-haired boy, who had clearly been listening in. He held out a textbook that had to be older than Nova. She reached out to take it, but as her fingers were about to touch the torn cover, it burst into flames.

"Fuck," the boy groaned.

"Language," Kate scolded.

The boy rolled his eyes. Nova was barely paying attention; the book was still literally on fire in his hands.

Kate grinned, following Nova's gaze. "Welcome to Alternate Academy, where the only things not falling apart, are probably already on fire."

"Doesn't that hurt?" Nova asked, as the flames licked at his fingers.

"Huh?" He followed her gaze. "Oh, no. Kind of comes with the territory."

"Oh sh-" Mr. Bellamy cut himself off, holding up his hands. "Nothing personal Mr. Evans, but if you could try to remember *not* to set our textbooks ablaze, I'd really appreciate it."

"Sorry sir," the boy said.

Mr. Bellamy softened. "It's fine, Luke, I'm only jealous I can't barbecue a burger without getting up from my seat."

The class laughed.

"Let's get back to it," Mr. Bellamy continued. "If someone else could please pass Nova a textbook, then we can begin."

A few minutes later, once Mr. Bellamy had set them off copying some equations from the board, Nova leaned closer to Kate again.

"What's his ability?" she asked.

Kate blinked. "Luke? I thought that was pretty obvious..."

"No, Mr. Bellamy."

"Oh right. He doesn't have one."

"Really?" For some reason that surprised Nova. "I guess I assumed everyone at Tidemarsh was an Alternate?"

"Most of the staff aren't," Kate explained. "Some of the kids who graduate go on to teach, but not many. That means Ms. Juniper needs to find normal people to work here. With the school being a secret, it's not like they can put an ad online that says: *Hey, do you like freaky magic stuff? Come teach at Tidemarsh!*"

"So how does she find them?"

Kate shrugged. "Ms Juniper. knows a lot of teachers. I think she used to work with regular kids years ago, so she must have contacts. I have no idea how she gets them to come here. All the staff have to live on the property, and they can't bring any family, so I guess most of them were already kind of sad and desperate to begin with. Pretty much all of the teachers here have been at the school forever. Which means it's either a good gig, or they have no other options."

"What happens if the kids lose control?" Nova tried to

imagine Mr. Bellamy waving a fire extinguisher at Luke if he fully burst into flames.

"They call for Elizabeth," Kate replied. "Or one of the teachers who does have abilities. And then there are the guards too, if things get really bad."

Nova's heart began to race. "The guards? There are guards here?" She had hoped the ones at the main gate were it. Only there to keep intruders out. She realised now that was stupid. A place filled with kids even half as dangerous as she was called for some kind of policing, some way for the teachers to remain in charge. Her stomach twisted into knots. What would happen if she lost control again? What did the guards do with Alternates who couldn't control their abilities?

Mr. Bellamy's voice echoed across the room. "Ladies, if you could wrap up your conversation within the next few minutes, I'd love to get back to science class."

Nova didn't get the chance to ask Kate any more questions. Mr. Bellamy kept them busy for the next 45 minutes. Nova hoped to talk to Kate some more in maths class, but on their way over she was intercepted by Elizabeth.

"Nova, "Elizabeth began, with a smile. "I need to borrow you, if that's alright?"

"Okay." It wasn't like she had much of a choice.

Elizabeth led Nova in the opposite direction, while Kate and Luke continued to class.

"How are you doing?" Elizabeth asked, as students bustled past on their way to their next period. "I know this place can be rather overwhelming at first." As if to prove her point, a horse with the head of a teenage boy trotted past.

"Liam, no transformations in the halls, you know that," Elizabeth scolded.

The boy's cheeks flushed, and he morphed completely back into a human. "Sorry Miss Perrin."

Elizabeth turned her attention back to Nova. "I see you and Katherine are becoming friends?"

"Yeah."

"I'm glad you're getting along. Katherine's a good girl... deep down." She stopped outside a door marked 'Headmistress'. "Our Headmistress, Ms. Juniper, likes to meet with all new students. I was going to catch you earlier, but something came up." She knocked on the door, then smiled at Nova. "Don't look so anxious, she's very nice."

"Come in," called a woman's voice from inside.

Nova followed Elizabeth into the room. It was large and bright, with a wide mahogany desk in the middle. The window at the back of the room overlooked the courtyard. The walls of the office were lined with bookshelves, groaning under the weight of hundreds of books, many of which looked ancient. There were paintings on the walls, mostly landscapes, in thick frames that might've been grand once, but were now dusty and cracked in places. Like the rest of the school, the place needed some TLC.

Sitting at the desk was a lady with frizzy greying-black hair, and purple-rimmed glasses hanging from a chain around her neck. She was writing something on a sheet of paper in front of her. Her eyes were a bright, piercing blue, striking against her dark skin.

"Hello," she said, warmly. "Do take a seat."

Nova and Elizabeth sat at the other side of the desk. The Headmistress finished writing and put her pen down.

"Nova Harris." The Headmistress said her name with a happy sigh, as if they were two words she never imagined herself saying. "It's such a pleasure to finally meet you."

"Thank you," Nova replied, though she was unsure why the Ms. Juniper would be particularly excited about meeting her. Unless, of course, she had a soft spot for people who accidentally made others explode.

"How are you settling in at Tidemarsh?" Ms. Juniper asked.

"It's..." Nova searched for the right word. "...different."

The old lady chuckled. "I know it can be hard at first, surrounded by so many others who are special. I promise; they'll soon feel like family, just as they do to me." She spoke to Elizabeth now. "Please make sure that Nova has all she needs. Perhaps you could ask her teachers to ease the homework load for a week or two, to give her time to adjust?"

"Of course, Ms. Juniper."

The Headmistress brought her focus back to Nova. "If you have any problems, or you need someone to talk to, my door is always open."

"Thank you." Nova tried to sound grateful, despite the wobble in her voice.

"Is there something wrong?" Ms. Juniper asked.

"No, it's...you're being really nice to me..."

"Did you expect me to be a horrible old hag of a woman?"

"No!" Nova's face grew hot.

Ms. Juniper's sapphire eyes sparkled playfully. "I'm only teasing you, dear." She leaned her elbows on the desk. "I like to think we're welcoming to all new students at Tidemarsh, however, you are extra special. We've been awaiting your arrival for many years now."

"Why? How did you know I was coming?"

The Headmistress's smile faded. "When your mother passed away in that terrible accident, we made arrangements to have you brought to us, as were her wishes should anything happen to her. Unfortunately, you and your step-father had already moved away before we arrived."

"We had to relocate a lot, for his job," Nova explained.

"Indeed. Whenever we felt close to finding you, we'd inevitably be too late. But we never gave up hope."

"Why did you keep looking?" Nova asked, struggling to keep up. "It's not like I'm anyone important."

M.s Juniper reached across the desk to squeeze her hand. "You are important to *us*. And I made a promise. I don't break my promises."

Nova could tell the Headmistress really meant that, and she felt a little warmer inside. Maybe this place really *was* one big family?

She felt brave enough to ask another question. "Did my mum think I had an ability? She died when I was five, and I didn't think kids started showing that early?"

Elizabeth answered that one. "Your mother wasn't sure whether you had an ability. They're not necessarily heredi-tary. As I mentioned yesterday, most of the children here have regular human parents, and most Alternates go on to have children who are completely ordinary. Liara wanted to wait and see if anything manifested. When she died..." Elizabeth paused, and Nova saw her expression cloud, as if the memory were painful for her. She took a breath, and then continued. "We knew she would want you to be with us, among her family, whether you were an Alternate or not."

"You would've taken me even if I couldn't...do what I can do?"

"It's not something we make a habit of," Elizabeth explained. "For your mother, though, we would've made the exception. But I always knew that any daughter of hers would be special."

This was the most anyone had spoken about her mum since she'd died. Nova hadn't even been allowed to attend the funeral, so hadn't even been in the same room as people who wanted to talk about her mother since she was a kid. She was starting to feel a lump form in her throat.

She changed the subject before she did anything embarrassing, like start crying in front of virtual strangers. "What makes people Alternates?"

"What makes some people double-jointed?" Ms. Juniper asked. "What makes some people able to roll their tongues? Why are some of us kind, and others cruel? We're all different, and that's what makes us such a wonderful species."

"Are you an Alternate?"

Ms. Juniper nodded. "Yes."

There was a pause, and the Headmistress laughed. "You're wondering whether it's polite to ask what I can do, aren't you?"

Nova gave a small smile. "Yes."

"It's not rude to ask," Ms. Juniper explained. "And I'm sure that most children here will show you their gift before you even get the chance to form that question. They do love to show off what they can do." She gave a little laugh, and then added: "But some of the students here are more reluctant to talk about how their ability manifests, and it's commonly understood that we don't press anyone for information in those circumstances."

"I understand," Nova said. She absolutely understood that part.

"As for me," Ms. Juniper said. "My gift is the ability to sense and locate other Alternates. I was the person trying to track you down for all these years, among the other children we discovered, of course."

"Thank you for finding me," Nova said. She didn't want to imagine where she'd be right now if Ms. Juniper hadn't led Elizabeth to her.

The Headmistress smiled. "I think it might be time to return to class. We've given you quite a lot to think about, and I imagine you need time to let it settle. You are always welcome to come back to either of us, any time, if you have any further questions."

"Thanks," Nova said, getting to her feet.

Ms. Juniper stood up. "I'm looking forward to seeing what you can achieve, dear. Your mother was an excellent student, and I already feel that you have great potential."

Potential for what?

The idea of ever using her ability again, let alone willingly practicing it, gave Nova an uneasy feeling in the pit of her stomach. How could Ms. Juniper and the other teachers possibly keep everyone safe? In fact, why would they even *want* her to use it again? The only thing that came from Nova's ability was death; not exactly a huge benefit to anyone at the school.

She was so preoccupied with these thoughts, that it was

only when she reached the door of her next class that she realised there was still one huge, unanswered question hanging in the air.

"Wait, what was my mum's ability?"

Elizabeth smiled widely. "I wondered when you might ask that again. Your mother's gift was rare. Over the years, we've seen many repetitions of the things the children here can do. Your friend Katherine, for example, is not the first person we've taught who can control insects, and we have several students, like Luke, who can manipulate elements such as fire or water. Your mother, however, is the only person either Ms. Juniper or myself have ever encountered who was able to freeze time."

"Freeze time?" Even in a place like this, the idea of that sounded too farfetched.

Elizabeth's grin widened. "Well, we always thought that sounded cooler. In reality, it came down to incredible speed. We've got other children here who are remarkably fast, but nothing compared to your mum. She was able to move so quickly that time stopped passing around her. She couldn't do it indefinitely; I believe the longest she could go was 10 minutes, but to be in the same room as her while she did it was extraordinary. She would disappear right in front of your eyes, and reappear somewhere else. It was like teleportation; however, she could tamper with things on the way." She chuckled at the memory. "She would play so many pranks on us – messing up our hair, moving cups when we were pouring our juice. You could never be sure it was her, because she got so good at sitting back in the same place, in the same position, as if she never left."

Nova shook her head. "I can't believe I never knew."

"She was very good at concealing it. It's something all Alternates learn." Elizabeth said. "She was so powerful; I was certain that any child of hers would be outstanding. Especially considering who their father-" she cut herself off.

"My father?"

Elizabeth's face flushed with colour. "You should get some rest; you've had a lot to take in." She made to walk away.

Nova wasn't about to let it go that easily, and stepped to the side to block Elizabeth's path. "Wait, you knew my father? What was he like?"

"We can talk about this another-"

"Was he an Alternate too? What was his ability?"

Elizabeth opened her mouth, then closed it again. After a couple of seconds she said: "You should get to class. I'll see you later."

Without another word she left, leaving Nova alone, her head spinning.

CHAPTER
SEVEN

The Tombs

Nova pushed what Elizabeth had said – or rather, what she had *not* said – to the back of her mind for the next few hours. She couldn't afford to be focusing on things she had no hope of finding the answer to on her own. Elizabeth wasn't going anywhere. She'd have to answer Nova's questions sooner or later.

Probably.

So, even though she'd learned more about both of her parents in five minutes than she had in her entire life up until that point, she forced her attention back on her classes.

Like science class, maths, english, and geography were all pretty much the same as they always had been. In fact, she frequently found herself forgetting Tidemarsh wasn't a normal school. That was, until Luke accidentally set a book on fire, some kid made his chair disappear with no idea how to get it back, or Kate recruited an army of ants to sharpen her pencil for her. Those things brought her back to her new reality pretty fast.

Nova's last class of the day was PE. At 3pm she found herself with 14 other girls, standing in the courtyard, wearing a pair of shorts that were slightly too big, and a t-shirt that hadn't been white in a long time. Their teacher was Miss Farley – the same woman who had come charging across the grounds earlier to break up the fight – who wore a blue tracksuit, her grey hair planted in a bun at the top of her head, and an expression that suggested she suffered no fools.

"Today you'll be running laps of the school," she announced to the class.

"How many?" Kate asked.

"Until I tell you to stop, Miss Stone," the teacher replied, briskly. A few wiry tendrils had escaped from her bun, but they did nothing to soften the hard features of her face.

Kate rolled her eyes at Nova. The girl standing on her other side put up her hand. "Miss Farley, can we use our abilities?"

Miss Farley's lips twitched into an almost-but-not-quite smile. "Where's the fun in that, dear?"

There were groans from several of the girls, and someone muttered: "Miserable old cow."

Their teacher either didn't hear or chose to ignore the comment. She brought her whistle to her lips and blew a long piercing blast. The girls set off, and it soon became clear to Nova that they were all a lot better at this kind of exercise than she was. Within a few minutes she was left far behind most of the others, though Kate kept the slower pace at her side.

"Everyone's so fast," Nova puffed. "How can they keep that up?"

Kate shook her head. "They don't, they just want to get out of Farley's sight."

"What do you mean?"

The question was answered when they turned the corner, and Nova realised that their teacher's desire for the students not to use their abilities had been completely ignored. With the woods to their right, and the lake on their left, they were out of her sight, and began to let loose. A girl a few meters ahead leapt from the ground and continued her journey by flying. Another shot off into the distance, nothing more than a blur, as though she had a rocket strapped to her back.

"Isn't that pointless?" Nova asked. "The teacher will know she used her ability."

"She'll go back to her dorm until the end of class," Kate explained. "Farley won't count how many times we pass her. Last week she was reading for the entire lesson, and didn't even look up."

Nova watched as a girl with bright red hair transformed into a horse, and galloped away.

"This is insane," she said. "I don't think I'll ever get used to this place."

Kate smiled. "You will. It was weird for me too, at first. Anyway, the thing to know about Farley is that she doesn't *actually* care about whether we use our abilities, or even if we do exactly what she's asked. She likes to lay down the rules, so it seems like she's strict, but she's been here like a million years, I'm pretty sure she's phoning it in now."

"Uh huh." Nova was finding it harder to talk. She'd never been great at cardio, and was trying to remember exactly how breathing worked.

Kate continued to chit-chat, unaware that her running partner was fast becoming a puddle of goo. "We can't all use our abilities, of course. I mean, what am I going to do, get ants to carry me? There are other girls who don't have powers that would help, and there are a few who are too afraid to use theirs."

I know that feeling.

"Want to take a short cut?" Kate asked. Without waiting for a response, she pulled Nova into the woods. They slowed to a walk, and continued through the mass of trees until the sounds of the rest of the class faded away, replaced with birdsong and the breeze rustling the leaves. It was cooler in there, and Nova sat down on the mossy ground gratefully. Her heart rate finally returning to normal.

"Not a runner, then?" Kate asked, a smile playing on her lips.

Nova wiped her forehead with the back of her arm. "What gave me away?"

"Most people aren't that shiny. Or red. Or, you know, dying."

"Wow, you didn't tell me you had super-perception too," Nova drawled.

Kate laughed. "We'll wait here for a while, then head out before the bell and act as if we've been running the whole time. You know, if you have any more sweat left."

Nova tossed a stick at her.

Kate grinned. "Sorry, that was my last one." She sat on a nearby log. "So, what did Miss Perfect want?"

"Who?" Nova asked.

"Elizabeth. Haven't you noticed how she never has a single hair out of place? Or a crease in her clothes? I think she sleeps standing up or something. If she even needs something as pedestrian as *sleep*."

"Maybe she makes all her imperfections vanish," Nova suggested.

Kate laughed again. "Hey, that's not completely unlikely." She put on an imitation of Elizabeth's voice. "Oh, hello Katherine, I hope you're well. I just need to borrow Nova for a teensy second if that's alright? Then I'll return to ironing my hair and dermaplaning away my pores." She returned to her normal voice. "Ugh, something about her totally rubs me the wrong way. No one can be that controlled, that *perfect*, all the time. Anyway, what did she want you for?"

"She took me to the Headmistress. Apparently, Ms. Juniper wanted to know how I was settling in."

"What's with the special treatment?" Kate asked.

"What do you mean?"

"Elizabeth collected you personally; that usually only happens when someone is a *big deal*." She said the words with mock-awe, then asked genuinely: "Do they have dirt on you?"

I guess they do.

Nova shook her head quickly. Maybe too quickly. "I think it's because of my mom," she said, changing the subject from anything that might lead to exploding stepfathers. She filled Kate in on what had happened in the meeting with Ms. Juniper; how she finally learned about her mum and her ability. Though she'd only known her a day, Kate already felt like Nova's confidant at Tidemarsh. Nova wasn't ready to tell her about what had happened with Gary or anything, but getting to talk about her mum, with someone who felt like she might be becoming a friend, sounded pretty good.

She told Kate about her mum's wish for Nova to come to Tidemarsh, ability or not, and that Ms. Juniper had supposedly been looking for her for a long time. When she got on to Elizabeth's sudden departure in the hallway, Kate frowned.

"And you have no idea who your dad is?"

Nova shook her head. "I never knew him, and my mum never spoke about him."

"Did you ask?"

"A few times when I was younger. She said he left before I was born, and we didn't need him. I never really worried about it too much. And when I was old enough to really understand and want to ask questions, it was too awkward. I had a stepdad, Gary, and he and my mum didn't talk about my real father." Gary's name left a sour taste on her tongue.

Kate scooped a beetle off the ground, allowing it to walk between her two hands. "Do you think Elizabeth knows something about your dad?"

"Something like what?"

"I don't know, but her reaction was weird. Like, if she knew him, why not say so? Leaving like that was totally suspicious."

Nova had to agree there.

"So, what happened to your mum?" Kate asked.

"She died in a fire."

Kate's face dropped. "Oh, I'm so sorry."

"I don't really remember it," Nova admitted. "Everything around that time is a blur. The doctor they made me talk to after it happened said it was a post-traumatic stress thing. For me, one minute she was there, the next it was just me and my stepdad." She cleared her throat, uncomfortable that they'd landed back on Gary again.

Nova glanced around, eager to change the subject. They had walked for a while to get here, and all she could see were trees and bushes. "Do you know where we are?"

Kate nodded. "I come here sometimes when I don't feel like running laps. Farley gets us to do it a lot. I guess it's easier than planning a real lesson." She leaned back, looking up at the sky through the leaves. "I like it in here. It's always quiet because most of the kids avoid the woods."

"Why?"

"They're scared."

Nova looked around. "Of what?" Though the trees were dense, there was plenty of light pooling on the ground around them. Wildflowers bloomed in several patches a few feet from where she was sitting, and the smell of the forest was comforting and inviting. In fact, it was hard to picture a less frightening place. "Why would anyone be scared out here?"

Kate looked thoughtful, then climbed to her feet. "I'll show you."

Nova followed Kate through the woods for several minutes, until a building came into view beyond the tree line. This one was different to those in the courtyard. It stood alone, and was built from charcoal-coloured bricks. The angles of the place seemed off; it sort of looked like it was leaning. There was a yard to the right, which was surrounded by a huge chain link fence, topped with barbed wire. One of the fences skimmed the edge of the woods, as though the forest was minutes away from fighting its way inside. All the windows of the building were frosted, and the heavy-looking doors were shut.

It was only a building, Nova knew that, yet somehow, she felt it was a bad place. Something about it made her stomach heavy, like a weight pressing down on her insides.

"What is that place?" she asked.

"It was a secure unit when Tidemarsh was a prison," Kate replied.

"And now?"

"Pretty much the same."

Nova turned to face her. "What do you mean?"

"Most kids brought to Tidemarsh get taken to the main school, like you did. But sometimes – if they did something really bad – they come here instead. We call it the Tombs."

Nova's skin prickled; she suddenly felt cold. "Why?"

"If you're locked up down there, you can never use your abilities. The kids sleep in cells, and barely ever see a window. It's like being underground. They can't get out. I guess someone thought it sounded like being in a tomb, and the name stuck. Anyway, no one likes coming into the woods because the further in you go, the closer you get to this place. The kids in there are dangerous."

Nova swallowed. "I thought you said we were *all* dangerous."

"Not like them. The kids they keep down there are the

ones the teachers would never be able to control. They're the ones who can't ever leave Tidemarsh."

"Why can't they leave?"

Kate held her gaze. "Because they've killed people. The kids locked away in the Tombs...they're murderers."

CHAPTER EIGHT

Show and Tell

"Nova, what do you do?"

The question had come from a girl who was sitting two beds away from Kate. She was around 16 or 17, pretty, with large doe-like brown eyes, and hundreds of tiny black braids. Like Nova and the other girls in the dorm, she wore one of the shabby nightgowns. Everyone was getting ready for bed.

For a moment, Nova forgot that she was at a school for fellow freaks, and wasn't sure she understood the question.

"I'm sorry?"

"Your ability," the girl said. "What can you do?"

Nova's stomach dropped. How could she answer that? *Oh, you know, nothing much. I occasionally make people explode from the inside when I get mad. How about you?*

Kate must've sensed Nova's unease from her own bed, where several dozen spiders had been roaming freely while she read a book, because she called over to the girl.

"Come on Ria, we all know you're only asking because

you want to show off to the one person in this room who hasn't seen what you can do at least a million times."

Ria folded her arms defensively, though she was smiling. "Wow, that's cold."

Kate spoke to the whole room now. "That's what you all want, right?" she asked, grinning. "A chance to put on your performance of '*Look at the Weird Stuff We Can Do*'?" She looked over at Nova. "Do you want to see it?"

"Absolutely!" Nova replied, eagerly. It wasn't only that it would take the focus away from her own horrific ability; she was genuinely curious to find out what the other girls could do. Other than Kate, and the one with the purple hair who had made her a toothbrush, she knew nothing about the other girls in her dorm or their abilities. They all looked totally normal on the surface, and she could figure nothing out based on their appearances alone.

"Well, you already know mine," Kate began. "Unless you want to see some more?"

Nova's eyes widened at the thought of more bugs in her close vicinity. "No, I'm good."

Kate laughed. "Fair enough." She addressed the rest of the room. "So, who wants to go next?"

Ria waited at least three seconds before stepping forward. "I guess I could."

"You can see how unenthusiastic she is," Kate joked.

Ria gave her a not-so-subtle hand gesture, and then approached Nova's bed. All the other girls watched with palpable excitement. All, that is, except Madeline, who was painting her toenails baby pink, and wearing an expression that suggested she was bored of everything and everyone else around her.

"You got a sock or something?" Ria asked Nova.

Nova grabbed one from her drawer, and handed it over. Ria encased it in her hands, covering it entirely, and then brought her hands to her mouth. She blew inside, and when she opened her hands up, the sock was gone. Instead, from out of her hands flew 10 white butterflies. They flitted around the room gracefully while several of the girls clapped.

Madeline rolled her eyes. "Just what this room needs: more bugs."

The others ignored her. A girl on the other side of the room called over to Ria: "The sock might've been more useful, though."

"My turn," said a skinny girl with short black hair. She hopped off her bed at the other side of the room, and hurried over to the middle.

"I'm Meredith," she said to Nova.

Everyone was silent as they waited. Meredith closed her eyes, took a deep breath, and then seemed to grow taller. But Nova quickly realised she wasn't taller; her feet were no longer on the floor. She was hovering in the air, a few inches at first, but getting higher and higher. Meredith opened her eyes, and spun in a circle gleefully. The others cheered, and she landed lightly on both feet. There were more cheers and clapping, and she gave a little bow, tucking a strand of hair behind her ear self-consciously.

"I've been working on the landing," she said.

"You can say that again!" Ria called over. "Last time we saw her do it, she came down so hard she practically went through the floor!" She pointed to a dented floorboard over by Meredith's bed.

"Speaking of going through the floor," began another girl. She was small, with hair right down her back in a long black braid. When she spoke, her voice was soft and gentle. "I think it's my turn."

"Are you sure Jas?" Kate asked. "Last time-"

"I can do it." The girl said determinedly, then gave Nova an awkward wave. "And I'm Jasminder, nice to meet you properly."

She headed to the middle of the room, which had clearly become the stage, and took a deep breath. "If you could all not talk...that will help."

Silence fell, and Jasminder turned, eyes focused on the wardrobe on the other side of Nova's bed. It belonged to Beth, the toothbrush-maker.

Jasminder strode towards it, expression fixed, and walked straight through the closed doors as though they were made of smoke.

For a few seconds, there was no sound, then a small bump came from inside.

"Jasminder, are you okay?" Ria asked.

"Yes," came a quiet voice. "Can you let me out?"

Beth unlocked the doors, and Jasminder climbed out sheepishly.

"I got in my head," she explained. "Over-thought it."

"Could've been worse," Kate said, reassuringly.

"*Has* been worse," Meredith joked. "Remember when you got stuck between the floor and the dorm below?"

A couple of the girls giggled at the memory, Jasminder included.

"Who's next?" Kate asked.

"She's seen what I can do," Beth said.

"I'm not sure I understand it, though," Nova added. "You made a toothbrush appear out of nowhere. Is that your ability?"

Kate laughed. "If that was it, it would be the absolute worst super-power in history."

The other girls laughed too, and Beth chimed in. "It's not that I can make toothbrushes appear, it's that I can move objects from one place to another. I don't know how it works exactly, but I suppose it's like dematerializing things from one place, and then remaking them in another."

"Wow," Nova said, suitably impressed.

"It's not as easy as that," Beth added. "I have to know exactly where the thing I want to move is. I have to know how big it is, and need to have held it in my hand to know the shape and weight. A few months ago, I snuck into the supply room and stayed there all afternoon." She grinned. "I touched pretty much everything, and tried to memorise where it was all stored. Now when someone needs a toothbrush or some tampons, I can bring them from there, to my hand."

Kate raised an eyebrow. "Wait...you touched all the toothbrushes and tampons?"

Beth waved her comments away, casually. "That's not important. Anyway, who's next? How about you, Madeline?"

"Pass," Madeline replied, without even looking over.

"Okay..." Beth trailed off. "Orlaith would you like to go?"

Orlaith was right at the other end of the room, in the bed opposite the one Nova had meant to have by the door.

She had shoulder-length brown hair, and spoke with a thick Irish accent. "I have really good hearing, it's not exactly a party trick."

"You can hear stuff really far away?" Nova asked.

Orlaith nodded. "Sort of. I have to know who I'm listening for, and train my ears to know to listen out for it. And my range isn't that great yet."

"She can hear when Elizabeth comes into the building," Beth said. "Which is pretty useful."

"Why?" Nova asked.

Beth grinned. "It's good to have a warning before she comes in."

There were only two girls left in the dorm who hadn't had a turn, the one with red hair, Laura, and a small blonde.

Laura went first. She didn't seem to harbour too much resentment towards Nova, at least, and bounded to the centre of the room holding a small potted plant. She stroked the leaves gently, and within seconds the plant started to grow. In less than a minute it was taller than she was, and it burst out of its pot, spilling soil all over the floor. Laura gave a small bow while the others clapped, but Madeline got to her feet.

"That's enough," she said, sharply. "Clean up that mess, and get the bloody butterflies out of here. I'm sick of you all treating this place like a circus."

"Can't Isabella have her turn?" Beth asked quietly. "She's the last one."

Madeline's gaze was icy. "If you think I'm letting her set those snakes loose up here, you're very much mistaken."

"Nova hasn't had her go yet," Orlaith said.

"I *said* we're done."

No one argued, and though the girl called Isabella seemed disappointed about not getting her turn, she didn't speak up. It was pretty clear to Nova that Madeline ran the dorm, and the others were quick to fall in line around her.

She guessed it didn't matter where she went, there would be bullies everywhere.

Don't Be Scared

Nova woke up drenched in sweat. She had dreamt of the corridor again; of the cold air, the dripping water, the screams. Tonight was different, though. Tonight she wasn't walking to the door; she was being dragged. In her dream, she had fought back, and felt the exhaustion weighing her down. Her chest was tight with fear, sweat and tears running down her face. Everything felt so real; the fingers digging into her arms, the cold, damp air, the wails from around her. She dreamt she was dragged towards the door at the end of the corridor, and when it swung open, Gary was standing there in the darkness. He beckoned her inside, grinning widely.

Nova had startled awake, sick to her stomach and freezing cold. At first, all she could hear was the sound of her own heart hammering in her chest. Then, slowly, the rest of the world slipped back in. Someone was snoring at the other end of the dorm. Beth's sheets rustled as she turned over in her sleep. Somewhere outside, an owl was hooting. As they had before, the memories from her dream slowly slipped away, though it took a few minutes longer than that for the tightness to leave her chest.

The clock on the wall said it was midnight. Nova laid back down and closed her eyes. It was no good. Though the dream was vanishing from her memory, something else was on her mind. She couldn't stop thinking about her conversation with Kate in the woods.

The killers go to the Tombs.

I've *killed someone.*

Kate said they can never leave.

What if Elizabeth had made a mistake? What if she and Ms. Juniper were talking right now about Nova and what she did? What if they decided she was too dangerous to live with others? If the Tombs were a place for kids who had killed people, it only made sense that she would end up there sooner rather than later. It would be like the dream. Only worse. She'd be locked away forever, without the release of waking up.

Nova sat up, swinging her legs out of the bed. It was as though a bucket of icy water had been tossed over her, bringing her to life and forcing her to get moving. Everything suddenly made sense: if staying at Tidemarsh meant being locked away in some dark corner of the woods, forgotten and trapped for the rest of her life, she'd rather take her chances with the outside world.

As quietly as she could, she stuffed her meagre belongings into her backpack, got dressed, and carried her shoes across the dorm. There was part of her, a big part, that wanted to say goodbye to Kate. But she couldn't risk it. She'd only known her for a day, and as much as she wanted to trust her, she couldn't be sure Kate wouldn't tell someone Nova was leaving. Maybe she'd even been told to keep an eye on her in case she tried to get away before her room in the Tombs was ready? Though the thought of that hurt, it made it easier to leave without saying goodbye.

In the hallway, Nova slipped into her shoes, and hurried down the stairs. She had to cross the next floor to reach the main staircase. On her way there, she was distracted by laughter coming from an open door up ahead on the left.

She peeked in. It was one of the boy dorms, probably the one directly under her own. There were three guys in the centre of the room fooling around with their abilities, while the rest cheered from the side-lines. The one nearest the door was making his bed levitate. Another had conjured a dark grey cloud, which he was directing around the room with his hand, while it rained water onto the heads of his dormmates. The third was spinning around in circles like a tornado, so fast that his features were indistinguishable. Everywhere he went, scraps of paper and clothing went flying. Someone else had brought to life a pair of pyjamas. They were walking around on their own, occasionally jumping into the air or performing a high kick.

Nova wanted to stay and watch, seeing the other kids do stuff like this still amazed her, but she made herself walk on. The longer she stood around, the more chance she had of getting caught.

When she reached the top of the staircase, however, she had no choice but to stop again. Her path was blocked by two people standing halfway down the stairs. One of them was Madeline. She was leaning against the wall, with her arms wrapped around a guy with dark hair. They were kissing as though the world were about to end. Nova grimaced at the sounds drifting up the stairs.

Despite the fact she had never kissed a boy before, she was pretty certain it wasn't supposed to be such a noisy experience.

The pair were so engrossed in exploring each other's tonsils, that Nova briefly wondered if she could sneak past without either of them noticing. Unfortunately, they chose that precise moment to break apart, and she had no choice but to turn tail and dart through the nearest open doorway, leading into one of the large bathrooms.

Nova stood with her back against the wall, listening to the sound of their voices. A few seconds later there were heavy footsteps going down the staircase, and lighter ones heading in her direction. The pair had clearly decided to call it a night. Nova moved further into the room, holding her breath, and waiting for Madeline to head back to the dorm.

But she didn't.

Before Nova knew what to do, Madeline was standing in front of her. Even in the darkness, Nova could see that her eyes were blazing with anger.

Nova swallowed. "Hi Madeline."

"What are you doing here?" Madeline snapped.

"Using the bathroom."

Madeline scowled.

"I mean, I'm not using it *right now*," Nova gabbled. "Right now, I'm just...thinking."

"*Thinking*?" Madeline hissed.

This was a trap that Nova often fell into. Most of the time she was a quiet person, but when she got nervous her mouth started talking without really consulting her brain at all. It rarely ended well. She got the feeling this was going to be one of those times.

"What are you thinking about, *Nova*?" Madeline said her name as though it left a foul taste in her mouth.

"I was thinking about...about going to the bathroom. Sometimes I have to kind of psyche myself up. Otherwise, I can be sitting for hours, and I read that's not good for you because it can make you get these huge-"

Madeline cut her off. "This is the *boys'* bathroom."

Fuck.

"Oh. Right," was all Nova could say to that.

"Were you spying on me?" Madeline stepped intimidatingly close.

"No."

"You better not have been, because you don't want to get on my bad side."

Do you have a good *side?*

Thankfully Nova was able to hold her tongue for that particular thought, and after Madeline allowed her cold blue eyes to bore into Nova's for a few more seconds, she stormed off in the direction of their room.

Nova let out a sigh of relief. Knowing what she did about Madeline's ability, she had half-expected to be forced to lick a toilet or something. As it stood, it didn't matter what side of Madeline's she was on, because she was leaving anyway.

She hurried out of the bathroom and down the stairs, stopping once again when she reached the bottom. The man and woman she had seen when she arrived – Mr. and Mrs. Driver – were sitting behind the front desk, watching the tiny TV. They hadn't seen Nova yet, because they had their backs turned, but there was no way she was going to be able to get past without being noticed.

Nova stepped into the shadows of a room to her left, trying to decide what to do next. She could probably crawl past the desk without being seen, but the front door of the building was directly in front of them. She bit her lip, trying to quell the panic stirring in her stomach.

"What's that?" Mrs. Driver asked.

Nova followed her gaze. There was water dripping from the ceiling.

Mr. Driver sighed. "B dorm."

"Come on, if we get there quick enough, we might be able to save the floorboards."

"I'll get the mop."

They got to their feet and rushed up the stairs and out of sight.

Not wanting to miss this glaring opportunity, Nova ran to the front doors, swung one open, and raced out into the darkness. She decided to cut through the woods, reasoning that it was her best chance at not being seen.

The trouble with walking through the woods at night, however, was that it was dark. Really dark. Thanks to the full moon and clear sky she could at least make out the trees a few seconds before she collided with them, but that was the extent of her visual range. It took her less than five minutes to get lost, and after another 20, she had turned herself around so many times that she had no idea if she was heading in the direction of the gates, or right back to the dorms again.

The time spent stumbling through the undergrowth had another effect; it made Nova realise how ridiculous her plan was. The walls were too high to climb, and even if she somehow managed that, she'd be cut to shreds on the barbed wire, and probably break her leg on the fall to the other side. There was only one way in or out that she was aware of – the main gates – and they were sure to be guarded and locked. The idea of blowing them up briefly flitted through her mind. If she had the power to make a person explode, surely a metal gate wouldn't be so much harder? The problem was, she had no idea how she had even used her ability in the first place. It wasn't like she'd been planning to turn Gary into a human firework. She didn't have the first clue how to focus the energy – or whatever it was – on an object.

And even if she somehow managed to blow the gates open, without turning herself to ash in the process, where would she go? Ms. Juniper knew how to find her again, and if she and Elizabeth had any doubts in their mind about whether Nova belonged in the Tombs, a daring escape where she blew up their gates wouldn't put her in their good books.

Nova came to a stop.

This is stupid. I need to go back.

Though Elizabeth had been weirdly mysterious about Nova's father, she had also been nothing but kind and welcoming. Sure, the thought of the Tombs was terrifying, however, there'd been no indication from anyone that Nova was going to be sent there. Elizabeth, Ms. Juniper, and just about everyone else – except Madeline – had been pretty great so far. Nova finally had a place where she could be herself, where she had people who *wanted* to know her. At Tidemarsh, she could mention her mum without feeling like she was saying an awful curse word.

She made up her mind: she was staying.

Unfortunately, at that moment in time, staying meant she would be living in the woods, because she had absolutely no idea how to get the hell out of there.

A twig snapped from somewhere in the darkness. Nova spun around. There was nothing there, and no movement from any direction. Still, something had made that noise.

She swallowed. "Hello?"

"Don't be scared."

CHAPTER TEN

The Naked Truth

Nova forced herself to stand up straighter, balling her fists at her sides despite her racing heart. It had been a male voice, though not one she recognised.

"I'm not scared, but you should be if you're planning to creep up on me."

"I wasn't trying to creep up on you," the voice replied. "I didn't want to frighten you."

"You probably should've thought of that before you decided to follow me through the woods, in the dark." She strained her eyes, still unable to figure out where the boy was.

"That's a good point," he admitted.

"Show yourself."

"Okay. But you should know...I'm naked."

Nova's defences gave way to confusion. "What?"

A boy's head popped out from behind a tree a few feet away. "I'm naked. As in, I have no clothes."

"Yes, I know what naked means. Why?"

"I can turn myself invisible, but not my clothes. So,

whenever I want to do it I, you know, leave my trousers and stuff behind."

Nova furrowed her brow, confused. "You don't look very invisible to me."

He was probably around her age. Skinny, dark-haired, and from the colour rising in his cheeks, clearly more than a little embarrassed.

"It wears off," he explained. "Sometimes I can make it last for hours, other times only a few minutes. It wore off earlier than I expected."

"What are you doing out here?" Nova asked.

"Following you."

Nova paused. "Most people wouldn't admit that."

He grinned. "I'm naked behind a tree, I'd rather be honest, than have you try to guess why else I might be back here with no clothes on."

"The fact that you were following me naked isn't exactly making me feel better."

"Like I said, it's the only way I can be invisible. Believe me, it wasn't like I was trying to decide what to wear and thought *nothing* was my best option."

He had such a ridiculous grin on his face that Nova almost wanted to laugh. Almost.

"*Why* were you following me?" she pressed.

"I wanted to know where you were going," he said, as if it was the obvious answer. "Not many people leave the dorms at night."

"Why?"

"I guess they don't want to get caught? And it's not like there's a lot to do out here in the dark, besides trip over tree roots and get spiderwebs in your hair. Besides, the others are out at night, and most people don't want to be anywhere near them."

Nova glanced around. "Others?"

"The kids from the Tombs. The worst ones at least. The guards don't let them out in the day in case any of us get too close. Even through the fence, I guess they think they're too dangerous."

"They let them out at night?" Nova asked.

"Only in their yard."

Nova didn't like the idea forming in her head, but found herself asking: "Can you show me?"

"Why?"

She tried to sound casual. "I don't know, I'm curious I guess." She couldn't tell him the real reason; that like those kids she had killed someone. That she wanted to see them, to see if they looked so different to herself.

The boy didn't seem sure. "I don't know, I don't like going over there. If anyone catches us-"

"You can make yourself invisible. And we'll stay behind the trees. They won't even know we're there."

"You can't be sure of that."

She raised her chin. "Fine, I'll go by myself." She made to march off, aware that she had no idea what direction to even walk in, when he called her back.

"Wait, I'll come. Just give me a minute. You won't find it on your own."

He closed his eyes, breathing slowly. Nova blinked and he was gone.

"Okay," came his voice, passing close by. "Let's go."

They walked through the woods in silence for a few

minutes. After a while, the invisible boy asked: "What's your name?"

"Nova."

"I'm Danny."

"Nice to meet you," Nova said. "Sort of."

"Yeah, you too. Sorry I'm naked."

"That's okay."

"Normally when I meet people for the first time I'm not," he added.

"I'd hope so."

"It's kind of embarrassing really."

"Maybe if we stopped talking about it?" Nova suggested, quickly.

"Where were you going?" he asked. "Before we spoke, I mean."

"Nowhere."

"That's true. You'd circled the same tree four times."

Nova stopped walking. "You watched me do that?"

"Yeah."

"Why didn't you stop me sooner?" she asked, scowling.

"I was trying to think of how to let you know I was there without completely freaking you out. Plus, you seemed kind of angry. I didn't want you to yell at me."

Nova started walking again. "I don't really yell."

That was true, she just blew people up, apparently.

Danny pressed again. "So where *were* you going? You know, before your tour of the tree?"

Nova had to give him something; she was forcing him to lead her through the woods after all.

"I was thinking about running away." She shook her head, "It's stupid."

"It's not stupid," Danny said. "I felt the same when I first came here."

"Really?"

"Yeah, of course. I mean, this place is *insane* when you think about it, right? We all get used to it, but when I first arrived, I wanted to get as far away as possible."

"Did you ever attempt it?" Nova asked.

An overhead branch seemed to move on its own, as Danny held it to one side so she could pass. "Once or twice. Invisible or not, I couldn't fit through the gaps in the gate. Once I reappeared with my head stuck in between the bars. The guard had to help me out...you know, after he stopped laughing."

Nova smiled.

"What's your thing?" he asked. "Your ability, I mean."

"I don't want to talk about it."

"Oh."

"It's..." Nova searched for the right words, but came up empty. "It's complicated."

"I understand, no problem."

"How long have you been here?" she asked, changing the subject.

"About six months. My parents always knew I was different, I mean it's hard to ignore a toddler who disappears in one place and reappears somewhere else. They tried to keep it a secret for as long as they could. If you don't know about Tidemarsh, about the others like us, then I guess you imagine all kinds of awful stuff happening if anyone finds out you have a magical kid. Then, a few months ago, some guys at my school were chasing me, trying to beat me up for not letting them cheat off my test. I was running, and I disappeared. But I couldn't bring myself back. I was invisible for like two weeks. That's how Elizabeth found me, the ripples from that must've been huge. She explained to my parents that she could help me learn to control my abilities, and they agreed to let me come here."

"Can they visit?" Nova asked.

"No. Ms. Juniper tries not to bring anyone into the school who doesn't need to be here. Everything about this place is secret. We write letters and stuff."

"Can you call?"

"Mobile phones don't work this far out. There are a couple of landlines we can use. I know my mum misses me, but I think my dad was relieved. He didn't have to try and explain my weird behaviour anymore. By the time I graduate from this place, I'll be able to control the invisibility."

They walked in silence for a while, then he asked: "How did your parents feel about you coming here?"

"My mum's dead."

"Oh...I'm sorry." He sounded like he was.

"She died years ago," Nova said. "I was living with my stepdad and his wife. But there was...anyway now I'm here."

They continued the rest of the journey in silence. Nova wondered if she'd said too much. Maybe Danny was putting the pieces together and had already figured out that she had done something terrible? Maybe he'd gone, and she was walking through the woods on her own?

She was proved at least half-wrong, when she heard his voice. "Over there."

"You can't say 'over there' when you're invisible. I don't know what you're pointing at." She tried to sound sharp, but it was hard to hide the relief she felt that he was still with her.

"Sorry, that log on the right."

Nova walked to the log, a couple of feet behind the edge of the woods. The Tombs were further down the hill, in a clearing, though part of the yard backed onto the tree line over to the right. As well as the lights from the windows, there were several lampposts in the yard, casting a silvery glow on the people within the chain link fence.

There were around 20 kids, all wearing white T-shirts and orange trousers. Some had large brown coats over the top, ill-fitting and clearly well-worn. A few of the kids were moving around, either pacing anxiously or slowly walking the length of the fence. Most were huddled in small groups.

"That's not all of them," Danny explained, as Nova sat on the log. "They let some of the less dangerous ones out in the early evening. These ones are only allowed out at night."

"Why are they kept in there?" Nova knew the answer, but she wanted to hear it from someone else.

"All of the kids in the Tombs have killed people, even the 'less dangerous' ones. Ms. Juniper won't turn them in to the police because she knows they'd either break out of jail, or kill more people trying. Plus, she doesn't want to risk our kind being found. No one's supposed to know about us. So, she keeps them here."

"Isn't that a huge risk?"

"The place is well-guarded. Most of the guards here are human, but there are a few Alternates too, and they can use their abilities to keep things under control. I heard one of the guards can even block other Alternates' abilities from working altogether. That's kind of cool. Anyway, I guess

Ms. Juniper thinks it's safer to keep the dangerous Alts close to the only people who could stand a chance fighting them."

Nova swatted away a mosquito. "Like Elizabeth?"

"Right. I mean, she could make them disappear if they got too much, couldn't she?"

"Why doesn't she?" Nova asked. "Someone told me those kids can never leave. What's the point in keeping them there?"

"Maybe Ms. Juniper wants to give them a chance?" Danny suggested. "And as far as I know, they *are* allowed to leave the Tombs if they can prove they can control themselves. Angela used to be one of them. At least, that's what I heard."

Nova thought for a moment. "You keep saying 'kids'. What happens when they grow up?"

"I don't know. Some people say they go somewhere else; like another prison but for older Alternates. Others say they stay here their whole lives. None of us know for sure."

The movements within the fence were nothing out of the ordinary. No one seemed to be using their abilities, like when the kids from the main school were together. Every now and then there was a burst of laughter, or raised voices, but there was nothing altogether exciting going on.

"We should go," Danny said. "I'm feeling weird, which means this is going to wear off soon."

Nova got to her feet. Her drive to run away had fizzled out, and all she could think about was getting back to bed.

"Wait," Danny said, sounding nervous. "I think I'm reappearing. Can you give me like, 10 seconds, then follow? I'd rather get a head start."

"Sure."

"Try and follow the path we came, and if you get lost call out. I won't be far ahead."

Nova heard Danny's footsteps fade away as he hurried back through the woods. She counted to 20, wanting to make sure he got far enough away, then got to her feet. She was about to turn and head back into the woods when something tickled her arm. Nova glanced down, eyes widening when she saw it was a horrifyingly huge spider. It was resting there on her arm like it owned the damn place. She tried to shake it off, lost her balance, tripped over, and landed on her backside. She stumbled to her feet, dancing around a little and finally managing to shake the spider free.

It was only then she realised she was past the tree line. Out of the woods. Out in the open. Her heart raced, and she stumbled back into the safety of the shadows, eyes scanning the fence. No one seemed to have noticed her. She took a breath, her heart slowly returning to normal.

It's fine. You're fine.

She saw him then; a boy inside the yard, standing close to the fence. He was looking straight at her.

He saw me.

Or did he? It was dark, and he was far enough away that Nova couldn't even see his face. How could she be sure he saw her? No one else had reacted to her fall, and she hadn't been far outside the tree line, a couple of feet at most.

There was no way he could see her. She was imagining it.

She turned, heading back the way she had come, doing everything she could to fight the feeling he was watching her leave.

CHAPTER ELEVEN

Coming Clean

When Nova woke up the next morning, it wasn't suddenly from a bad dream, but slowly, with the sunlight from the window warming her face. For a moment, she felt utterly relaxed. She was warm, comfortable, and completely at ease.

Her moment of serenity was shattered when she rolled onto her side and saw someone standing inches from her bed. She jolted upright. "You almost gave me a heart attack!"

Kate crossed her arms, causing Colin the tarantula to almost lose his footing on her shoulder. "I didn't want to wake you. I thought you might need sleep after your busy night."

Nova swallowed, her throat suddenly dry. "What do you mean?"

"Your night-time stroll through the woods. Come on, Nova, did you think I wouldn't know? I have eyes everywhere."

This took a minute to process, and then Nova understood. "The bugs?"

Kate nodded. "I heard you leave, and sent a couple of friends to check you were okay." She paused, eyes flicking around the empty dorm before asking: "Why did you go to the Tombs?"

"I...wanted to see the place up close. Call it morbid curiosity." It sounded even less believable out loud than it had done in Nova's head.

Kate snorted. "You're a terrible liar." Without waiting for a response, she motioned for Nova to get up. "Come on, we need to get ready, or we'll miss breakfast."

Nova sheepishly got dressed, and the two of them left the dorm.

"Did the bugs tell you where I was?" Nova asked, as they headed downstairs.

"They don't *tell* me anything," Kate replied. "It's more like images, a feeling. It's hard to explain."

It didn't sound like she wanted to explain, either. Kate was clearly angry at her for sneaking out. Nova couldn't believe she'd only been at Tidemarsh one day, and already upset the first real friend she'd had since...well...ever.

They went into the bathroom, which wasn't quite as busy as it had been yesterday. Nova found an empty sink at the end of the row. Her mind was racing with what she could say to get Kate back on side, as she reached into her new wash bag without looking. Her fingers brushed against something slimy, and she whipped her hand out as though it had been scalded. Slowly, she looked inside. Instead of her toothbrush, there was only a long, black slug.

Nova turned to Kate, trying to keep the hurt out of her voice. "Did you put this in here?"

Kate glanced into the bag. "No, it wasn't me." She turned, yelling across the bathroom: "Beth!"

Beth hurried over. "Oh shoot," she groaned. "I thought I'd finally got it figured out." She scooped the slug out of the bag and tossed it casually towards the showers, ignoring the scream of the girl whose stall it rolled into. Then she took Nova's hand, ran her own over the top, and another toothbrush appeared.

"I don't know why. Sometimes they just turn into slugs," she said thoughtfully, and then gave Nova a smile. "Hopefully it sticks this time."

Once Beth had walked away, Nova looked at Kate with wide eyes. "I don't want to put that in my mouth."

Kate wrinkled her nose. "I don't blame you."

After going to the front desk and getting a new toothbrush, Nova quickly showered and got dressed. Then she and Kate headed over to breakfast.

"I'm sorry," Kate said as they sat down at an empty table. "I didn't mean to be so moody with you earlier."

"It's alright," Nova replied.

"No, it's not," Kate insisted. "I was upset because when I saw you had gone, I thought maybe you were running away."

Nova sighed. "I was. Well...I thought about it."

"You don't like it here?"

Nova looked down at her breakfast. "It's not that. To be honest, the people here are probably nicer than anyone else I've been around for a while."

"What, then?" Kate asked. "And why did you go down to the Tombs?"

Nova glanced around. There was no one else at their

table; it was safe to talk. "If I tell you, you have to promise not to tell anyone."

"I promise," Kate said.

"And you have to promise you'll still like me."

"Of course."

"And promise you won't look at me differentl-"

Kate rolled her eyes. "Oh my god, just tell me."

Nova took a deep breath. "When Elizabeth found me, it was because I'd used my abilities for the first time. And I...I killed someone."

To Kate's credit, she didn't even flinch. "Who?"

"My step-father."

"How?"

"I blew him up."

Kate gritted her teeth. "Ouch."

"Yeah."

"That's your ability?"

"I guess so."

"Wow." Kate turned back to her tray, taking a bite of her toast. "Did you start the maths homework yet?"

Nova blinked. "That's it? You don't have any more questions?"

"About your stepdad?"

"About...about *any* of what I just said?"

"No," Kate answered, simply. "You're not in the Tombs, so clearly Elizabeth doesn't think you're a psycho." She cocked her head to one side, thoughtfully. "That's why you went down there, right? To see if you're like the crazies they keep locked away?"

"I guess."

Kate furrowed her brow. "You're not like them, though. You know that, right?"

"How can you be so sure?"

"Did you enjoy it? Killing him?"

"No," Nova answered quickly. Maybe too quickly.

Kate shrugged. "Then you're not like them. Those kids, they're damaged. They see hurt and pain, and they laugh. They enjoy the destruction. I've only known you a day, but I can tell you're not like that." She gave a small smile. "So, relax, you're not getting locked in the nuthouse any time soon. And no more running away, got it?"

"You'd miss me?" Nova teased.

Kate's grin widened. "Don't get cocky."

Their conversation was interrupted by Luke, who dropped into the chair opposite Kate and offered to brown her toast some more. He turned it to ash within seconds, and Nova spent the next 10 minutes listening to the pair of them argue about it.

She supposed Kate was right. Although she didn't feel particularly sorry for what had happened to Gary, she hadn't enjoyed it.

Not really.

Something from the night before popped into her head, and she interrupted the argument at the table. "Do either of you know a girl called Angela?"

Luke arched an eyebrow quizzically. "Angela?"

"Yeah, someone said she came from the Tombs."

Kate sighed – clearly not thrilled that Nova was already back to that place – but turned in her chair to look around the room. "She's the one over there with all the hair."

Nova followed her gaze. At the furthest corner of the

room, sitting on her own, was a skinny girl with thick, frizzy, black curls. She appeared to be in her own world, speaking slowly even though she was sitting alone. At first, Nova wondered if Danny was with her, then spotted him laughing with some boys at a different table.

"Who is she talking to?" Nova asked. "Are there other people who can become invisible besides Danny?"

"How do you know Danny?" Kate asked, arching a brow.

"I met him last night. In the woods."

Luke's eyes widened. "You were in the woods last night?"

Nova ignored him. "Who's Angela talking to?"

"No one," Kate answered. "Danny's the only invisible kid at Tidemarsh right now."

"So, she's talking to herself?" Nova asked, watching Angela's lips move rapidly. Whatever she was saying, she was saying it in a hurry.

"She's always talking to herself," Luke replied. "She's weird. Who knows why they ever let her out of that place."

"They don't keep kids down there because they're *weird*," Kate snapped. "If they let her out, then she's not dangerous, and if she's not dangerous, then she can be up here with the rest of us."

Luke didn't look altogether convinced, but said nothing.

The three of them finished breakfast, and then took their trays over to the drop-off. As they passed Angela, Nova heard snippets of the things she was muttering.

"Through the skin...right inside...doesn't feel like anything...warm though..."

Angela put her hand through the table, as if it wasn't even there, and then pulled it back again. After a few seconds she noticed Nova watching, and a cloudy expression crossed her face.

"What?" she asked, irritably.

Kate took Nova's arm. "Come on, let's go."

The girls left Luke talking with some other guys at a nearby table, and walked across the courtyard to their first class. The day was mild, though the sky had already turned grey. The air felt heavy, as though a storm was closing in.

"You don't want to get on Angela's bad side," Kate said.

"Why?" Nova asked, watching as a boy up ahead walked to class on his hands. Was that an ability, or a party trick?

"You said it yourself," Kate replied. "She used to be in the Tombs."

"You said she's not dangerous; otherwise they wouldn't have let her out."

Kate shook her head. "I just said that to stop Luke being cruel about her. I still think she's dangerous. You saw the way she was muttering." Kate shuddered. "Just between us, she gives me the creeps."

Nova didn't have much more time to think about the strange girl that morning. Her classes were intense, and kept her mind off Angela, Elizabeth, and her own escape attempt from the night before. Later though, halfway through English, a kid arrived with a note for the teacher. Nova had been summoned to Elizabeth's office.

Everyone turned in their chairs to look at her, as if trying to decipher what terrible thing she had done to be pulled out of class so suddenly. Nova got the distinct impression that, though Elizabeth seemed perfectly nice, a lot of the kids at Tidemarsh either didn't like her, or were afraid of her.

Nova got to her feet, and followed the boy out of the room.

Why did Elizabeth want to see her? Did she know about Nova's night-time stroll through the woods? Her visit to the Tombs? What actually happened to kids who left their dorm after lights-out?

At the end of a long hallway, she and the boy stopped outside a door. It had Elizabeth's name stamped onto the frosted glass.

"Good luck," the kid muttered, and Nova noticed for the first time that he had another eye right in the middle of his forehead.

How the hell did I miss that?

"T-thanks," she said, unsure which one she should actually be looking at when she spoke to him. It didn't matter, he turned and headed in the opposite direction, leaving her alone in the corridor. Nova took a breath, and then knocked on the door.

"Come in."

The office was smaller than Ms. Juniper's, though equally bright and cheerful. There was a small desk with a computer, several filing cabinets, a bookcase, a door to what she assumed was a wardrobe, and a slightly worn-looking green sofa.

Elizabeth was at her desk, typing on her computer. There was a small tray in front of her, containing an untouched croissant and a glass of orange juice.

"Good morning," she said. "Thank you for coming."

Nova wasn't aware she'd had much choice in the matter.

Elizabeth gestured to the chair on the other side of her desk, "Please, take a seat."

Nova sat down, stomach still churning. What would happen to her if Elizabeth knew where she'd been last night? If she knew she'd been planning to escape? Was it a big deal? Danny had been out too, and he didn't seem too worried. Maybe it wasn't even against the rules?

That felt unlikely.

Elizabeth finished what she was typing, then put a hand on the tray. The whole thing disappeared.

"Not hungry?" Nova asked.

Elizabeth glanced down at where the tray had been, as if she hadn't realised she had vanished it. "Oh, no. I already ate. Ms. Juniper is constantly getting the kitchen to send me extra food. She says I don't eat enough." She lowered her voice to a whisper, as if sharing a secret. "That woman is like a dog with a bone sometimes." She smiled. "Nova, I owe you an apology."

"For what?"

"For behaving so poorly when you asked me about your father. It's only natural that you'd have questions, and it was absolutely wrong of me to handle it like that."

Relief flooded Nova's veins. She wasn't in trouble. Elizabeth didn't know about last night. She wanted to talk about her dad. Nova wanted that too.

"That's alright," she said, shoulders relaxing.

Elizabeth tipped her head. "You're too kind. But you have questions, and I'd like to answer them. Let me start by explaining my reaction yesterday. I knew your father from our time together at Tidemarsh. In fact, he and your mother were among my closest friends."

"He was an Alternate too?"

"Yes."

"What could he do?"

Elizabeth smiled again. "He could fly."

Nova wanted to be happy about learning this. She wanted to enjoy finding out about her father, yet it felt like her time for curiosity had come and gone many years ago. Elizabeth may as well have been telling her about a stranger.

"He and my mum were friends?" she eventually asked. "From the way she spoke about him, or didn't, I guess I thought he was someone she barely knew."

"They were friends, and then they were a couple." Elizabeth looked wistful. "It was like they were made for each other. Liara never laughed so much as she did when they were together. And when Rick looked at her...it was as though the rest of the world was black and white, and she was technicolour."

"I don't understand," Nova said. "If they were so great together, where is he? Why wasn't he there when I was growing up? Why did he leave?" Her words were coming out faster, and much more sharply, than she had anticipated. Perhaps she cared more than she thought? Maybe it wouldn't be so bad to have a father out there?

Elizabeth took a breath. "He didn't leave. He died, only a few months before you were born."

The brief bubble of hope that had been growing in Nova's chest disappeared with a pop. "Oh. How?"

"He was killed by another Alternate. It's...still too

painful to talk about. I will tell you, I promise, but I need a little more time, if that's okay?"

"Okay," Nova said, absently. "Why didn't my mum talk about him? Why did I never see any pictures? I mean, until a minute ago I didn't even know his *name*."

Elizabeth sighed. "On that, I can only speculate. After he died, your mum and I lost touch for a while. She cut herself off from our community, and none of us wanted to push her while she was vulnerable and lose her entirely. She would write letters occasionally but refused to see anyone in person. I knew she needed space, so I wrote to her instead. She let me know that you'd been born, and about her hopes for your future, but she never spoke of Rick, and so I never asked. I guess losing him was so painful that she found it easier to pretend he never existed in the first place."

"She was really good at that," Nova muttered. "She didn't talk about him at all, other than to tell me he left and we didn't need him."

Elizabeth reached across the desk, squeezing Nova's hand. "I'm not saying I *agree* with her choice, only that I understand why she did it. After a few years of rarely hearing from her, she told me she was getting married. I never received another letter. When I tried to visit, you had already moved away." She chewed her lip. "I wondered if maybe your stepfather had forbidden her from speaking to us anymore."

"Maybe," Nova muttered. "He was an idiot. I don't know why she married him."

"People make bad choices for love," Elizabeth said, thoughtfully.

"I guess they do."

They sat in silence for a few minutes, before Elizabeth asked: "Is there anything else you'd like to know right now?"

"Do you have any pictures of him? My dad."

Elizabeth smiled. "Yes." She reached into one of her desk drawers, and brought out a photograph, sliding it across the table. In the picture was Elizabeth, Nova's mom, and a boy. All of them looked around 16 or 17. They were grinning widely, with Nova's mum in the middle, and Elizabeth and Rick on the outside, with their arms around her shoulders.

"He has brown eyes," Nova said. Hers were brown too. Her mother's had been blue.

I have my dad's eyes. Even the thought sounded weird.

"You look a lot like him," Elizabeth said.

Nova swallowed. "I think I need some time to process this, if that's alright?"

"Of course, take as long as you need. You can come back and see me any time."

Nova put her hand on the photo, stroking her mother's face. "Can I borrow this?"

"Keep it. When you're ready, I'll show you the others."

Nova pocketed the picture. "Thanks." She got to her feet, and walked back to the door.

"Nova," Elizabeth said. "I know you must feel very alone, without your mum or dad, but I want you to know that we all care for you a great deal. If you let us, we can be your family."

CHAPTER TWELVE

Better Than Freaks

"Good morning, everyone. We have a new student in our mastery Class. This is Nova." The teacher smiled warmly. "It's so lovely to have you here with us."

The other kids, all sitting on chairs in a circle in the centre of the room, regarded Nova curiously, and her stomach sank. Most of them looked no older than 13 or 14. She supposed most of the students her age were probably a lot further along in their Alternate education, and no longer required an 'Introduction to your Abilities' class. There were a few kids who looked closer to her age, but she was clearly one of the oldest ones there.

"Please, take a seat," Miss Garrett said, gesturing to an empty chair in the circle, and taking her own spot between red-headed twins. She was probably one of the youngest teachers Nova had seen at Tidemarsh so far, with a pretty face and bright green eyes. Her brown hair reached her shoulders, and she wore a silver stud in her nose. "Why don't you start by talking us through your ability?" Her voice was soft, almost motherly, despite how young she looked. She reminded Nova of her old kindergarten teacher.

Nova wrung her hands together on her lap. "I'd rather not."

Miss Garrett gave her a sympathetic smile. "That's normal, sometimes what we can do feels intense and frightening. Try to think of this room as a safe space. Perhaps the rest of the class could talk about their own abilities, to help you feel more comfortable?" Without waiting for a reply, she gestured to the boy on Nova's left. He was wearing thick black motorcycle gloves, even though it was stiflingly warm in the classroom, and looked closer to her age than any of the other kids.

"Jason, why don't you start?"

Jason shrugged. It was clear he'd rather do anything else.

"Show us, then," one of the twins called over.

Miss Garrett's eyes widened. "Oh, I'm not sure that's-"

"Yeah, show us!" jeered the other twin.

Jason yanked off one of his gloves, and reached behind him to put his hand on the nearest table. The instant he touched it, it turned to sand, which hung in the air for half a second, before landing in a pile on the floor.

"Ta da," he muttered, slipping his glove back on.

Miss Garrett could barely keep the disappointment out of her voice. "Thank you, Jason. Perhaps next time you could choose something smaller for your demonstration?"

He shrugged again.

The teacher moved on, though slightly less upbeat than before. "Okay, Sarah, how about you go next?"

A girl with long braids closed her eyes. After a couple of seconds her braids began to get shorter and shorter, as if they were being sucked into her head. Then they were gone, with long golden curls shooting out to take their place. There was still a single braid in the middle, and the girl scowled when she caught sight of it.

"I still can't do the whole head," she muttered.

Next was a girl who could stretch her limbs, though hadn't quite mastered getting them back to their regular size. Her left arm was still halfway across the room when Miss Garrett moved on to the next student. That was a boy who could turn into a horse, though his head remained human, which was rather terrifying to look at.

There was a girl who could shoot bubbles from her fingertips, which let out an awful smell of rotting eggs when they popped, and a boy who could apparently speak every single language that had ever existed, but couldn't control which one he used each time he opened his mouth.

Nova was starting to understand why she was in this class.

The next person should have been one of the red-headed twins, but Miss Garrett ignored him, and instead spoke to his brother.

"Mark, why don't you talk us through your power?"

"Sure thing," replied the one she'd ignored.

"I can make copies of myself," said the one called Mark.

"The most I've ever made is 10," the other said.

"It gets harder the more I make," said another one, who was identical to the first two, and stepped right out of Mark's body. Another followed.

"I can make them all talk, but they're not solid."

Mark got up, and his three copies followed. He tapped on the wall, but when the others tried to do the same, their hands went straight through. He clapped his hands, and one after another they flew back into his body and disappeared.

Nova was so caught up trying to process what she'd seen, that she barely registered they were back round to her again. Everyone was waiting expectantly.

"I don't know exactly how to explain what my ability is," she began, carefully. "Only that it feels dangerous. It's worse when I'm angry and it's made me...people have got hurt."

Miss Garrett nodded. "It's very common for our powers to manifest themselves when we feel extremes of emotion: anger, fear, happiness. All of those are what we call triggers. What we learn here, in mastery Class, is not simply how to manage our abilities during these triggering moments, but also how to use them at will, not simply when we feel we have no choice."

"I'm not sure my power is one I want to use ever again," Nova said, quietly.

"Everything has its use," Miss Garrett said, gently. "For today, though, let's take a break from practical work."

The door to the classroom swung open, and Angela – the girl who had been talking to herself at breakfast – walked inside.

"Sorry I'm late," she said dreamily. "I didn't want to come."

Miss Garrett, unaffected by this comment, gestured to another empty chair. "That's alright Angela, it's always lovely to have you." She brought her attention back to the class. "Let's start with something simple. Pair up, and list together the emotions or events that you feel are triggering for you. These can be big or small, and you don't have to share anything you're not comfortable with."

Everyone hurried to find a partner, and Nova soon realised that their haste was because none of them wanted Angela. In fact, Mark paired with himself to avoid being left with her, and within a minute it was only Nova and Angela still seated.

Miss Garrett looked over. "Why don't the two of you work together at that desk by the window?"

Nova stepped over the pile of sand and walked to the empty table. Angela trudged over too, dropping down into the seat opposite. Neither spoke for what felt like a very long time. Minutes ticked by; five, 10, 15. Their paper was startlingly blank, and Nova watched those around her talking animatedly and scribbling down ideas.

"I guess we should do this," she said, trying to keep her voice upbeat.

"Probably," Angela mumbled.

"We don't want to be the only ones with nothing at the end of class."

"Nope."

"I'm Nova, by the way."

"Okay."

This conversation was trickier than Nova expected. She took another stab at it. "And you're Angela?"

"I know."

"I know...it's just that usually when...never mind."

"What's your ability?" Angela asked, sounding more bored than curious.

"I don't like to talk about it."

"Why?"

Nova chose her words carefully. "Because it makes me uncomfortable."

"Why?"

Nova decided she liked Angela better when she didn't talk. "Because it's dangerous."

"Have you killed anyone?"

Who just asks someone that?

Angela had already lost interest, her eyes glazing dreamily. "I've killed someone. It was weird. Good-weird."

Nova glanced down at their blank paper. She got the feeling they weren't going to excel in today's class. Maybe it was worth following a different route.

"Is that why you were in the Tombs?" she asked.

"Yes."

"How did you get out?"

"I didn't want to be bad anymore."

Nova glanced around, then asked: "What's it like in there?"

Angela's whole body stiffened in an instant. Without another word she got up and left the room.

Miss Garrett was standing where the pile of sand had been, but it was gone, and the table was back. She watched Angela leave, sighed, and then gave Nova a reassuring smile.

"Don't worry, it wasn't your fault."

But Nova knew that wasn't true.

Later that evening, when she and Kate arrived back in the dorm building, there was a stream of kids darting through the door to the right of the stairs. There were excited voices coming from inside, and the girls followed the crowd.

The room was small, with several patched but comfy

looking sofas pointed at a TV that had to be at least 15 years old. The seats were all taken, and there were more kids were sitting on the floor. Nova saw they were watching the news.

"What's going on?" Kate asked Luke, who was standing behind the nearest sofa.

"Something's happened," he said, pointing to the screen as the newscaster cut to some footage. A building was on fire, blazing out of control, and appeared only seconds from falling down. Someone was yelling in a language Nova didn't recognise from behind the camera. A man ran into the building, straight through the flames. Nova gasped, and several of the kids on the floor covered their eyes.

A minute or so passed, and the room was silent as they watched the flames at the door. The TV crackled, and the picture disappeared. Several kids cried out, and a boy banged on the top of the TV.

"Why is everything in this place such a pile of shit?" he mumbled, banging once more.

The picture returned, as the man came back out of the burning building. He was holding a small child to his chest, wrapped in a blanket. His own clothes had almost completely burned away, but his skin was unmarked.

"How is that possible?" Kate asked.

"He's one of us," a girl said from the carpet.

The footage ended, and it was back to the studio. The female presenter said: "Despite an extensive search for the man everyone is calling 'The Firewalker', no one has been able to find out who he is, or how he managed to survive walking into the flames." She gave a little smile. "Doctors report that the boy is doing well in hospital, thanks to this hero."

"Do you know what this means?" Danny asked. Nova hadn't realised he was standing beside her, even though he wasn't invisible right now. "He's one of us. He showed himself to the world, and they think he's a hero!"

Kate snorted. "Is that what we are? Superheroes?"

"It's better than freaks."

CHAPTER THIRTEEN

Rise And Shine

Nova was being dragged down the long, dark, corridor. The screams around her were louder tonight. She fought back, tears streaming down her cheeks.

"Let me go!" she yelled. Her captor, dragging her through the shadows, ignored her pleas. She was being pulled towards the door at the end of the corridor, and she fought back. She knew what was behind it.

"I'm sorry," came a voice from the darkness.

It was no use fighting. The person dragging her forwards was stronger. They reached the door and it swung open.

"Hello sweetheart."

Nova sat up. She was drenched in sweat, heart racing. In seconds she was out of the bed and dressed. The dream had felt so much more real; the walls pressing down on her, the choking darkness, Gary's grinning face. There was no way she was going back to sleep. She needed to get outside, to see the sky, to feel fresh air on her skin. To breathe.

She headed down the stairs as she had done the previous evening. Thankfully, they were free from Madeline and her boyfriend tonight. When she reached the bottom, however, she saw Mr. and Mrs. Driver behind the desk, watching the tiny TV. Tonight, there was no flood to distract them. How would Nova get outside?

She glanced around, searching for inspiration, and noticed a door under the staircase. It was either another exit, or a broom cupboard. There was only one way to know for sure. She tiptoed over and edged it open. It wasn't a cupboard; it led to a long thin corridor. She hurried through.

She passed doors with signs that said 'maintenance', 'laundry', and 'office'. Finally, at the very end, she found the back exit of the building.

Getting outside was exactly what Nova needed. The cool air whipped her hair across her face, blowing away the last fragments of the dream. The sky was cloudless, despite how heavy the day had felt, and as Nova looked up at the huge expanse of nothingness and stars above her, she felt slightly giddy. She liked it. When she was a kid, after the hardest days, she used to sneak out of her bedroom window and lie on the garage roof, staring up at the night sky. It reminded her she was only one tiny dot in a sea of other tiny dots: insignificant to the universe itself. It always made her feel like none of her worries or stresses were really so huge.

Though she had planned to head back inside after getting some air, Nova found herself walking in the opposite direction; over to the woods. It was like her feet were in control, and she was simply along for the ride. In the back of her mind, she knew exactly where she was going. Why did she feel like she had to see the Tombs again? Maybe it had something to do with speaking to Angela. She wanted to look at the kids in the yard one more time, to remind herself that she was where she belonged; that she wasn't meant to be in that prison.

Despite the darkness, and her notoriously hideous sense of direction, Nova managed to retrace her footsteps from the night before, and was back at the fallen log within no time.

There were kids outside in the yard, around the same number as yesterday. Were they the same ones? Danny said it was the most dangerous residents who came out this late, so it was likely to be the same group. Like yesterday, they were walking laps, or standing in small clusters, though there were a few on their own.

Nova wanted to get close enough to hear them speaking to each other. She wanted to know what killers talked about. Keeping to the cover of the trees, she moved closer, until she was at the portion of the fence that met the tree line. She found a spot a few feet from the chain link, sheltered by the darkness of the woods, where she could watch and listen without being seen.

To her disappointment, after nearly an hour, none of the groups had moved close enough to the fence for her to overhear anything.

What were you hoping for? A bunch of kids talking about how fun it is to murder people, just to prove to yourself that they deserve to be down here more than you do?

Nova brushed the dirt from her legs, and got to her feet. After one last look back at the fence, she returned to her dorm. This whole thing had been ridiculous. She shouldn't come back again. She wouldn't.

Probably.

She was woken up the following morning by Orlaith yelling from across the room.

"Elizabeth is coming!"

"Are you sure?" Beth asked.

"Definitely! We've got 30 seconds, tops!"

The room erupted with movement. Girls jumped out of bed, and seemed to be running in all directions. Nova had no idea why they were so panicked, and all she could do was watch.

Ria was scrabbling around under her mattress, and came out with several packs of cigarettes. She held them in her hands and yelled: "Someone get me a jar!"

Orlaith called over to her. "Don't! The last time you did that the damn things tasted awful after you turned them back!"

"You want Elizabeth to find them?" Ria snapped.

"I've got a jar in my wardrobe."

There was a thud, and Nova looked over to Kate's bed. On the floor next to it, rubbing his head and wearing only a pair of boxer shorts, was a boy Nova vaguely recognised from their maths class.

He groaned. "Kate, what the hell?"

"Shut up and get out!" She tossed his t-shirt and jeans at him.

He yanked them on hurriedly. "Can we do this agai-"

"Go!"

Orlaith yelled: "She's on the stairs!"

Kate swore loudly. Jasminder ran over, putting a hand on the boy's shoulder. "Here, let me."

His eyes widened. "Wait-"

He didn't get the chance to finish, because at that

moment he fell through the floor as if it wasn't there. There were sounds of commotion from the room beneath them.

"I'm pretty sure that's his dorm," Jasminder said, thoughtfully.

Kate pulled her hair into a ponytail. "He'll be fine."

Beth and Laura were hiding bottles of a glowing green liquid in Beth's wardrobe, and Isabella was shushing a cardboard box, which was making an alarming hissing sound. Even Madeline looked nervous as she shoved something hastily under her pillow.

"Quiet!" hissed Orlaith.

Everyone was back in their beds in seconds. Nova copied the others and pretended to be asleep as she heard the door open.

"Good morning, girls," came Elizabeth's voice.

There were dramatic yawns and eye rubbing around the room, as each girl slowly sat up.

"What time is it?" Beth mumbled, sleepily.

"I'm so tired," yawned Meredith.

Nova wasn't sure if Elizabeth was buying it. If she doubted their sincerity, though, she wasn't saying anything yet.

"I'm sorry to have to start the day like this," Elizabeth began, ignoring the lone butterfly that had somehow avoided the jar and fluttered past her head. "However, I need to talk to all of you about something serious."

Nova swallowed. Did Elizabeth know that she'd snuck out again last night?

"You are all well aware that leaving the dorm after lights out is strictly against school rules."

Nova steadied her breathing, preparing herself for

whatever came next. How bad could the punishment be? Kids didn't get sent to the Tombs for sneaking out after bedtime, right?

"You are also all aware that the pool is out of bounds when there is no teacher to supervise. This is for *your* safety."

The pool?

Elizabeth crossed her arms. "If anyone in here knows *anything* about where the water in the pool went, I suggest they speak up."

Nova's muscles relaxed. It wasn't about her; she was in the clear.

She looked over to Kate, planning to pull a face at the idea of some kid draining the pool for a prank, but her friend's focus was on the floor next to her bed. There, out in the open like a flattened snake, was a lone boy's sock.

"Well?" Elizabeth asked. She began to walk down the centre of the room. "Does anyone know anything?"

Nova watched as the sock began to move. There had to be ants or spiders, or something small underneath it, carrying it back towards Kate's bed. At the rate it was moving, however, and the speed Elizabeth was walking, there was a good chance she'd see it before the bugs got it out of sight. Nova had to do something; she wanted to help.

Elizabeth was a few feet away, when Nova asked, innocently: "How could the water disappear?"

Elizabeth paused, her expression softening as she turned toward Nova. "There are some children at Tidemarsh who can control elements, such as water. In theory, it wouldn't be too difficult for them to pull off."

The sock was almost out of sight. Nova continued. "I don't think anyone in here has that ability, though?"

"Maybe not," Elizabeth agreed. "But that doesn't mean there isn't anyone in here who knows something."

The sock was gone, which was lucky, because at that moment Elizabeth glanced over at Kate. "Some of the girls in this dorm have lots of...friends."

Kate kept her face impassive, almost bored, watching the butterfly as it did another circuit of the room. When no one else said anything, Elizabeth sighed.

"Very well. If any of you learn anything about what happened last night, please come to my office today. You all know how much I value honesty." She walked back to the door, which was good timing, because green sludge was beginning to drip out of the bottom of Beth's wardrobe. Beth met Nova's eye, gritting her teeth.

"Enjoy your day, girls," said Elizabeth, reaching for the door handle.

The butterfly flew past her, set to do another lap of the room, when she caught it in mid-air. She glanced at it briefly, then held it up. Nova saw that it was no longer a butterfly, but a cigarette with wings.

"Shit," Ria muttered.

Elizabeth put the cigar-fly in her pocket. "Ria, I'll see you in my office before class."

"Yes Miss Perrin."

Elizabeth left the room. The dorm was silent while the girls waited.

"She's gone," Orlaith said, a minute later.

The girls began talking, pulling their contraband out of its hiding places, and getting ready for the day. Beth and

Laura opened the wardrobe gingerly, as a flood of green liquid washed over their feet.

"This is safe, right?" Beth asked.

"Sure, yeah, I think so," Laura replied. "I mean, I've not tested it on human skin yet, but-"

"Laura, are you kidding me?"

Isabella was cooing at the shoebox, which had started hissing again, and Madeline slipped something that looked suspiciously like a phone out from under her pillow and into her pocket.

Kate came over as Nova got out of the other side of her bed, not wanting to risk the 'probably safe' green goo.

"Thanks," Kate said.

"No problem."

"That was close. We're not exactly allowed to have boys in the dorm."

Nova laughed. "I gathered that from the way you shoved him out of your bed."

Kate grinned. "I owe you one. I promise I'll return the favour somehow if you have a male guest."

Nova stifled a snort. What were the chances of that ever happening? Boys found her aloof at best, weird most of the time, and – on occasion – kind of scary. Even in a place like this, filled with people exactly like her –

Correction: not exactly like me. None of these girls accidentally blow people up.

She doubted she'd be fighting them off. She didn't have that cool, attractive, I'm-on-top-of-my-superpowers thing going on that so many of the girls here had. She was just as awkward and uncomfortable as she always had been.

Kate misread her reaction. "You're not into boys?

That'll make things easier if you decide to bring anyone back. Though take my advice: don't hook up with anyone in this dorm, you don't want that kind of drama."

"Oh, no, it's not that. I just don't exactly have a lot of experience..."

Or, you could say "no experience whatsoever".

Kate winked. "New school, new start. Though, to be honest, the pickings aren't exactly rich here. Don't expect to meet anyone who will change your world."

"He wasn't anyone special?" Nova asked, quirking her head towards the part of the floor the boy had disappeared through.

"No, but I'm not looking for love," Kate winked. "So that makes things a lot simpler."

CHAPTER FOURTEEN

A New Friend?

It had been pointless going down to the Tombs. Nova knew that. But for some reason, she returned the following night. Her experience was the same, a bunch of kids quietly spending time outside without doing anything remotely dangerous or interesting. Nova stayed an hour and then went back to her dorm. When she arrived, she found Kate also sneaking back to bed. Neither asked where the other had been, though Kate gave her a smile that suggested she had a theory.

At breakfast the following morning, she shared it.

"So, did you follow my lead and lower your standards?"

"Huh?" Nova asked.

"Last night," Kate said. "That was the walk of shame, right?"

Nova was confused. "The walk of what?"

"The walk of...never mind. I'm asking if you were with a boy."

"No, I told you, guys aren't into me."

"You've not had a boyfriend before?" Kate asked.

Or kissed a guy. Or even held their hand.

"No."

"Based on my evening, please believe me when I tell you, you're not missing out. I sometimes wonder if these guys have taken a single biology class in their entire lives." Kate grinned, then took a sip of her juice. "So, what *were* you doing last night?"

Nova crinkled her nose. "You're not going to like it."

She was right; Kate hadn't liked it at all. As soon as Nova mentioned the Tombs, her friend had groaned in frustration. Kate talked for 10 minutes about how dangerous this new hobby was, and Nova promised she'd try her best not to go back again.

Unfortunately, she wasn't trying very hard. It was now Friday, and for the fourth night in a row Nova had found herself in the woods. Kate hadn't been in bed when she left, so Nova hadn't had to face her questions at least. All she could do was hope she'd still be out by the time Nova got back. Then she'd never know. Unless a worm told her or something.

Nova reached her spot by the fence in record time, and made herself comfortable sitting with her back against a tree. It had a groove in the bark, which meant she was practically tucked inside it, concealing her even more from view.

She watched as some kids passed by close to the fence, talking cheerfully. Nova had begun to recognise them now. It was definitely the same group she'd seen each time she'd visited. This little troupe was led by a girl around her age with long, cherry-red hair. She was the only one talking. The three following her were silent, and wore sour expressions. They passed by Nova without so much as a glance in her direction. She knew they would walk laps for the whole time they were outside, she had seen them do it the night before. In fact, most of the kids seemed to stick with the same habits. The ones who walked, did it for the entirety of their time outside, likewise the ones who sat on the benches stayed there. The groups didn't mix, and the loners stayed alone.

He was there again. She was pretty sure he was the same boy she'd spotted when she'd come down with Danny. She had seen him the previous two evenings as well, though not paid him much attention. The only reason she noticed him now, was because it dawned on her that he'd been standing in the same place every night, around 20 feet from where she was sitting. He was facing her portion of the fence, but unless he had night vision – which, when she thought about it, wasn't exactly out of the question – she was confident he didn't know she was there.

Why is he alone? Doesn't he have friends?

He was standing in front of one of the spotlights, with the light shining behind him. It cast shadows on his features, so all Nova could gleam about his appearance was that he was tall, broad-shouldered, and kind of creeping her out. She didn't know if it was the fact that she couldn't see his face, or that he never seemed to move, but something about him set her on edge.

She drew her eyes away, watching the other kids within the fence wander around aimlessly. Some came closer to where she was sitting tonight, and she was able to get a better look at them. She had noticed from her previous visits that alongside the orange trousers, white t-shirts, and brown coats that seemed to make up their uniform, almost all of them had thick metal collars around their necks. She had no idea what they were for.

Their conversations were mostly pretty standard for a bunch of teenagers; who they liked, who they didn't, what they hoped to eat the following day. There were, however, occasional treats.

"I'd love to stab her through the eye and see if she's still smiling then."

"And then I told him I'd burn his house to ashes if he didn't give me the last chip, and he laughed! You should've seen his face when the fire started."

What Nova found the most strange – other than those charming statements – was that the kids who talked about violence and killing were the only ones who sounded mildly cheerful. The rest spoke in low, flat voices; like they'd had the happiness stamped out of them a long time ago.

She didn't stay for as long that evening. The air was cold, and her bum quickly went numb. As she got to her feet, Nova told herself it was stupid to keep coming down to this place. Elizabeth and Ms. Juniper said she belonged with the other kids up the hill, so that needed to be good enough. Besides, she wasn't wandering around talking about how great it had been to blow Gary to bits. That had to be proof enough that she wasn't like these kids.

Feeling slightly more positive, she turned away from the fence, ready to walk back through the woods and leave the Tombs behind her for good.

That was when she heard the voice.

"You're leaving early today."

Nova spun around, scanning the yard. There was no one close enough to talk at that volume and have her hear.

No one except him. Her friend, the boy in the shadows. He was near enough to have said it.

Her mouth felt as though it was full of sand. Right now, she had three options: run away, talk back, or stand there like an idiot.

She chose option three.

The boy moved from his position, coming over to the section of the fence a few feet in front of her.

"Hello," he said.

Nova could finally see him clearly. In her head, she'd unconsciously built up a picture of 'the creepy boy who didn't move', but that picture looked nothing like the person in front of her. He was tall, with dark hair that reached his shoulders, and piercing eyes that were either blue or grey. Nova couldn't tell for sure in the low light. His sharp cheekbones and jawline made him look almost like a statue; like he'd been chiselled out of marble by someone whose only instruction was 'make him handsome'.

And they had done a good job. Nova was fairly confident that – had he walked into her old school – he would've had every girl following him around with puppy-dog eyes within 10 minutes.

However, there were some dents in the otherwise perfect packaging. This boy clearly hadn't seen the sun in a long time. His skin was pale, which emphasised the dark circles around his eyes, as if he hadn't slept in weeks. That, coupled with the fact that he had barely blinked since he had said hello, gave him an intensity that made Nova uneasy.

His voice was smooth. "My ability isn't telepathy. If you'd like us to talk, you'll have to open your mouth."

At that moment Nova – the person who could never shut up when she was nervous – found herself lost for words.

"Are you going to speak?" he asked. When she didn't respond he added: "No one can hear us."

As if on cue, there were sounds of commotion by the back doors of the Tombs. Two of the kids were fighting. There were no abilities involved; they were wrestling each other, throwing punches and kicks while a small crowd gathered around them, cheering and laughing.

"If you'd like to chat, now is the perfect time," the boy continued, holding his hands up.

"Chat?" Nova's voice was a croak.

"Talk. Gossip. Chew the fat. I don't mind what you want to call it."

Nova swallowed. "Why do you want to talk to me?"

"You've come here four times, mostly on your own. I have to assume you have questions about the Tombs?" He cocked his head curiously. "This place doesn't scare you?"

"I don't want to get caught," Nova admitted. "If the guards see me down here-"

"I'm not sure it's the guards you should be afraid of," he said, his lips twitching for half a second.

Nova's heart felt like it was about to smash its way out of her chest. Was he threatening her?

"What do you mean?" she asked.

He paused, then answered simply: "Most of the students at Tidemarsh are frightened of *us*. They don't come down here. It makes me wonder if you're brave, or something else." He had a strange way of speaking; clipped and old-fashioned. Like he'd just stepped off the set of a period drama.

Nova's feet were lead. It didn't matter whether she wanted to leave or not; right now, she wasn't going anywhere. "Should I be afraid of you?" she whispered.

He grinned. "I think the more interesting question is: should *I* be afraid of *you*?"

"What?"

"Alright freaks, back into your caves!" It was one of the guards. The fight had been broken up. The other kids began to head back to the doors.

The boy took a step back.

"Wait," Nova said, stepping forward and curling her fingers around the chain link fence. "I don't understand."

"I'll see you tomorrow," he said, turning away and following the others.

"I'm not coming back," she insisted.

The boy didn't reply.

CHAPTER
FIFTEEN

No Running, No Splashing, No Electricution

"Are you okay?" Kate sounded concerned as she and Nova headed down to breakfast the following morning. "You're really quiet."

"I'm fine," Nova muttered.

"You're a terrible liar, you know?"

"I'm not."

"You are," Kate insisted. "You go all pale and blinky. And your voice gets weird."

Nova hastened to change the subject. "What do you think we're having for breakfast? I hope it's not that egg thing again, because I swear last time, I found..." she trailed off, noticing for the first time the red marks around Kate's lips They looked almost swollen. "What's that on your face?"

It was Kate's turn to fluster. "Nothing."

Nova blocked her friend's path on the stairs, leaning in to take a closer look. "Around your lips. Are those...are they burns?"

Kate made to step past. "I think we were talking about *you*. Or breakfast. Either one of those."

Nova wasn't going to give in that easily, and blocked her escape again. "How did you get burns around your mouth?" She gasped as the realization hit. "*Luke*! Were you kissing Luke?"

Kate sighed. "Yes." She carried on down the stairs, and Nova hurried to keep up.

"When did this happen?"

"Last night."

"Are you going to see him again?" Nova asked.

"Sure, in biology on Monday."

"Is he your boyfriend?"

Kate laughed. "Oh please."

"Do you like him?"

"Enough to kiss him it seems."

"Why didn't you tell me?"

Kate arched a brow. "I'm not sure you can throw that particular stone."

She had a point. If Nova was planning to keep quiet about her chat with the boy from the Tombs, she couldn't exactly expect her friend to spill her guts about her own night-time activities.

The cafeteria was emptier than usual. It was Saturday, and most of the other students were sleeping in, or had taken breakfast early to make the most of the sunshine. Kate and Nova grabbed their food and sat at their usual table.

"So," Kate said. "Are you going to tell me what's bothering you? Or do I need to get the mind-reading kid in here?"

Nova's eyes widened. "There's a kid who can read minds?"

"Yeah, she's creepy."

Nova gave in. There was no real reason to hide what had happened from Kate.

"You know where I've been going each night?" she began.

Kate buttered her toast briskly. "Of course, it's driving me insane."

"Yesterday, one of the kids down there spoke to me."

Kate stopped buttering. She glanced around, then leaned closer, lowering her voice. "Which one?"

"I don't know, he wasn't wearing a name tag."

"Didn't you ask him his name?"

"It was kind of a one-sided conversation," Nova admitted.

"What did he look like?"

"Tall, dark hair, kind of intense."

"Was he handsome?"

Nova rolled her eyes. "Really? That's your question?".

Kate grinned. "What did he say?"

Nova tried to find the words, but they eluded her. "It wasn't so much what he said, but what he *didn't* say."

"Deep," Kate said, sarcastically.

Nova continued. "It was strange. It was like he knew something about me. I don't know..." she trailed off. It sounded so stupid out loud.

"Do you think he was messing with you? I mean, those kids don't get to see new people that often. Maybe he wanted someone to talk to who wasn't a crazy murderer." Kate bit her lip. "Sorry, that sounded kind of-"

Nova cut her off. "It's fine."

"What are you going to do?"

"I'm going back there tonight." Though Nova hadn't admitted it to herself until that point, she knew she had no choice. She had to find out more about the boy, about how he seemed to know she'd done something terrible.

Kate groaned. "I really don't think that's a good idea. If he's one of them, he's dangerous. He could be planning something."

"He's behind a fence, what could he possibly do?"

"You'd be surprised."

The conversation was dropped when Ria and Orlaith joined their table. Once they had finished breakfast, Nova and Kate decided to spend their morning at the pool. Nova hadn't had a chance to use it yet, and apparently the water was back now. She had always enjoyed swimming. Barbara and Gary had constantly looked for ways to get her out of the house, and when they had lived near the beach, they would often drop her off in the morning, and return as it got dark. Nova had learned to love the water, otherwise she'd have been in for a rough time. Instead, they became some of her best memories – at least since her mum had died – because she hadn't needed to walk on eggshells all day. She'd swam, laid out in the sun, and when the owner of the ice cream shop came to recognise her, he'd come out every few hours with drinks and ice cream. It had been a good way to spend the summers.

The winters had been less fun, but she had gotten used to it. A good book and a warm coat had got her through those days.

When she and Kate arrived at the pool, they found it

bustling with kids. But, like everything at the Alternate Academy, things weren't exactly 'normal'. Among the people in the water, Nova could see a shark, a sea lion, a duck, and a dolphin. Several birds were flying overhead, and a huge shaggy dog almost knocked her into the pool as it charged past and threw itself into the deep end.

"The animal Alternates are always showing off," Kate said, hanging up her towel on one of the hooks on the wall. All of the kids had the same faded, scratchy white towels. Nova wondered how many years they had been floating around. They smelled clean, at least. She wore a dark blue one-piece swimming costume, as did the other girls around the pool – the ones that weren't animals, that is – and the boys wore dark blue trunks.

"I don't know," Kate continued. "Maybe some of the animal Alts can't control it, but most do it for attention."

It was certainly working – the kid who'd transformed into a shark had at least six girls squealing in delight as he or she swam in circles around them.

Animals weren't the only form of entertainment in the room. At the other end of the pool Nova could see the boy from the cafeteria, who had left puddles everywhere, shooting fountains of water into the air from his hands. The girl from her mastery Class was turning those fountains into bubbles, which floated up to the ceiling where they popped, and rained back down as water again. Either she'd gotten a handle on the egg smell, or the room was too big to notice.

Another boy and girl were having a race, running across the surface of the water as fast as they could, while the shark snapped at their toes. A girl in the shallows, who looked no older than 10, was creating huge waves by pulling up the water like a blanket and tossing it aside.

Miss Farley, the PE teacher, was sitting on a high life-guard chair, with a whistle in her mouth and her nose in a book. Every now and then she'd blow the whistle – for what appeared to be no reason other than to remind everyone that she was there – and it quickly became clear that she was more interested in her novel than what any of the kids were doing.

Nova and Kate swam for a while, but ultimately Nova was too distracted by the chaos to do anything other than sit on the edge of the pool and watch.

"I'm not sure I'll ever get used to this," she said, as a huge wave crashed into a nearby wall and exploded into a thousand tiny bubbles.

Miss Farley blew her whistle. "No splashing," she called absently, her eyes never leaving her page.

"I know, it's a bit much," Kate agreed, pulling herself up to sit beside her. "I felt the same when I got here too."

Nova realised she'd never asked Kate about her arrival at Tidemarsh. "Did you know you were different before you came?"

"Yeah," Kate said. "I'd been manipulating insects for as long as I can remember. Even my mum knew, but she never really questioned it. I guess she just thought I had a way with bugs." Her expression clouded. "She was usually too busy to notice what I was doing anyway."

Nova wasn't sure whether to ask what she meant, but Kate continued.

"Elizabeth found me after I set a swarm of bees on this girl who pulled my hair. I was 12. She came to my house the next day and told my mum I was special, and she could take me to a school where I could get a great education, all for free, and no one would try to hurt me for who I was."

"What did your mum say?"

"She was relieved, I think. I guess she'd got kind of sick of the house being full of insects. And she'd started to worry what would happen if anyone found out what I could do."

"Do you see her much?" Nova asked.

"I call her every few weeks. She's...things aren't like they used to be."

Nova lowered her eyes to the water rippling around her legs. Kate was always so strong and confident that she hadn't even considered her friend might have her own stuff going on. She felt guilty for not asking about her family sooner.

There was a sudden splash as Kate was plunged into the water. Nova heard a familiar laugh over her shoulder, and quickly slipped into the pool before Luke had the chance to push her too.

Kate came to the surface, scowling as she pushed her wet hair from her face. "Luke! You're such an idiot!"

He grinned. "Come on Katie, lighten up."

"Don't call me that." Kate waded to the side of the pool, as Luke sat on the edge. Her mascara had left black splotches under her eyes, and Nova wiped them away for her.

"Thanks," Kate said.

"I can warm you up if you like?" Luke asked, playfully.

"No thanks, I'm not sure third-degree burns look good on me."

Luke's cheeks flushed pink, though he waved off her comment. "I'm getting better every day. By graduation I'll be able to light a cigarette from 20 feet away."

"You don't smoke," Kate said.

He shrugged. "It'll be someone else's cigarette."

"Are you coming in?" Nova asked him.

"No."

"Can't swim?" Kate drawled.

"Har. Har. Getting in the water usually means I can't use my abilities for an hour or so," Luke explained.

Kate widened her eyes dramatically. "And how would you cope without the power to accidentally set someone on fire?"

Luke grinned, and belly-flopped into the water, unceremoniously splashing the girls, and then attempted to dunk Kate under again. She tried to look angry, but Nova could tell she was fighting back a laugh.

The trio hung out for a while, chatting, and watching the other kids using their abilities. Everyone seemed to be having a great day, but as Nova scanned the room, she noticed one girl sitting on a bench in the spectator area. She was the only person not in a swimsuit, and had a gloomy air about her.

"What's her story?" Nova asked the others.

Kate followed Nova's gaze. "Erica?"

"Why isn't she in the water?"

"Because she doesn't want to kill us all, probably," Luke answered.

"Her power involves electricity," Kate explained. "She can usually control it day-to-day, the most you might get is a minor shock if you surprise her or make her mad, but it's different in the water. The last time they tried her in the pool was during a PE lesson. It was just her and one of the teachers." Kate's expression turned grim. "Miss Shaw got burned pretty bad."

"They fixed her up though," Luke added. "She's fine now."

Kate continued. "Since then, Erica's not allowed to go swimming."

"Electric-Erica," Luke mused. "No, *Electrica!* If we're going for superhero names, that has a ring to it, right?"

Kate nodded. "Sounds good, Burn-Boy."

"I was thinking more: Flame-God."

"God implies a level of skill you absolutely don't have."

Nova couldn't focus on their bickering, still watching the sad girl on the bench.

She knew what it was like to have an ability you feared.

CHAPTER
SIXTEEN

Hope That's Not A Nickname

Nova left the pool without the others. Seeing Erica, another Alternate who had hurt people without meaning to, brought back what the boy from the Tombs had said. Did he know something about her? Why did he think she was dangerous? She needed a change of scenery, needed to clear her head.

As she made her way towards the dorms, she saw Angela sitting on the main steps to the front door. They hadn't spoken since Nova's question in mastery class had caused her to storm out, and Nova wasn't sure she was ready to deal with whatever reaction seeing her again might cause. Instead, she decided to head into the building through the back door.

Unfortunately, unlike the last couple of times she'd used it, today the corridor wasn't empty. Madeline was there, with the same boy she'd been with the other night. Seeing him now, though, Nova realised he wasn't a boy. He was a man, no younger than 20, and possibly much older than that.

Remembering how Madeline had reacted the last time she had stumbled upon the pair of them, Nova tried to back up quietly. Today, however, luck wasn't on her side, and she stepped on a mop leaning against the wall. It clattered to the floor, and Madeline's eyes snapped in her direction. She broke off the kiss, glaring at Nova.

"You! Were you following me again?"

"No," Nova said, hurriedly.

Madeline scowled. "You just happened to be right here, right now?"

"I...yes."

The man met Nova's gaze, only for a second, before focusing on his shoes. Madeline, however, stared her down, taking several slow steps closer.

"Nova, you're going to forget what you've seen here, got it?"

"Yes. Of course. Already forgotten. Madeline who?" Nova let out a nervous laugh, and immediately wanted to punch herself in the face.

"Don't cause me any trouble. You won't like what happens. I'd tell you to sleep with one eye open, but it won't be me you need to worry about; it'll be what you do to yourself." Madeline's eyes blazed with even more intensity. "Got it?"

Nova was too scared for even her usual blabbering, and simply nodded.

"Good." Madeline bumped her shoulder on her way back to the door. The man followed, pointedly not meeting her eyes. Nova let out her held breath, and scuttled back to her dorm.

I really need to start paying more attention to my surroundings.

That night, Nova waited until the dorm was silent, and then waited a little longer. When she was fairly sure everyone was asleep, she got dressed and snuck out. Kate was in bed, though Nova couldn't tell whether she was actually sleeping or not. Either way, her friend didn't try to stop her leaving.

Nova hurried down the stairs, out through the back door, and into the woods. After several days of making the trip, she knew the route well, and arrived at the Tombs in good time. While checking out the yard from the safety of the trees, she spotted him, standing by the portion of the fence that met the tree line; the place where they had spoken the day before.

Is he waiting for me?

Nova tried to settle the uneasy feeling in her stomach. She wasn't sure how ready she was for another conversation with this boy. Everything about him put her on edge. Talking to a guy who looked like he belonged on the cover of a magazine would've been enough on its own. Talking to a guy who looked like he belonged on the cover of a magazine, who was also locked away for life for what was probably a horrific crime involving more than a little bit of murder? Nova was pretty sure that was enough to make anyone anxious.

She readied herself to walk over, when she saw someone else sitting a few feet away from her, on the log she had first sat on with Danny. It was Angela.

Nova couldn't exactly head down to the fence to talk to her mysterious new friend with Angela watching, but she wasn't ready to go back to the dorm either. Would it be crazy to approach her after what happened the last time they spoke? She had to admit, she was kind of curious about what brought the strange, distant girl down to the Tombs. Especially given her reaction to the mere mention of the place.

Nova took a few steps closer. "Hi," she said, tentatively.

Angela jumped to her feet, spinning around to face her defensively. Her shoulders were tense, as though she was preparing to be attacked. Though Nova had been mildly terrified of her ever since their last conversation, she felt the need to hold up her hands reassuringly.

"I'm not here to hurt you." The words felt ridiculous, and yet they seemed to do the trick. Angela's stance relaxed, and she sat down on the log again.

"That's good," she said, dreamily.

Nova dithered, before finally settling on joining her. "I didn't know you came out here."

"Yes," Angela replied. "I find it comforting when I can't sleep."

"Because you used to be there?"

"Yes."

"Do you miss your friends?" Nova asked.

"Yes, and my mother."

"Oh, no, I meant from down there." Nova pointed to the yard.

Angela scowled at the building. "No one has friends down there."

"What's it like?"

"Dark. Cold. Loud. Sometimes quiet. Too quiet."

Nova was confused. "So, you don't come here because you miss it?"

Angela turned her head, her voice had lost all softness now. "I come here because it comforts me to know they're still locked away in that place. I like seeing them trapped. They can't hurt me from in there." Her eyes flicked to the fence where the boy was waiting. "Carver," she murmured.

Nova followed Angela's gaze. "Is that his name?"

"He's a bad one."

"Why?" Nova asked. "What did he do?"

Angela didn't answer, and stared at the boy for a moment. "He's looking over here. Is he waiting for you?"

"What did he do, Angela?" Nova repeated.

It was clear she wasn't going to answer. Angela got to her feet, slowly, the softness returning to her voice. "You shouldn't talk to him. You should run away. I'm going away." She walked back through the trees, leaving Nova sitting in the dark, alone.

Nova knew she should follow; go back to the dorm and never come back to this place. Talking to one of the prisoners was a really bad idea. She knew that. Yet, after a quick check that the guards were down by the doors to the building, she made her way over to where the trees met the fence.

I really hope 'Carver' is his last name, and not a nickname he got from chopping up bodies.

His voice drifted over when she was a few feet away. "I thought she might talk you out of coming back."

"Angela?"

"Yes."

"What makes you think she'd try?" Nova asked.

Carver smirked. "She doesn't like me."

"She said you're dangerous."

"Aren't we all?" His voice was like velvet, which made his statement all the more unsettling.

"Some more than others," Nova said, tentatively.

Another smile. "Very true."

Nova saw that he, like the rest of the Tombs' residents, had one of the metal bands around his neck, half-hidden by the collar of his brown jacket. He must've noticed her looking, because he zipped his jacket up fully.

Nova cleared her throat. "She said your name is Carver."

"It is."

Silence hung between them.

"Don't you want to know my name?" she asked.

"Would you tell me if I said I did?"

"I...don't know," she admitted.

"Then I won't ask, and we can avoid an uncomfortable moment for you."

Nova glanced over her shoulder, checking the coast was clear. "Last night you asked me what I did. Why do you think I *did* anything?"

"Do you know what this building is? Why they keep us here?"

Is that a trick question?

She must've pulled a face, because his lips twitched. "So you *do* know, and still you keep coming. That makes me wonder if you have a reason to think you belong here."

Nova said nothing. How could he possibly know that? Was it so obvious?

Carver continued. "And that begs the question: what

could a girl like you have possibly done to think you deserve to be locked away down here?"

"*A girl like me*?" That rubbed her the wrong way.

He chuckled. "Don't take it personally, you don't exactly look the type."

"Maybe you don't know me," she said, standing up straighter.

There was a spark in his eyes, only for a second. "Not yet."

A mosquito hit Nova's cheek. She brushed it away absentmindedly, still scowling at Carver. Then another bug hit her cheek. And another. Something clicked.

"Kate," she murmured, glancing behind her. If her friend was sending bugs, it meant something. "I have to go."

Without waiting for his response, she turned on her heel and hurried back through the woods, tripping over roots and undergrowth in her haste.

By the time she made it to the courtyard she was sweating and out of breath, but kept going around to the back of the dorm building. She raced through the corridor and up the stairs, all the time wondering what Kate was trying to tell her. Then she arrived at the door to her room, and it was all too clear.

Elizabeth was waiting.

CHAPTER
SEVENTEEN

The Tour

Elizabeth was wearing a white robe. Perfect, of course, without a single crease or loose thread. She crossed her arms as Nova slowed to a halt. "Busy night?"

Nova didn't answer. What was there to say? She'd been caught.

"I know where you've been," Elizabeth said. "I know that you went there yesterday too, and the night before. These visits need to stop, Nova." She uncrossed her arms, softening her tone. "You're impulsive, like your mother. She was my best friend, and you're so much like her it scares me."

"Why?" Nova asked.

"Because she was always one to leap before she looked, and it *always* got her into trouble. I don't want that for you." Elizabeth sighed, running a hand through her perfectly straight hair. "Listen, tomorrow morning, I'll take you down to the secure building. You can see what's inside, and hopefully that'll put an end to your fascination with that place once and for all. Okay?"

"Okay."

Elizabeth smiled. "Good. Now get to bed, and don't let me catch you outside the dorm after lights out again."

Elizabeth was true to her word. Bright and early the next morning, she found Nova in the cafeteria and walked her down to the Tombs.

The place was exactly as it had been described, which was pretty damn awful. There were hardly any windows, and the few that punctured the cracked and dented walls were frosted and barred. The place was lit with fluorescent tube lights, which gave the whole building a sickly, greenish glow. The walls were white, or had been once, and there were no paintings, plants, or anything at all which might've provided some colour or cheerfulness.

Elizabeth took Nova through a maze of identical hallways, and stopped outside the door of what appeared to be a classroom. There were 10 single desks facing a blackboard, and a bookshelf filled with books that were even older than the ones from science class.

"The students here earn privileges through good behaviour," Elizabeth explained. "If they prove they want to learn to control their urges, to stop putting themselves and others in danger, then they are rewarded by being able to resume their education. If they learn to control and use their abilities safely, then they can leave the secure building."

Each of the single desks was coated in a layer of dust. Clearly, no one had used the room for a while.

Elizabeth followed Nova's gaze. "It doesn't happen often, unfortunately. Most of the children here can't or won't learn to control their impulses. More often than not, they simply don't want to. It means we have no choice but to keep them confined, for their safety as well as everyone else's."

"What about Angela?" Nova asked.

Elizabeth smiled. "There are a few success stories. Angela is working very hard to learn how to control her ability, and we decided that she was no more of a threat to others than the rest of the children back at the main school."

She took Nova to the cafeteria next. It was small, containing only eight tables.

"We let the children out in groups," Elizabeth explained. "Most eat two to a table, with a maximum of 12 in the room at any time. However, there are some students who must eat alone in their rooms"

"Why?"

"Having certain students in a room such as this is risky. We do all we can to keep everyone safe, and sometimes that means keeping them away from open spaces." She looked around. "I know this building seems gloomy, or even frightening, but everything we do here, we do for the good of our students."

The doors at the other side of the room opened, and several kids came in. They took their trays and walked to the tables, each wearing the kind of vacant expression adopted by people so used to the same routine that they barely even need to be awake to do it. Once seated, a couple of them began talking quietly to each other, while the four guards at the other side of the room watched. The guards had thick black belts around their waists, and hanging from each was a walkie-talkie, a baton, and a gun. Nova shivered at the idea of someone watching her have breakfast with a gun inches from their hand.

A couple of the kids noticed her and Elizabeth, but no one asked any questions. They were all wearing those same metal collars.

"What were those things around their necks?" Nova asked, once they had left the room and were moving down the next hallway.

"The collars impede the use of abilities," Elizabeth explained.

"They stop them working?"

"It's more of a deterrent. An electric shock is administered when abilities are used. The stronger the ability, the stronger the shock."

They're electrocuting kids?

Elizabeth sighed. "It's not something we enjoy, but there's only so much we can do to protect ourselves and the other students. Most of our guards aren't Alternates. You can imagine how difficult a human would find it to face off against a child who can throw balls of fire, or liquefy matter. At that point, I imagine their gun would be rather comforting." She shivered. "The collars mean the guards can look after the students without the need for more extreme measures. In fact, most of the students here don't attempt to use their abilities, because they know what happens if they do, and so the collars are harmless to them."

"What if they do something by accident?" Nova asked.

"We try to limit that by ensuring there are few triggers. Many of the children take mild sedatives to help them avoid getting angry or upset."

Nova's head was spinning. Shock collars? Drugging kids? What kind of place was this?

They entered a new corridor, where the walls were lined with heavy doors. Each had a number stamped onto it, and a slot through which trays could be passed. Up ahead, a guard opened one of the doors, number 32, and two girls stepped out. He motioned for them to start walking, and followed them through a door at the end of the hall.

Nova peeked into number 32. It contained a bunk bed, toilet, sink, desk and chair, and a small bookcase. The walls were decorated with hand drawn pictures, taped haphazardly onto the concrete. There was a tiny rectangular window at the top of the back wall. Her stomach sank. It was a cell.

"This is where they live?" she whispered.

"The building was never converted," Elizabeth said, a sad tone to her voice. "We didn't expect to be housing anyone in it. At first, it was one or two dangerous students, brought to us after terrible accidents. When it became clear we wouldn't be able to help them master their abilities, our only other option was to keep them confined. Unfortunately, their numbers have increased over the years."

They continued through the door at the end of the corridor, and found themselves in a check-in area, not unlike the one from Nova's dorm. Several guards were chatting behind the desk, and there was a row of empty chairs lining the wall on the right.

"What kind of accidents?" Nova asked.

"I'm sorry?"

"You said the kids came after terrible accidents. Like what?"

Elizabeth stopped walking, turning to face her. "Nova, I know why you keep coming down here. You feel like you belong in this place because of what happened to your stepfather. You're wrong. The children in this building made choices. Their initial crimes may have been accidental in some cases, but each of them showed absolutely no desire to learn to control their powers, and no remorse for what they did. They hurt and kill, and they do it because they enjoy it. You're not like them."

Nova swallowed. "I told you I didn't feel bad about what happened with Gary. You said I should keep that a secret. That's because you know they'd put me down here, isn't it?"

Elizabeth opened her mouth, but was interrupted when a guard hurried over.

"Miss Perrin. There's been an incident. We may need your assistance."

"Christopher?"

"Yes, ma'am."

Elizabeth sighed, and then pointed to the chairs lining the wall. "Nova, please wait here. I'll be back in a few minutes."

Nova took a seat as Elizabeth followed the guard back through the doors. She had hoped her mind would be put at ease after this visit, that she'd hear something that would stop her obsession with the Tombs for good. She hadn't.

Like the other kids here, she had killed someone, and she didn't feel a whole lot of regret about it. She knew she *should* feel bad; she'd killed the man who'd raised her ever since her mother died. The man her mum had clearly loved enough to marry. Loved enough to entrust him to look after her.

But Nova hadn't loved him. Years of being made to feel like she was a burden for simply existing, like a worthless object he'd been left with and couldn't dispose of, meant there had been no room for feelings of gratitude or love.

And then there was the other stuff. The drinking, the weird way he'd sometimes speak. The strange looks he'd started to give her that had made her feel uncomfortable in her own home, in her own skin. Something had changed, and in that dynamic shift she'd begun to put as much distance between herself and Gary as possible.

None of that was the reason she'd killed him, though. She'd done that because he stole something that meant more to her than anything in the world. It was stupid, and her anger caused her to lose the very thing she'd been desperately trying to save.

Nova shook away the thought, glancing over at the guards by the check-in desk. Two of them appeared to be in their 40s, and the other was younger. Familiar, though she couldn't work out where she recognised him from.

The doors at the end of the hall opened. She looked over, expecting Elizabeth.

It was him. Carver. He walked ahead of his guards, with hands cuffed behind his back. He wore the same white T-shirt and orange trousers as the others. Now that he was without a coat, Nova saw that his arms were covered in tattoos, though she wasn't close enough to see them clearly. The harsh strip-lights illuminated several cuts and bruises decorating his pale skin. His hair was ruffled, and his lip was split. Despite that, he walked confidently, as if the guards were the prisoners, and he was leading them to their own cells. He caught sight of Nova and smirked. Her cheeks burned, and she dropped her gaze to the floor before anyone noticed.

The doors at the other end of the hallway opened, and when she looked up again, he was gone.

Elizabeth reappeared, straightening her jacket. "Sorry about that. Shall we continue?"

"What's down there?" Nova asked, pointing to the doors through which Carver had been taken.

"That's the old maximum-security wing," Elizabeth said.

"What is it now?"

"It's where we keep the most dangerous residents, the ones with no chance of rehabilitation. The cells are stronger, and it's more heavily guarded than anywhere else in the building."

"Can I see?"

Elizabeth shook her head. "Absolutely not. Come on, let's take you back to your dorm."

Neither of them spoke again until they had reached the dorm building. At the doors, Elizabeth sighed, turning to Nova and placing a hand on her arm.

"I hope, now that you've seen that place up close, you can understand why you don't belong there?"

"I guess."

"There's no guessing involved. You're a good girl, you belong here, with us."

Nova wasn't sure what to say to that.

Elizabeth gave her arm a gentle squeeze. "I'll see you soon. Enjoy the rest of your day."

Nova said goodbye, forcing a smile despite the heaviness in her chest. She wanted to do what she was told. She wanted to make Elizabeth happy, yet she couldn't fight the feeling that – whether she liked it or not – she wasn't done with the Tombs yet.

CHAPTER
EIGHTEEN

Madeline's Mistake

Nova was being pulled along the dark corridor. The sound of dripping water surrounded her. Greenish lights flickered. Someone, somewhere was screaming. Was it her? Gary was smiling, leering at her as the sting of metal hit her neck. A collar; heavy, choking.

"I'm sorry."

It wasn't Gary's voice. Who was it?

She startled awake. The things she'd witnessed from the Tombs – the flickering lights, the collars – were being pulled into her dreams. As if her imagination alone wasn't bad enough.

Nova swung her legs out of bed, glancing at the clock. 1.00 AM. Her morning with Elizabeth felt a long time ago, and she barely gave it a second thought as she got dressed, pulled her mass of curls into some form of ponytail, and left the dorm.

Kate's bed was empty again, and Nova wondered if she was with Luke. She felt a pang of something almost like jealousy. Not because she liked him in that way Luke, but because even at a school filled with kids as freakish and weird as she was, she was still too afraid of herself to even imagine having a boyfriend. How could she risk letting someone get close? What if she hurt another person? She couldn't stand the idea of another face joining Gary's in her nightmares. Unless she somehow managed to get her ability completely under control, or found some magical way to get rid of it altogether, she would have to be single forever.

She headed down the stairs and through the back door. Elizabeth clearly had some way of knowing Nova had been sneaking out, and because there didn't appear to be any cameras in the dorm building or outside, Nova had to assume she'd been spotted through a window. Tonight, instead of heading out of the back door and walking straight across the courtyard, Nova kept to the back of the buildings, sticking to the shadows, and taking the long route past the main building and the pool. It would take longer, but if she avoided being seen, it was worth it.

Once she reached the end of the wall, her only option was to make a break for the woods, running at full speed until she reached the tree line. Blanketed in the darkness of the trees, she stopped, taking a minute to catch her breath. Had she done enough to avoid being seen? She hoped so. Elizabeth had been nice so far, but that still didn't mean it would be wise to get on her bad side.

Walking the familiar path to the Tombs, she soon arrived at the spot where she had stood with Danny on that first night. Carver was standing further down, where the fence met the woods. Was he waiting for her? A small shiver ran through her body. Though she was afraid of him, something about him fascinated her. What did he do to end up on that side of the chain link? In fact, what did he do to end up in the most secure wing of the building? Why did Angela think he was one of the worst people down there?

Nova was almost at the spot where Carver was waiting, when she heard movement behind her. She turned; there was nothing there. A few seconds later she heard it again. It was a voice, whispering.

Did someone follow me?

She went back on herself, following the sound. Behind the next tree, Nova discovered the source of the sound. It was Madeline and her boyfriend making out.

How does this keep happening to me?!

It was no wonder Madeline thought Nova was following her. She wasn't going to wait around to be caught this time, turning and scuttling back the way she came.

But, because life wasn't fair, Nova tripped over a tree root and landed heavily in a pile of dead leaves.

As she lay there, looking up at the sky, hating herself and her big clown feet, she heard the inevitable sound of footsteps.

"You!"

"Hi Madeline," Nova said, still on the ground. "How's it going?" She got to her feet, brushing herself off. As she locked eyes with Madeline's boyfriend, she instantly recognised him. He was one of the guards from the Tombs; she'd seen him at the desk when she was waiting for Elizabeth.

She must've looked a fraction too long because he muttered, "She knows who I am."

Nova hadn't thought it was possible for Madeline to look angrier. She was wrong. Madeline took several steps closer, gritting her teeth so hard Nova half-expected them to shatter. "I warned you."

"Wait," Nova spluttered. "This isn't what you think."

"Oh really? What other explanation can there be for you being out here in the middle of the night?"

Nova didn't have an answer for that.

Madeline sneered, closing the distance again. "I told you what would happen if you crossed me. I guess you need a demonstration?"

Nova shook her head. "No... I didn't mean to-"

"Get on your knees."

It took Nova less than a second to do what she was told. The moment the words left Madeline's mouth; she could do nothing but drop to the ground.

"Good." Madeline never broke eye contact. "Slap yourself."

Nova did it, striking her cheek hard and fast. It stung like hell.

"Again."

Nova did as she was told.

Madeline smiled. "Don't leave out the other half of your face, Nova."

She slapped herself twice more, and now her skin felt like it was on fire.

The guard took Madeline's arm. "That's enough."

"She *saw* us."

"She gets the point."

Madeline shook him free. "We need to be sure." She knelt on the ground in front of Nova. "I don't want you to forget how you felt tonight." She smiled again. "Scoop up some dirt."

Nova dug her fingers into the cool earth.

"Maddie..." the guard said.

She ignored him. "Good. Now eat it."

Nova brought the soil to her mouth and shovelled it inside. It was gritty, wet, and caked together as she tried to chew. She didn't want this, yet it was still happening. It was as though someone else was controlling her body, and she was simply watching.

She struggled to swallow, retching as she did, but finally, her mouth was empty.

Madeline stood up, absentmindedly picking a single fallen leaf from the shoulder of her jacket. "Good. *Now* we're done."

She walked away. The guard waited for a few seconds, then followed.

Nova was still on her knees. Her face stung. There was dirt under her nails and between her teeth. The taste in her mouth was awful. Slowly, she got to her feet, and turned to go back to the dorm.

She hadn't realised how close they were to the fence. Carver was only a few feet away, watching silently. His expression was impassive; without sympathy or emotion. Shame prickled in the corners of Nova's eyes. She couldn't bear to look at him anymore. What did he think of her now? That she was weak? Stupid? He probably thought it was the best entertainment he'd had in months. Nova didn't wait to hear what he had to say. She ran.

She wished she'd never got out of bed, wished that she'd been able to manipulate time like her mom, wished she could fly away like her dad. Wished she could shove Madeline's face into the dirt and wipe the smile away. Wished for anything to make this whole thing go away. She was angry, so angry.

She tripped again, landing on all fours, and crying out with rage. Her hair fell over her eyes. Her hands stung from whatever she had landed on, and her cheeks stung from Madeline's punishment. Pure, sizzling fury bubbled up inside her. She closed her eyes as it swept through her body, and felt the energy burst from her skin and ignite the very air.

She screamed.

When Nova opened her eyes, she saw that every tree within 10 feet of where she stood had huge cracks and splinters. Several creaked, as if they were seconds away from falling. She stumbled to her feet and ran.

At least I didn't blow up a person this time.

When she got back to the dorm building, Nova spent 20 minutes brushing her teeth, and holding a cold wash-cloth to her face. She couldn't believe she'd been so stupid. She vowed there and then never to go back to the Tombs again. All it had done was cause her trouble. If she had to stay at Tidemarsh, then she was going to focus on learning to control this horrible ability, so that she could never hurt anyone, or anything, again.

And she was going to stay the hell away from Madeline.

It turned out, that part would be harder than she thought. A few hours later, Nova woke to the sound of screaming. She sat up, looking bleary-eyed around the room. The clock said 7 AM. The sky outside was dark, with the first drops of rain smattering against the window.

Kate was sitting up in her bed too, yawning as she searched for the source of the noise. It didn't take them long to find it. Madeline was standing in front of the mirror beside her bedside table, screaming as though she were being murdered.

Nova supposed that, in her mind, it was almost as bad as that. Her long, beautiful hair, lay in pieces on the floor beside her bed and on her pillow. Her scalp was an uneven mess, with her hair no longer than an inch in most places.

"What happened?" Beth asked, hurrying to Madeline's side.

"Can't you see?" Madeline screeched. "Someone cut my hair!"

"Why would they do that?"

"How the hell should I know?" Madeline dropped onto her bed with her head in her hands.

Several other girls crowded around, talking in soothing tones.

"It'll be alright."

"Hair grows, it'll look better in no time."

"I could try to bring it back," Beth suggested. "I mean, I've never done anything like that, but maybe if I touch the hair then-"

"Are you kidding me?" Madeline interrupted. "Do I look like I want a head full of slugs right now?"

Kate padded over to Nova's bed, Colin sitting faithfully on her shoulder, while the others fussed over Madeline. "Can you believe this?"

"Who do you think did-" Nova began, but she was cut off when she saw Kate's eyes widen. Her friend pointed to Nova's bedside table. Poking out of the top of the closed drawer was a lock of blonde hair. Nova clapped a hand to her mouth. Kate opened the drawer to reveal a large pair of scissors, the hair – wrapped in a blue ribbon – and a small, folded piece of paper.

Kate picked up the scissors. "What did you-"

Nova shook her head. "I swear, I don't know how that got there."

Without another word, Kate grabbed the hair, scissors, and note, and rushed to her part of the room. She flung everything into the drawer of her own bedside table, and quickly shut it again. Seconds later, Madeline's voice carried across the room.

"It was Nova!" Madeline got off of her bed and marched over. "You did this!"

"Why would she do that?" Orlaith asked.

Ria agreed. "She has no reason to hurt you, Maddie."

Several others chimed in in agreement.

"She was asleep, we all were."

"Nova isn't like that."

"You're just upset."

Madeline shook her head. "I know it was her. It *had* to be."

Kate stepped in front of Nova, crossing her arms. "Prove it, or back off."

Madeline let out a roar, leaning over and flinging the sheets off Nova's bed. When that yielded no evidence, she moved to the bedside table, yanking the drawer open and rooting around inside.

"Are you done?" Kate asked.

"She hid the scissors, she must have!" Madeline's eyes narrowed as she rounded on Kate. "I bet you helped her."

Kate didn't flinch. "You want to search my stuff too?" She gestured to her part of the room, where there were at least 10 large spiders, roaming the bed and floor, and an enormous millipede wandering across the bedside table. "Be my guest."

"I won't forget this," Madeline hissed, storming away.

The other girls split up, some following Madeline, others heading to their own beds to start getting ready.

Kate waited until Madeline had left the room, towel wrapped around her head, before coming back over. She held the folded piece of paper in her hand, and passed it to Nova discreetly.

Nova opened it up, heart racing.

"Now she *gets the point."*

"What does that mean?" Kate asked, reading over her shoulder.

Nova had a horrible feeling she knew exactly what it meant.

A Crazy, Stupid Idea

Rain hammered against the windows of the classroom. It had been getting heavier all day, and by lunchtime had become a full-blown thunderstorm.

Nova was in History class, learning about great people from the past who were rumoured to be Alternates. It should've been fascinating finding out that Marylyn Monroe could talk to fish, Shakespeare could turn himself invisible at will, and Abraham Lincoln regularly flew loops around the White House, but all she could think about was the note.

Kate, helpfully, wasn't the most reassuring.

"I still can't believe the scissors and hair were in your drawer. Do you think someone was trying to frame you?"

"I don't know," Nova answered, for at least the hundredth time that morning.

"It doesn't surprise me that Madeline has an enemy here. I mean, she's a terrible person. What I can't work out is what it's got to do with you?"

Nova hadn't told Kate about what happened the night

before; how Madeline had humiliated her. She knew she should. She liked Kate, trusted her, but for some reason couldn't bring herself to say it. Maybe it was because she was ashamed about what Madeline had made her do. Or maybe she was scared about what Madeline would do to her next if she knew Nova had been telling people about the guard.

Or, just maybe, it's because then you'd have to tell her that Carver – an incredibly dangerous Alternate from the Tombs – found a way to escape and leave a macabre gift in your nightstand?

It had to be him. No one else could've known what the guard said. Or seen what Madeline had made Nova do. The real question was: *why*? Why had he done it?

Kate was still talking. "Whoever it was, they'd have to be brave to risk cutting Madeline's hair. What if she had woken up?"

"Mmm," was all Nova could murmur in reply.

"It was kind of brutal too. Don't get me wrong, most of the time I'd like nothing better than to fill her underwear with maggots, but cutting off her hair? That's, like, her *soul*." Kate shuddered.

Nova was only half-listening. If it was Carver who did it – and she was 99.9% sure it was – she needed to find out his motivation. Was he trying to get her into trouble? Or – and this was probably more terrifying – was he trying to help? If that was the case, what did he want in return? A boy like that surely didn't do anyone any favours without expecting some kind of payment.

"I have to go back down to the Tombs," she mumbled.

Kate put down her pen, giving her a pitying look. "Why would you do that?"

"I can't explain right now. It's about what happened. I need to check something."

"Elizabeth told you not to go down there anymore."

Nova raised an eyebrow. "Oh, and you do everything you're told?"

"Me sneaking out every now and then to meet boys is hardly the same as you risking everything because you're curious about a building full of crazies." Kate sighed, softening her tone when she spoke again. "Look, I get it. You're confused about your powers, you don't know where you fit in around here, and your subconscious has latched on to that place. But seriously Nova, you need to let it go." She narrowed her gaze. "And you need to stop obsessing over that boy."

Nova was incredulous. "I'm not obsessed."

"Uh-huh."

She pretended to focus on her notebook. Kate didn't understand; she wasn't going down there to flirt with Carver – she wouldn't know how to do that if she tried – she was going down there because she needed to look him in the eye and ask if he was responsible for what happened to Madeline. She couldn't tell Kate that, not yet. If she knew Nova thought he was responsible, that he could somehow leave the Tombs and get into the dorm, she'd flip out. She might even tell Elizabeth. Nova needed to be sure, then she'd decide what to do with the information.

Kate groaned. "Fine, but don't say I didn't warn you." Another flash of lightening lit up the dark sky, and she added: "What makes you think they'll even be out tonight? Only an idiot would go outside in weather like this."

That evening, Nova discovered that she was, in fact, an idiot.

She had only been outside for 30 seconds, and was already soaked to the skin, freezing cold, and hating whichever part of her brain came up with this ridiculous idea. But it was too late to turn back now, so – bracing herself against the roaring winds – she charged towards the woods.

The hideous weather meant it took longer than usual to reach the Tombs, and when she arrived it was for nothing. The yard was empty.

Of course it's empty. Why would they let the kids out in a storm like this?

Nova lingered for a few minutes, trying to decide what to do next. Going back to the dorm felt like such a defeat, but if Carver wasn't outside, there was no way to talk to him.

She wasn't sure why she felt so disappointed that she wasn't going to be able to speak with him tonight. A conversation about Madeline's hair could wait until tomorrow. It wasn't like the guy was going anywhere. Why was she so reluctant to return to bed?

There was obviously something about the mysterious boy that had made coming out in such a horrendous storm seem like a good idea, and it was more than just the fact he was ridiculously good-looking in that 'I might kill you' kind of way. He seemed to know things about her, more than the other kids at Tidemarsh. It made her feel vulnerable, and she had to find out what he knew and how he knew it. Was he just good at bluffing, or did he have real information that could get out and cause her problems?

There was a bang ahead and to the left, and Nova turned in the direction of the noise. It was a door, swinging back against the wall of the building. Her mind started racing. She had an idea. A crazy, stupid, dangerous idea. She needed to talk herself out of it. She *wanted* to talk herself out of it.

Before she could even begin to try, she was running to the door. She slipped inside, pulling it closed behind her with a gentle click.

Nova was in a storeroom. The walls were lined with shelves, and there were more standing units in the middle. They were filled with canned food, boxes of flour, pasta, and a hundred other things. The light was on; flickering with every clap of thunder.

Great job, Nova. What's your plan now? Stroll the building and politely ask one of the guards to show you where the handsome scary guy is kept?

Finding an open door was a ridiculous stroke of luck. Winging it, though, would only get her so far. Nova shook her head; this was all too intense. If she was caught in this building, she could get into the kind of trouble she didn't even want to imagine. She needed to get back to her room, put on some dry clothes, and hope that the weather tomorrow would be good enough for her to come back. She could talk to Carver then.

Nova turned, rattling the door handle.

It wouldn't open.

She tried again. It was no good, it didn't budge. There

was a keypad on the wall, and Nova felt a gut punch when realised she needed a passcode to get out.

"Fuuuuuck," Nova hissed, kicking the door as her heart began to race. This achieved nothing more than hurting her toe, and she swore again. There had to be another way out. She glanced to the other side of the room, where there was a second door. Thankfully, this one wasn't locked. She creaked it open an inch, revealing a hallway. Slowly, listening for any sounds of movement, she opened it a little more, then a little more. It wasn't anywhere she recognised from her visit with Elizabeth, though every hallway had looked pretty much the same, so she couldn't be sure. Either way, she wasn't exactly drowning in choices. She'd have to pick a direction and take a chance.

Nova opted for left, and set off. Water dripped from her clothes onto the tiled floor, and she shivered. Why was this building so much colder than the others? Thinking longingly of the dry clothes back in her dorm, she picked up the pace.

She walked for several minutes, and so far hadn't run into any guards. Even though technically she wasn't one of their prisoners, Nova was pretty sure that getting caught down there on her own would get her into more trouble than she needed. The sooner she could get back outside, the better.

The more time passed, the more Nova began to feel uneasy. She still had no idea where she was going. Every corridor was identical, and none of them contained signs that said: '*Exit this way if you're here by mistake*'. At each junction she was going with her gut, and she knew from experience that it didn't have the best track record.

"-our biggest problem is losing power."

The male voice came from the corner up ahead. Nova darted into a room to her left, pressing her back against the wall.

"What happens then?" asked another man. They were getting closer.

"The locking mechanism on the cells is electronic. If the storm knocks out the power, the Alts can open their doors."

There was panic in the second voice. "What about the back-up generators?"

"They take half a minute to kick in. That gives the monsters 30 seconds to figure out their doors aren't locked no more. If they get them open-"

Their voices faded as they passed. Nova was alone again. She took a breath, trying to slow her racing heart. That was too close. She waited a few more seconds, then stepped back out into the hallway. At the junction, she took another left. There was a heavy looking pair of metal doors up ahead, and she almost laughed with sheer joy. She remembered those from her visit with Elizabeth; it was where the guards had taken Carver. That meant the building exit wasn't far away.

One of the heavy doors began to open, and Nova ducked inside a darkened room on the right. Through the gap in her door, she could see a man in a guard uniform leaving Maximum Security. He called to someone behind him.

"Hey Cartwright, make sure you push it closed behind you. The thing's warped, won't shut on its own anymore."

A second guard appeared, and pushed the door shut

behind him. They walked past the room Nova was in and out of sight.

She took a few seconds to steady herself, then made to leave the room. Suddenly the heavy metal doors opened again, and she slipped back into the safety of the shadows. Two more guards passed.

"We'll have to be quick, if they catch us away from post..."

"Stop worrying. We'll be 10 minutes, tops."

Once their footsteps had faded, Nova hurried out into the corridor. As she neared the doors to Maximum Security, she saw one of them hadn't closed properly.

If you wanted to speak to Carver, you could get inside right now.

Shaking away the ridiculous thought, she continued towards the exit. She was seconds from reaching the door when she heard the voices on the other side. There were guards coming. Nova turned on her heel, charging back the way she came. There were voices coming from that way now too. She was trapped.

Nova had no other options. She pulled open the door to Maximum Security and threw herself inside.

She waited, heart racing, but no one followed. She hadn't been spotted. The guards were still out there, though, she could hear them talking. There was no way she was getting out the way she came in.

Nova was stuck, in the most secure wing of a building no one was supposed to be able to leave.

CHAPTER TWENTY

Bad Luck

Nova walked through a long, dark corridor, lined with cells on either side. There were no windows. The cells were glass-fronted, with heavy metal doors to the right of the glass, and lit with a dull green light.

She kept her eyes focused on the path ahead, hoping that the prisoners were asleep. There was nowhere for her to hide in the open corridor, and the last thing she needed after avoiding being spotted for so long, was to have someone start yelling for the guards. She couldn't quite believe her luck that there didn't appear to be any cameras.

There was a peel of high-pitched laughter to her right, drawing her attention. A girl with bedraggled, dirty, white-blonde hair, stepped forward and pressed her hands against the glass wall of her cell. Without saying anything, she bit her own arm, sending blood trickling down her skin. She pulled away, grinning with bloodstained lips. She looked like a macabre parody of a little girl who had put on her mum's lipstick.

Well, that's probably the worst thing I've ever seen.

Nova hurried away. There were more voices now. The kids weren't asleep. They knew Nova was there. Some of them were laughing, some yelling, and one was screaming. She reached a turn at the end of the corridor, hoping for a way out, and let out a frustrated sob when she saw it led to more cells. Her heart raced, and she stopped walking to put a hand to her chest, breathing slowly to try and calm herself down.

This was, without a doubt, the most dangerous situation she'd ever found herself in. How could she have been so stupid to end up in such a mess? What if there was no way out of this place? What would happen when the guards found her?

"Hello there."

The voice came from a boy in the cell to the right. Unlike the other kids in Maximum Security, he didn't have a hair out of place, and his clothes were without a single crease. His cell, like the others, was sparse; containing only a bed, a toilet, a small desk, and the chair on which he was sitting. He had a book in his hand, the title of which was written in characters Nova couldn't read; she thought they might be Japanese. He put it down now that he had her attention.

"Lovely evening, isn't it?" he asked. His eyes were almost as dark as his hair, yet contained no warmth.

Nova licked her dry lips. Her voice was quiet. "How can you tell? There are no windows down here."

He smiled. "It's always a lovely evening when a beautiful young lady visits us." He tipped his head to one side. "You're not with the guards. Are you here to break us out in some daring rescue?"

"I'm afraid not."

His grin spread. "What an interesting choice of words. Tell me, what *are* you afraid of?"

He got to his feet, walking to the glass. Nova took a step back.

"Is it this?" he asked. In less than a second his skin darkened, peeling off in long, gory strips, dropping to the floor with a gentle *phut*. Nova's stomach dropped, and she let out a single whimper.

"Or this?" A huge spider appeared where he'd been standing, so big it barely fit inside the cell. It pressed a hairy leg against the glass, snapping its pincer mouth hungrily. Then it was gone.

Standing in its place was Nova's stepfather.

"No," came Gary's voice. "I think it might be *this*." His grin widened. "Want to spatter the walls with my blood again, sweetheart?"

Nova wanted to scream. Or cry. Or run away. But her legs were lead and her lungs empty. Suddenly there was a crack of thunder, and all the lights went out at once. Maximum Security was plunged into absolute darkness.

Along with the dark, silence fell over the place like a blanket. The only sound Nova could hear was her own breathing.

After a few seconds, there was something else; a heavy mechanical clicking. This was what the guards had been talking out. The electronic locks had failed.

Get out get out get out.

The words came screaming into her head, and though it was pitch black, Nova knew she had to run. She turned, charging off in the direction she'd come.

The air was filled with the sound of rusted metal scraping across the concrete floor, and of excited voices.

They're opening their cells.

Get out, Nova!

She collided with someone in the dark, ricocheted off of them, and crashed into the wall. She lost her balance, landing on her hands and knees on the cold floor.

Her head hurt. Her heart pounded. She was surrounded by footsteps, movement, whispers, laughter, and screams. The emergency lights on the walls flickered to life, and a dim red glow lit the hallway. Nova got shakily to her feet. There were people all around her. The one who had turned into Gary was back to his real form now, and out of his cell. He watched her get up.

"Oh dear. What a frightening situation to find yourself in," he said, grinning.

There was a commotion from the other end of the corridor. Two guards were backing away, towards the main doors, as several prisoners advanced on them. One of the guards fired his gun into the air, then did it again as the kids got closer.

Nova wanted to yell, to call for help, but her voice caught in her throat. What if they didn't come? What if it drew more Alternates over? Other than the one who had turned into Gary, they seemed too busy to even care that she was there.

The guards backed up through the doors, and heaved them shut. But it was too late. They were gone, and she was trapped. Several of the kids slammed their arms against the heavy metal, but it made no difference. Those things weren't going to budge.

Many of the prisoners were wearing the metal collars, though some – including the dark-haired boy – were not. They took advantage of that by using their abilities on the door, walls, and each other. One sent a barrage of rocks flying into the wall. Another squirted a thick, purple liquid from his fingers, and directed it under the doors. There was a girl flying up and down the corridor, occasionally picking up the other kids and dropping them, laughing hysterically as she did.

Nova backed up, away from the boy who was still watching her with a smirk on his face, moving further down the corridor. By now, some of the others had started to notice the only person not dressed in orange and white. Slowly, they drew closer. The girl who'd screamed and bitten herself, smiled, showing off her bloodied teeth. She stumbled closer, unsteady on her feet.

"I'm going to peel the flesh from your bones," she whispered. "I'm going to eat you right up." She giggled, high pitched and childlike. She was wearing a collar, but Nova was sure that a girl who'd bitten into her own arm hard enough to draw blood without so much as flinching, would have no problem killing her the old-fashioned way. Standing next to her was a boy with a shaved head, whose fingers slowly reformed into the shape of knives.

Nova's throat was sandpaper, her heart beating so fast she could hardly breathe. Her legs, once again, felt like they were nailed to the floor. She was helpless.

But you're not helpless.

She had an ability, and it was as deadly as any of the kids down there. She took a breath, forcing herself to stand up straighter.

"Don't come any closer," she stammered. "I don't want to hurt you."

She sounded about as threatening as wet toilet paper, and unsurprisingly, several of the kids laughed. Others regarded her with glazed expressions, as if she'd said nothing at all.

"I mean it!" Nova insisted. "Keep away."

"How?" The dark-haired boy asked, calmly. "*How* would you hurt us?"

"M-my ability. I've killed before."

Another girl, who looked no older than 10, snorted. "If that's true, why aren't you down here with us?"

The screamer was at the front of the crowd, giggling again. The boy with the dark hair took a step back, watching Nova curiously. Another boy, white-haired and pale, bared his teeth, which were sharpened into points. They all began to talk over each other.

"She ain't dangerous."

"I'll bet she breaks real easy."

"Do you think she'll scream?"

"I bet she'll cry first."

"I like it when they cry."

The screamer took another step closer, holding up her hand like she was in a classroom. "I get to go first."

Nova stumbled back, trying to keep her eyes on all of them. "I'm warning you..."

They weren't listening, and she was running out of places to go.

"I get the second slice," said the boy with knife hands.

Nova's back hit something. Not the wall this time. She spun around.

Carver!

Relief flooded her veins. Seeing him was almost like finding a friend. They'd spoken at the fence, and not once had he said he wanted to peel her skin off. He felt like a safer bet than any of the others.

But something was different. Without the fence to separate them, he didn't seem the same. He was taller than Nova remembered, and stronger looking. He regarded her without even a hint of a smile, his face hard and impassive. His eyes flicked to the group. She followed his gaze. The others were close, but had stopped approaching, watching him apprehensively.

Are they scared of him?

The screamer stepped forward. "Let me cut her, Carver. Let me taste her. We can share."

He paused for an agonizingly long time, as though seriously contemplating the request. Nova was too afraid to speak. She pleaded with her eyes, begging him wordlessly not to hand her over. She didn't know if sticking with him would be any safer, but at that moment she was willing to take a chance.

Finally, he took hold of her arm.

"No," he said to the crowd, his voice as firm as his grip. "She's mine."

He pulled her away, down the corridor, and over to the very last cell, shoving her inside. The stone floor was uneven, and Nova lost her footing, stumbling, and falling onto her knees. Again. She didn't try to get up this time, instead crawling to the furthest corner. Carver entered the cell, pulling the door closed behind him.

None of the other kids tried to get in, despite howls of

disappointment from the girl. It was just the two of them now, in the small, dark room. Carver slid his back down the door, sitting with his gaze fixed on her. The noise outside increased; thunder, screams, and the sounds of hands pounding on the doors and walls as the kids fought to get out of Maximum Security. Nova gritted her teeth, pushing herself further back into the darkness.

"You picked a bad night to visit, Nova."

CHAPTER
TWENTY-ONE

Not Yet

The cell was dark, but thanks to the red emergency light shining through the glass wall, Nova could see Carver well enough. He was sitting with his back against the door. She was close enough now to see that the tattoos on his arms were pictures and symbols, though she wasn't sure what any of them meant. His arms were muscular, as if he did push-ups every day. She supposed in a place like this, there wasn't much else to do.

Was he sitting in front of the door to stop her leaving? Or to prevent the others from getting inside? Was he trying to keep her safe? Or keep her for himself?

Nova wished she could turn her stupid brain off.

Though she had been in the room for a while, her heart refused to slow, and beads of sweat prickled on her forehead. Carver's cell was the last one at the end of the corridor, and most of the other kids had gone back towards the entrance of Maximum Security. The sounds of them yelling, hammering on doors, and trashing their cells, was quieter now at least. The plink plonk of water dripping somewhere nearby was almost soothing. She forced herself to take a breath, to try and slow the pounding in her chest. For now, at least it seemed she was safe.

Carver's cell was probably the most depressing out of all of those she'd seen. There was a single iron bed with a thin sheet and no pillow, a toilet with no lid, and a desk with no chair. There were no pictures, no plants, no books, no windows. Nothing at all to provide any joy or comfort. Nova was pretty sure that spending any length of time down here would make even the calmest person want to start smashing things.

Not Carver though. He was sitting there, eyes facing forward, appearing almost bored with the entire situation. Like having her there was an inconvenience to him. She found herself fighting the overwhelming urge to apologise for taking up his valuable time.

There was a clap of thunder, and the emergency lights flickered. Nova hadn't considered that her night could get much worse, but being plunged into complete darkness, while trapped in a room with a murderer, would probably be a start.

You're a murderer too, don't forget.

"What do you think of my humble abode?" Carver asked, breaking the silence that had hung between them for a long time.

Nova took another glance around, trying to keep her face impassive. "It's...uh...not as small as some of the others."

A smile pricked at the corners of his lips. "That's true."

She searched for something else to say. "And it's...very clean."

"Not much to dust in here. Saves me a lot of time."

Now that they were talking, Nova plucked up the courage to ask the question playing on her mind. "How did you find out my name?"

"I asked someone," he said, simply.

"Who?" she pressed.

"Someone who knew it."

Nova rolled her eyes before she could help herself, then looked at the floor, cheeks blazing. Carver was being nice for now, but she had no idea what might make this guy angry. He was obviously locked away down here for a reason, and it would be wise to stay on his good side.

She tried to keep the conversation flowing. "Is Carver your first name?"

"No."

"What is it?" she asked.

"I don't usually share it."

"Why?"

"Names are worthless down here." He thought for a moment. "Though if you're curious, I suppose it couldn't hurt to tell you mine."

"Why the change of heart?"

Carver shrugged. "There's a 50/50 chance you won't survive the night. You may as well know my name."

"Thanks," Nova muttered, sarcastically.

He gave a small smile, just enough to soften his features. It made him a lot less intimidating. "Kit."

"That's nice. It's short so it's easy to-"

"You don't need to compliment my name," he interrupted. "Your thoughtful words about my cell are more than enough." He gently knocked his head on the door behind him. "Most of the others won't try to come in here, but there are a couple who might attempt it."

Nova swallowed. "Why would they do that?"

"To get to you."

"You're trying to keep me safe?"

"They would've torn you to shreds. Eaten you, maybe." His voice was very matter of fact, as if describing a problem with a car, and held no emotion whatsoever.

"And that would...upset you?" Nova began.

He paused, as if really considering this. "I don't know."

Interesting response.

"Can I ask you another question?" she asked.

His eyes stared straight ahead. "Yes."

"Will you answer it?" she pressed.

"That depends."

"On?"

"On whether I like it."

"Why are they like that?" Nova gestured to the few kids still outside the cell. A couple of them were pacing, and a girl with red hair was curled in a corner crying.

Kit's face darkened. "They've experienced things you can't possibly imagine."

"I can try," Nova said

"No. You can't."

She pushed a little more. "Are you like them?"

"I don't cry, or bite myself, or throw my excrement, if that's what you mean."

Nova was undeterred. "Have you experienced things I couldn't possibly imagine?"

"Yes."

"The same as them?"

"Yes."

"But you're not..." Nova trailed off.

Something sparked in Kit's eyes, and he finally looked at her. "I'm not *crazy*?"

"I didn't say-"

"It's what you were thinking." He watched her thoughtfully for a moment. "That's an unpopular opinion. Most of the people here think I'm the worst of them all."

"Why?"

"Because I've killed," he said, calmly.

So have I.

"So have they," Nova countered. "Elizabeth said all of the kids in here have killed people."

A muscle ticked in his jaw. "Then I suppose I killed the *wrong* people. And it would be wise not to believe everything Elizabeth says." He spoke in such a formal way, almost like he was from the past. Nova had never met anyone who talked like that before. Where had this boy come from?

A question for later, maybe. For now, she asked: "Why shouldn't I believe Elizabeth?"

"Because she's a liar."

"What do you mean?"

He sighed. "I've answered a lot of your questions, and they're starting to bore me."

Formal twang aside, the way he spoke was cold, as though he didn't care at all about whether he sounded rude. Nova supposed that being locked in a cell on your own for almost 24 hours a day would do that to anyone.

"Can I ask one more?" she asked, gently.

He paused, then gave a small nod.

"Did you cut Madeline's hair?"

A smile played on his lips. "No."

"But you know who did?" Nova continued.

"Yes."

"Did you tell them to do it?" she asked.

"In a sense."

"Why?"

He furrowed his brows. "I would've thought that was obvious?"

Nova thought about this. "Because of what she did to me?"

"Correct."

She was confused. "You don't know me. We'd barely spoken before tonight."

"I don't like bullies."

That seemed a strange thing for him to say, considering where he was, the people he was surrounded by, and the way everyone seemed to be terrified of him.

"You did it to help me?" Nova ventured.

"I did it because she deserved it. The fact it made you happy was merely a coincidence."

"Why would you think it made me happy?"

He met her eye. "Didn't it?"

"No," Nova kept her voice firm. "You cut her hair off, you humiliated her."

"And she made you eat dirt. That seemed rather humiliating too."

Nova shrugged. "I guess I don't do revenge."

"Then it's lucky I did it for you." He surveyed her for a second, then added: "Maybe you should consider it sometime? I saw what you did to the trees. Seems to me like revenge would be something you'd be very good at."

Nova didn't know what to say, and so the two of them slipped back into silence. More time passed. She watched the girl outside the cell for a while. She had stopped crying now, and was sitting with her back against the wall. Her cheeks were stained red, and Nova realised with horror that the girl cried blood. The girl looked over, making eye contact with Nova.

"Don't look at her," Kit said.

Nova immediately brought her gaze to the floor in front of her. "Why?"

"Trust me, even I can't protect you from that one."

Nova swallowed, and nodded. She spent the next few minutes/hours/days – she still had no idea how much time had passed – examining the dents and scratches on the floor by her feet. As well as being terrified, she was bored out of her mind. It was cold, and the stone floor was uncomfortable. She shifted, her joints popping loudly.

"You can sit on the bed if you like," Kit said from his spot across the room.

"I'm fine," she lied. She decided to try and get him talking again. Anything to take her mind off her discomfort. "How did you know I was there in the woods that first night? When we spoke, you said you'd seen me before."

"I did."

"Is that your ability?" she guessed. "You can see things other people can't?"

"No. You're very bad at hiding. You literally fell out of the woods."

Nova rolled her eyes again, less nervous about his reaction than she had been before. He hadn't killed her yet, and she was feeling more and more sure he wasn't going to.

"Okay," she continued. "Then what *is* your ability?"

"I'm sure you can work it out," he replied.

Was he messing with her? She had absolutely no idea what he could do. It didn't seem to be something obvious, unless she was even more oblivious than she thought.

Embarrassed, she moved onto a different topic. "There was a boy out there, the one with black hair. He did something..." she paused, not really sure how to explain it. "He changed into things. Horrible things."

Kit smirked. "That would be William. Delightful, isn't he? I bet he was thrilled to see you."

"Why?"

"He hasn't had anyone new to scare in months. I imagine you were very interesting."

"Is that what he can do?" Nova asked, glancing back to the corridor. William wasn't there, he must've been further down, by the main entrance. "He can turn into the things people are frightened of?"

"Not exactly; he can make you see your deepest fears. The interesting part, though, is that they're all in your mind. If I were to watch him project your fears, you would see what most frightens you, but I would see William standing in front of you as he usually looks. Even he doesn't know what he's showing you." Kit quirked an eyebrow curiously. "What did he make you see?"

"I don't want to talk about it."

Kit sighed. "You know, conversations with you are rather one-sided. The point of saving you was so I would have someone interesting to talk to, but if you're going to be this dull..."

"What, you'll put me outside?" Nova snapped.

There was a banging on the glass. The girl who'd said she wanted to peel off Nova's flesh held up her bloodied hand and waved. Nova's skin prickled. Kit got to his feet wordlessly, and faced the glass. Nova couldn't see if he mouthed any words, or whether his presence was all it took, but the girl backed off, and soon they were alone again.

"Not yet, I suppose," he muttered.

CHAPTER
TWENTY-TWO

Not Scared Of You

The storm had died down. Nova hadn't heard a thunderclap for a long time.

"Are you wondering how you'll get out of here?" Kit asked. He had been walking slowly back and forth in front of the glass for a while. Nova sensed it was a habit he had. She wondered how many times he'd paced this cell.

"Of course I am." She'd been driving herself crazy over it. Even if she somehow managed to get out of Max without being ripped to shreds by the other kids, the guards would be on high alert after the cells unlocked. There was no way she'd be able to escape their notice. What would happen when they caught her? What was the punishment for sneaking into Maximum Security?

There probably isn't one yet, you're the only person stupid enough to do it.

Kit offered no words of encouragement, continuing his slow pacing.

"You've got a lot of tattoos," Nova said, trying to take her mind off of her impending doom.

He didn't say anything.

"What do they mean?" she pressed.

"They have to mean something?"

"Most people's do."

"Maybe I'm not like most people."

That's obvious.

Nova continued. "Usually, when people get tattoos that don't mean anything, it's stuff from movies. Or designs they like. But yours..." she trailed off. Kit's tattoos were strange. Many were symbols that didn't appear to be from any language she'd ever seen, yet weren't intricate enough to have been chosen for their aesthetic merit. They were all done in black, made up of different lines, shapes, or – occasionally – numbers. They had to mean *something*.

Whatever it was, he clearly wasn't willing to share it.

"Did they hurt?" she asked, lamely, desperate to keep the conversation going. It was hard to keep this guy talking, though at least it kept her busy.

"No."

"I heard tattoos hurt," she continued.

"They don't."

"Maybe you've got a high pain threshold?"

"There are far more painful things than tattoo needles. Trust me."

Nova's eyes were drawn to the collar around his neck. She gestured to it. "That?"

He snorted. "That's nothing."

"William wasn't wearing one."

"Lucky him."

Nova got to her feet, peering through the glass wall at

the few kids outside. "Elizabeth said the collars are meant to stop the Alternates in the Tombs using their powers."

"That's right."

"Not all of the kids are wearing them, though. Shouldn't everyone have one?"

Kit scowled. "You'd like us to be shackled like dogs?"

Nova's eyes widened. "No! I didn't mean that. I...I just wondered why some people have to wear them and some don't?"

He held her gaze for a minute, eyes cold. Eventually he spoke. "The collars are uncomfortable whether they're shocking you or not. It can make sleeping difficult. If you go long enough without using your ability, you earn the chance to have it off at night, providing your power isn't one that could damage your cell or anyone outside it. All William can do is scare the other kids, and even then, it's only the ones he can see. It's not really something the guards care about. Not so much fun for the person in the cell opposite his, but other than that he's harmless when he's locked up."

"You still have your collar," Nova said. "Does that mean you used your ability recently? Or is it too dangerous?"

He grinned. "Both."

He sounded almost like he was proud of that, and Nova wasn't sure what to make of it. She nodded towards the glass. "The kids out there, they started using their abilities on each other as soon as they were out of their cells."

"I don't doubt it."

"Why would they do that?" she asked. "Aren't they friends?"

He sounded confused. "Why would they be friends?"

"I would've thought after being locked down together here maybe-"

"You thought wrong," Kit said, coldly. "I'm sure you all have a wonderful time up at the main school, going to class and bonding at the pool and making memories." He said the words with disdain. "Down here, if you're still breathing, if someone hasn't tried to stick a blade of some kind in your back or put broken glass in your food, you're having a good day. I don't blame the others for taking the opportunity to have some fun."

Nova scowled. "Hurting people is fun?"

He held her gaze. "If they're the *right* people."

"Is that what you do?" Nova asked. "Does your ability let you hurt people?"

"If you want to know what I can do, then first you tell me about you."

"You saw what I did to the trees, isn't that enough?"

"Perhaps I want to hear it."

"Why?" Nova asked, irritated. "Because you're bored? Or because you want to make me feel bad?"

He frowned, as if he didn't understand. "Why would talking about your ability make you feel bad?"

Sounds of commotion in the distance ended their conversation. There were raised voices – adult voices – yelling at the kids to get back into their cells. Nova instinctively backed away from the glass. This was it. She was about to be discovered.

"Sounds like your knights in shining armour are here," Kit drawled.

Now it was Nova's turn to start pacing. "Oh god, what's going to happen to me?"

"I'm sure it'll be fine," Kit said. "Maybe they shout at you, maybe you get expelled, maybe they stick you in one of these cells for a couple of years. Maybe you move into the empty one over there and we spend the rest of our lives in the darkness, with only each other for company. What's the worst that could happen?"

"That's not helping at all." Nova moved back to the glass, craning her neck to try and see what was happening. It was no use, thanks to the angle, and the sharp turn in the corridor a few cells down, there was nothing to see yet. But it wouldn't be long until the guards arrived.

Kit came closer. "Maybe the guards aren't your biggest problem."

"What do you mean?" She was still trying to see if there was anyone coming.

"*Maybe* you should be more afraid of me."

She moved away from the glass, facing him now. "Very funny."

Kit's eyes locked with hers. The coldness had gone, replaced with an intensity she found impossible to look away from. They weren't blue, as she had originally thought, but a bright, vibrant grey. At that moment, trapped in the dark, looking at nothing but those eyes, she couldn't even bring herself to blink.

"What if I've been biding my time?" he asked, voice low. "It could be that I want to kill you with an audience." His face was inches from her own, his breath warm on her cold skin.

"You won't hurt me." Nova said, as much to herself as to him. "You've had all this time and you haven't even touched me."

He closed the gap between them even more by bringing his face closer to hers, whispering now. "Isn't anticipation half the fun? You know I'm locked up for a reason. We're all psychopaths down here, right?"

Another scream from the corridor. The guards were getting closer.

Nova swallowed. "I'm not scared of you." She didn't know if it was a lie or not.

An unreadable expression crossed his face. He took a step back. "When they come in, go with them. Don't speak, don't make a scene. Understand?"

There was such urgency in his voice, that all Nova could do was nod, even though she didn't understand what was happening at all.

Kit took a few more steps away from her, until his back hit the wall. "This place isn't what you think," he muttered.

"What do you mean?"

The door to the cell opened before he could say anything more. Nova turned around as a guard stepped inside. He walked forward, face expressionless, took hold of her arm, and lead her from the cell.

They walked in silence past the other kids, now locked away, past the empty check-in desk, through the corridors, and to the main door of the building. The guard opened the door, pushed her outside, and closed it again.

Nova stood outside the Tombs in the drizzling rain, as the sun began to peak over the horizon, with no idea what the hell had just happened.

Ant Mail

"Stop. This is too much."

Kate leaned back against the bench. She and Nova had taken their breakfast out to the courtyard so they could speak without being overheard. The storm from the night before had given way to bright sunshine, and the smell of the damp grass was pleasant and comforting. They had the courtyard to themselves, other than a couple of kids playing chess by the steps to the dorm, and Angela, who was meandering around as if she had no idea where she was or what she was supposed to be doing.

Kate ran a hand through her hair, loose today and cascading down her back like a waterfall.

"Let me get this right. You *broke into* the Tombs, snuck through the place until you found Maximum Security, then hung out in Carver's cell all night?"

Nova put down her uneaten waffle. "No. The Tombs had an open door, so I didn't break in. Going into Max wasn't exactly planned, it just sort of happened. And I didn't *hang out* in his cell. He stopped me from being killed, and then somehow got me out of there."

"And the guard didn't say *anything*?"

Nova shook her head. "It was so weird. It was like he wasn't even there. Like he was a robot, you know?"

"And no one else saw you?"

"I guess the other guards were busy getting the place locked down again. There don't seem to be any cameras down there either."

Kate shrugged. "What do you expect? The Alternate Academy is hardly drowning in funding, remember?"

"I half-expected Elizabeth to be standing over me when I woke up this morning, to yell at me or worse," Nova said. "But when I saw her in the cafeteria all she did was wave. It sounds impossible, but I'm pretty sure no one has any idea I was even down there."

"Do you think the other kids will tell?" Kate asked. "They all saw you last night."

"Saw me, threatened to kill me, *tried* to kill me..."

"Exactly. Aren't you worried they'll blow your cover?"

Nova considered this. "I don't know. I mean, for starters, it's not like any of them know my name, or anything about me. And if they did say something, I don't even know if anyone would believe them."

"Lucky for you," Kate said. She exhaled loudly, leaning back on the bench and absentmindedly stroking a butterfly that had landed on her arm. Colin was in one of the flower beds, finding breakfast. "This is all so insane. The fact that you got out of there with no repercussions is one thing, but to be honest I'm more surprised that Carver didn't kill you."

"You've heard about him?" Nova asked.

"Well, yeah. When you said you had a boyfriend down in the Tombs, I never thought-"

"He's not my boyfriend," Nova interrupted.

Kate waved her hand dismissively. "Whatever. He's been down there since he was a kid. I heard he killed a bunch of people, all in one go."

"How?"

"No clue. All I know is that it was a big deal. And it happened *here*, so it must've been teachers or students or both. That's probably why everyone is so scared of him."

Nova's cogs were turning. "If you've heard about him, that means other kids might have..."

Kate groaned. "I can see where this is going. Don't do it, Nov."

"There's something about him," Nova insisted. "He knows things he's not telling me. I mean, what do you make of what he said about Tidemarsh not being what I think it is?"

"I think he was saying whatever he could to make you want to go see him again."

Nova shook her head. "I can't shake the feeling he's important, somehow."

Kate narrowed her gaze. "Are you *sure* you're not into him?"

"You said he killed a bunch of people. He *told me* hurting people is fun. How could I like someone like that?"

A familiar voice came from Nova's left: "You can still like people who scare you."

"Danny!" Nova scowled, waving her hand, and meeting invisible flesh.

"Hey! A couple of inches lower and that would've been really unpleasant for both of us."

Kate got to her feet, causing the butterfly to take flight, and scowled in the direction Danny's voice had come from. "Have you been listening to our conversation?"

"Only the last part," Danny said. "And I'm right, you can be attracted to people who scare you. Like me with you."

Kate rolled her eyes. "It's not going to happen, Danny."

"We already kiss-"

"Fine, it's not going to happen *again*."

Nova folded her arms. "Did you hear anything else?"

Danny paused before answering. "No. Well, only about you having a crush on Killer Carver. But that's it."

Nova groaned, swiping her hand through the air again. Danny avoided her swing this time.

"I don't have a crush on him," she insisted through gritted teeth. "I only want to find out what he knows."

"How?" Kate asked, sitting back down.

"Maybe you could send him a note?" Danny suggested. "That way you don't have to physically go down to Max again." He paused. "Okay maybe I heard the whole thing."

"You're such an idiot," Nova muttered.

"He might have a point though," Kate said. "Write him a note, see what he says."

Nova considered this. "How would I get it to him?"

Kate grinned. "Leave that part to me."

And so that was how Nova found herself in the library that afternoon, trying to put together the perfect note for Kit. So far, it wasn't going well. She reread her latest attempt.

Hi Kit, it's me. Nova. From last night. And the fence. What did you mean when you told me not to trust Elizabeth? Do you know something about her? Are you psychic? Please tell me, because it's driving me insane. Also, I suck at writing notes, and this is useless. Oh, and my friends think I have a crush on you because I can't stop talking about you, so that's awesome for me.

Nova scowled, screwing the paper into a ball. She'd been at it for over an hour, and somehow that was her best attempt. Numerous others had been tossed into the overflowing bin next to the desk, as she grew increasingly angry at her appalling lack of communication skills. This was a terrible idea. She seriously doubted that Kit was going to pour his heart out into a note, and tell her all the juicy secrets he apparently knew about the school. He'd barely answered her questions when they spoke in person, so asking him to write everything on a piece of paper no larger than a five pound note was ridiculous.

Nova would need to change tactics. She pushed the balled-up paper aside and grabbed a new piece.

We need to talk. Meet me by the fence tonight. I have questions and I really need you to answer them!

She crossed out the last part and rewrote it.

I have questions, and you owe me answers. Nova.

She read it a couple of times. Not too bad. It made her sound confident. Yes, she'd have to do the opposite of what Kate wanted, and go back down to the Tombs, but at least this way she could be relatively sure he'd be at the fence waiting for her. It was better than heading down and hoping for the best. Plus, maybe he'd actually be ready to talk about stuff if he had a warning.

"Hey," Kate said, as she sat down on the edge of the table. "Finished?"

"I think so."

"Great." Kate held out her arm, and hundreds of ants scuttled out from under her sleeve and down onto the table.

"They were just...there?" Nova asked.

"I brought them from outside."

Nova blinked. "That must've felt weird."

"I'm used to it."

"Hey guys." Luke was standing a few feet away, his arms full of books.

"Hey," Nova said. "What are you doing here?"

"I volunteer at the library."

Kate gave Nova a sideways glance. "Is that a good idea? Having someone sorting through books who occasionally bursts into flames?"

Luke shrugged. "They didn't exactly have a long list of candidates. It was me or the girl who makes tiny black holes." He eyed Colin, perched on Kate's shoulder. "Are you allowed to bring that thing in here?"

"*He*," Kate corrected, "likes to explore during the day. If you want to put him back in the dorm, though, be my guest." She took the spider off her shoulder and held him out to Luke.

He recoiled. "I'm good." His eyes flicked to the table behind the girls. "What's with the ants? They like exploring too?"

"They're delivering a message," Nova said, turning back as the last one scuttled off the desk. "But doing a terrible job, it's still here." She grabbed the piece of paper and held it up. "They left the note." Then her stomach dropped; the desk was empty. "Wait. Where's the other one?"

Kate sounded confused. "What do you mean?"

"There was another note, I balled it up because it was awful." Nova shook the scrap of paper in her hand. "*This* is the one I needed them to take."

"Why didn't you throw the other one in the bin?" Kate asked.

"I guess I didn't expect your ants to ignore the perfectly smooth piece of paper in favour of the one that looked like a piece of rubbish!" Nova's voice was getting higher. She got to her feet, searching the floor around the desk. It was no good, the ants had disappeared. "Can you call them back?"

"It doesn't work like that."

"Are you kidding? You're meant to be the bug girl!"

Kate arched an eyebrow. "First; that's the worst superhero name ever. Second; do you have any idea how hard it is to get a hundred insects to do what I want?" She didn't wait for a response. "I usually need to be close to make them behave in complex ways, so for something like this I have to imprint things in their brains. I need to tell them where to go, who to look for, and what to do when they get there. I only have your directions and a vague description of what the guy looks like to go on. I had to do all of that while I was holding them. I can't call them back with a whistle like a dog." Kate softened her tone. "I'm sorry, the ants won't come back until they've done what I told them to."

Nova dropped back onto her chair, defeated. "Okay, I get it."

"How bad was the note?" Luke asked.

"Bad."

"Who was it for?"

Kate waved him off. "Don't you have some books to set alight? Get out of here."

Secret's Out

Nova couldn't bring herself to go to the Tombs that night. Not after the disaster of the note. In fact, if it had been up to her, she would've dug herself a hole, climbed inside, and stayed there for the rest of her life. She couldn't bear to even guess what Kit must have thought of her after reading it.

Kate said he hadn't replied, despite the ants bringing him a pencil, which Nova supposed was a small mercy. At least she didn't have to read whatever cutting words he had to say after that abomination of a note. There was a part of her, though, that couldn't help but imagine why he had chosen not to write back. Maybe he was too busy laughing? Or perhaps he was so embarrassed on her behalf that he decided to cut all ties? Either way, she remained in her bed until morning.

Breakfast came and went without much excitement. She and Kate got their trays, and purposefully talked about anything that wasn't related to the Tombs or Carver. Luke appeared and tried – unsuccessfully – to make Kate's bacon a little crispier. Then Danny arrived – fully clothed and visible – to ask if the girls wanted to watch a movie in the TV room later.

The conversation passed Nova by, as she pushed her scrambled eggs around her plate. She caught sight of Madeline, sitting a few tables over. Nova had taken the hair/evidence into the woods the previous afternoon with Kate and a box of matches. She had been too scared of it being found to throw it in the bin, though she had to admit, it had felt kind of sacrificial to set it alight; like she and Kate should've been naked, chanting, and throwing eye of newt into the flames.

Nova saw that Madeline had somehow got her long locks back, and looked as beautiful as ever.

"How did that happen?" Nova asked the others, finally breaking her silence.

Kate followed her gaze. "She went to Laura."

"From our dorm?" Nova asked. "The one who makes plants grow?"

"Right. She convinced her to see if her ability worked on humans as well as plants."

"Looks like it did," Nova noted.

Luke grinned. "I heard it worked too well."

"What do you mean?" Nova asked.

"See for yourself."

Nova glanced back over at Madeline. At first, she couldn't understand what Luke meant, then she realised; Madeline's hair was longer than it had been a moment ago.

"It's constantly growing," Luke explained. "I heard she's had to cut it, like, six times already."

"And it keeps getting full of weeds," Danny added.

"My heart bleeds," Kate drawled, getting to her feet. "Shall we go?"

Nova's first class was mastery, and she was once again doing everything she could to avoid using her ability. She sat at a table in the corner, while the other kids spread out around the room, working under the watchful eye of Miss Garrett.

Jason, the one who turned everything to sand, was practicing holding ping pong balls without gloves on. His eyes were unblinking, and he bit his lip anxiously as he balanced the ball in the palm of his right hand. Miss Garrett was counting the seconds before it inevitably dissolved into a small pile of sand.

"That was five!" she said, cheerfully. "A personal best! Let's try again." She grabbed a new ball from the pack and dropped it into his hand.

Mark, the kid who could multiply himself, was trying unsuccessfully to make one of his doubles move a cardboard tube across the table. The girl with extending limbs was getting some help from a couple of the other students pulling her arm back inside, after she'd tried to get it out of the window and over to one of the flower beds in the courtyard.

"Don't step on it!" she yelled out of the window at the kids below. "Drag it over and toss it through the window. And see if you can find my watch!"

"Is something on your mind?" Angela asked. She was sitting in the chair opposite Nova, resting her head on the desk as if trying to take a nap, and asked the question without even looking up.

"Yes." Nova replied, honestly.

"Okay."

"Are you going to ask me what it is?"

"No."

Nova stifled a smile, her first of the day. There was something about Angela she was starting to really like. She was dreamy and distant, but at least she was honest. Angela didn't say or do things because she was *meant* to. She said and did whatever felt right at the time.

"Are you going to try and use your ability today?" Angela asked.

"Not if I can help it," Nova replied.

"How are you two getting on?" Miss Garrett asked, appearing at their table. As neither of the girls had expressed an interest in joining in with the others, they'd once again been given the tedious task of further exploring their triggers.

So far Angela's sheet of paper contained nothing but a crude drawing of a man with knives in his eyes, and Nova's was blank. She tried to casually cover it with her arm, forcing a smile.

"We're fine, thanks."

Miss Garrett opened her mouth to speak, when there was a scream from the other side of the classroom. Jason was standing in front of a pile of sand. A *large* pile.

His eyes were wide. "I told Mark to drop the ball, but he passed it. He touched my hand and...*I told him*!"

A ripple of realization spread through the class. The sand was Mark.

Was.

Miss Garrett hurried over. "It's alright," she said, kneeling in front of the pile. "It's alright, step back please."

Jason did as he was told, and Miss Garrett held her hands over the sand. For a moment, nothing happened. The whole class was silent. Then, the sand began to vibrate, rumble, and lift upwards. It formed the outline of a person, which – in only a few seconds – solidified into Mark.

"What happened?" he asked, then grimaced, spitting some sand onto the carpet.

Jason exhaled loudly, then pulled his gloves back on. "I'm done."

"Jason-" Miss Garrett began.

He ignored her, storming out of the room.

"I think that will do for today," Miss Garrett said. She was pale, and wobbled as some of the other kids helped her to her chair. "Could someone please take Mark to the nurse?" she added. "I'd like her to check him over. The rest of you are dismissed."

The girl who could make the bubbles and the one with the extending arms led Mark away, and the rest of the class filed out.

"How did she do that?" Nova asked Angela, as they headed to the door.

"It's her ability, to fix the mistakes we make."

"Is she alright?" As the girls passed her desk, Nova could hear their teacher breathing heavily.

Angela lowered her voice. "I think it's harder to undo things like that. She just brought Mark back from the dead."

By the next morning, Nova had come to a decision. She wasn't going to obsess over Kit, what he thought about the hideous note, or the cryptic comments he'd made about Elizabeth and Tidemarsh. It was time to pick a side; she could either continue fumbling her way through life, making bad choices, and following unreliable hunches, or commit to the school. She could learn how to control her abilities, get a good education, and – when she graduated – live like a normal person.

So that was what she was going to do.

When Miss Farley instructed her class to run laps of the grounds again – while she read her book on one of the benches – Nova told herself that she was going to work hard and not slip into the woods to kill time with Kate. That, however, was before she remembered how terrible she was at running. Soon enough, the two girls had left their classmates and snuck beyond the tree line.

I guess no one's perfect.

Kate wiped her brow with the back of her hand. It was a particularly hot day, without even the faintest whisper of a breeze. "You've got mastery again tomorrow, right?" she asked.

"Yeah," Nova said, grimly. "For all the good it's done me so far."

"You still don't want to use your ability?"

"How can I? I could blow anything, or *anyone*, to pieces."

Kate shrugged. "Miss Garrett can bring them back."

"Can she always do it? Bring people back from the dead?"

Kate thought for a moment. "I think it has to be recent, like within the last minute or so."

"Well, even if she can undo it, I'm pretty sure it'd still be unpleasant for whoever I rip apart."

"They'll get over it," Kate said with a wink, as she helped a caterpillar into a nearby bush.

There was a voice from somewhere behind them: "So that's your power? You blow things up?" Luke stepped out from behind a tree, grinning.

"Luke, what the hell?" Kate scowled.

Nova's face burned. Up until this point, she'd managed to keep her ability a secret from most of the other kids. What would Luke think of her now he knew how dangerous she was?

But his smile was soft, and he held up his hands. "Relax, we won't tell anyone."

Kate raised an eyebrow. "*We?*"

Danny's head popped out from behind a different tree. "Hey."

"What are you two doing here?" Kate asked.

"The same thing as you," Luke replied, simply. "Skipping PE."

"Mr. Henderson wants us swimming across the lake," Danny said. "I'm a terrible swimmer, and Luke dies if he goes in the water-"

Luke rolled his eyes. "Funny."

"We thought we'd hang out in here for a while."

"So, Nova," Luke began, taking a seat on a tree stump. "What's the biggest thing you've ever blown up?"

"Is it loud?" Danny asked.

"Does it hurt?" Luke added.

"Could you, like, blow up a bomb, and make the explosion twice as big?"

"What does it feel like?"

"What would happen if you blew something up in space?"

"Have you ever blown up a person?" Luke asked.

"And we're done," Kate interrupted, taking Nova by the arm. "We're out. Enjoy your day boys."

Kate had told Nova to ignore Luke and Danny. She said they were idiots who said the first things that came into their heads, and had four brain cells between them. Nova wanted to laugh. She wanted to not care about their ridiculous questions. But she couldn't. And that night, Nova couldn't sleep.

Have you ever blown up a person?
Have you ever blown up a person?
Have you ever blown up a person?

The words had been echoing around her head since lights out. Even though she'd thought about the accident every day, hearing the words made it feel so raw. She had *killed* someone. Gary wasn't breathing anymore, because of what she did. Gary was dead.

That night, she didn't dream of the corridor, or the darkness, or the screams.

She dreamt about that day.

CHAPTER TWENTY-FIVE

That Day

"What are you doing?" Nova asked.

Gary spun around. Clearly, he'd not been expecting her to come home yet. In his defence, Nova usually went to the library after school and stayed until they locked up – anything to hold off coming back to this house – but today it was being repainted, and she'd had to come straight home instead.

After a long, meandering walk – in which she'd circled her street twice – Nova had arrived at the house. They'd only been living there a few weeks, though it was pretty much the same as the others they'd lived in. Nova had lost count of the number of times they moved. Usually it was to a small place in the middle of an okay neighbourhood, in a grey little town. Moving to London this time had been better – at least there was more for her to do to keep her out of the house – but at home things were the same as ever. She was given the smallest room, and then pretty much left to her own devices. Gary and Barbara actively avoided her, and as long as she kept out of their way, they could continue their lives as if she didn't exist, which was everyone's preference.

When she'd opened the door of her bedroom today, though, Gary had been standing by the window with his hand in her jewellery box. She didn't have much in the way of jewellery in there; a couple of pairs of earrings, a watch she'd won in a claw machine, and the thing her stepdad was currently holding: a silver locket that had belonged to her mother.

"Why do you have that?" Nova's voice cracked; she already knew the answer.

"Relax," Gary said, dropping the locket into his pocket. "It's only for a few days."

Nova swallowed, blinking back the tears that were already pricking at the corners of her eyes. "That's what you said about the other stuff." Her mother's bracelets, earrings, necklaces. Everything that had been worth anything had been pawned, piece by piece. It was supposed to be for a few days. Nova had never seen any of it again. She had put up with it all, but not this, not the locket. Not this one last bit of her mom.

She took a step into the room. "Gary, please."

"You've never called me Dad," Gary mused. His pupils were huge, and his voice had a thick tone that she knew too well after all these years. Was it beer today? Whisky, maybe? It had become his new favourite. There was still a bottle or two downstairs. Or perhaps it was something else.

She didn't reply to his comment about her never calling him Dad. He didn't seem to expect one anyway. He closed the jewellery box gently, and moved to the door.

Nova blocked his path. "Give it back."

Gary snorted, and made to walk past her. She blocked him again.

"It's the only thing of Mum's that I have left," she said, her voice pleading.

Gary leaned forward and did something he'd never done before: he ruffled her hair.

"Don't worry kiddo," he said. "I'll get this one back, I promise." He winked, then put his hands on her shoulders and firmly moved her aside so he could pass.

At first, Nova simply stood in the doorway. Then, as the familiar feeling of loss settled heavily on her chest, something snapped. She turned, storming after him. He was halfway down the stairs when she caught up.

"Gary, give it back," she insisted.

He waved his hand dismissively without turning around. "Enough, we've talked about this."

"No, you *talked* about it," she countered, as they reached the bottom of the stairs. She followed him to the kitchen, her voice getting louder. "I didn't stop you when you pawned everything else Mum left me. I didn't stop you when you emptied the bank account she'd set up for me-"

"Hey, you think raising a kid is cheap?" His voice was sharp now.

Nova ignored him. "You make me do everything around here. I cook, I clean, I do everyone's washing. You let your wife treat me like dirt, I can't say my mum's name without being yelled at-"

"That's enough!" His face was red.

"-and I put up with it all!" Nova was shaking now. She took a breath, and lowered her voice. "You can keep treating me like crap, I don't care. But that locket is *mine. You can sell*

219

your own stuff to drink or get high, or whatever it is you need money for, and give that back to me right now, or-"

He slapped her, hard. Nova recoiled, clutching her hand to her face. Her eyes were wide. He'd never hit her before. He'd yelled, made fun of her, talked down to her, and generally treated her like she was less than nothing. But he'd never hit her.

Gary took a few seconds to compose himself. When he spoke, his voice was icy. "Now, listen here, you ungrateful shit, I won't let anyone speak to me like that. I'm going to chalk that one up to teenage hormones, or that it's your lady time or whatever, but if you ever talk to me like that again, you won't like what happens."

Nova's vision rippled. Her anger was subsiding, giving way to humiliation. She fought against it. She wouldn't let him see her cry.

Gary didn't blink. "Do you understand that?"

"Yes," she whispered.

"Good." He smirked. "You're like your mum. She used to get that wounded bunny look too when I showed her what was what. She learned quick enough though. Sometimes all a woman needs is a little tough love."

That was what did it.

It had been building, of course: the locket, the slap, the insults. And before that, the years of being treated like a servant, an outsider, unwanted and unloved. Maybe if he'd left it there, Gary might've survived. But when Nova thought of her mother, her loving, kind, beautiful mother – who cried when she accidentally killed a spider, and whose embrace had always made Nova feel like they were the only two people in the world – being broken down by someone as weak and cruel as Gary? That was the nail in the coffin.

Had she known what she was about to do? No.

Would she have stopped if she had? Probably not.

It didn't matter. At that moment Nova had no control over her actions, and as the anger built inside her with more speed and ferocity than she had ever felt before, it was all she could do to close her eyes as it ripped through her and tore Gary into a million nasty little pieces.

Nova woke up with her heart racing. She sat up in bed. It was still dark, and everyone else in the dorm was asleep. With a shaking hand, she took a sip of water from the glass on her bedside table.

It had felt so real. She could still smell his breath from when he had yelled at her, feel the sting of the slap against her cheek. The warmth of his blood spattering against her skin. Nova hadn't allowed herself to think about that day, or really take the time to think about it at all since it had happened. Now the memories were forcing their way through the walls she'd built up.

He deserved it.

No one deserves to die like that.

He was a bad person.

Am I a bad person too?

Nova's thoughts were interrupted by a noise to her left. Fingers closed around her arm.

"Get dressed."

CHAPTER TWENTY-SIX

Apple Crumble

"I really could've done without a late-night heart attack," Nova said with a yawn, as she traipsed through the woods.

Kate looked back at her, grinning. "I thought about something gentler, but honestly, scaring you was too much fun."

"Thanks." Nova pulled her coat a little tighter. It was the standard black coat that everyone at Tidemarsh got given, but was a couple of sizes too big, and made Nova feel like she was a kid borrowing her mum's clothes. "What are we doing out here anyway?"

"You'll see, come on, we're nearly there."

The Tombs came into view up ahead, and for one horrible moment Nova thought that was where they were going, but Kate changed direction, and headed further into the woods. After walking for a few more minutes, they arrived at a clearing, surrounded by trees on all sides. Moonlight shone onto the ground, illuminating two figures waiting for them.

"You're late," Luke said.

"You're boring," Kate retorted.

He flipped her off with a smirk.

"What are we doing?" Nova asked.

"I decided we all need to blow off some steam," Kate said. "And this is the best place to do it." She turned her attention to the guys, narrowing her gaze. "These two have promised not to ask ridiculous questions about your ability or, you know, be the idiots that they are."

"Yes we have," Danny said, cheerfully.

"So, I agreed that they could join us." Kate gestured to their surroundings. "We're safe here."

"No one can see us," Danny explained. "And because we're within the school grounds, if we use our powers, the ripples get lost among everyone else's."

"Which means no one will know it's us," Luke added.

That explained why no one had come looking for Nova when she used her ability in the woods after her confrontation with Madeline.

"You want to use your abilities?" Nova asked, unable to keep the anxiety out of her voice. She wasn't worried about her friends; they clearly had more control over what they could do than she did, and other than Luke, they weren't really that dangerous. But if they were goofing around with their powers, it would only be so long before they wanted her to join in, and that wasn't something she could do.

Kate squeezed her hand. "You don't have to do anything you don't want to; you can watch us." She glanced around. "We could use some more light. Luke, do you mind?"

There was already a pile of logs and sticks laid out on

the ground, and with one touch Luke set it ablaze, bathing them in a warm orange glow.

"Okay, let's get started," he said.

Nova took a seat on a nearby log, as Luke began rummaging through a backpack. He pulled out various fruits: bananas, apples, pears, and a large bunch of grapes.

"Hungry?" Kate asked, sarcastically.

"Har har. Next time you can be in charge of victims." He put an apple down on the ground, crouched next to it, and placed one finger on its side. A couple of seconds passed, before the fruit burst into flames.

"My turn," Kate said, taking an apple of her own.

"Going to turn it into a ladybird?" Luke asked.

"If I ever learn to turn things into insects, you'll be the first one I transform into a slug. Oh, wait, too late."

Danny and Nova laughed.

Luke grinned. "Ouch, why don't you say how you really feel, Katie?"

Kate winked, then turned her attention to the apple. Nova watched as slowly it wriggled, then began to get higher and higher. At first, she thought it was levitating, then she saw the tower of ants building up underneath, lifting it into the air. Once it got to a couple of feet off the ground, it began to rotate, and then dropped to the floor. The ants disappeared within seconds.

"That felt good," Kate said.

"I know what you mean," Luke agreed. "If I don't get to use my power – like, really *use* it – for a few days, I start to feel kind of tense."

Kate was nodding. "Like you need to stretch, right?"

"Exactly."

Danny piped up. "Hey, I have an idea, why don't we have a contest?"

"What kind of contest?" Kate asked.

"The first person to get rid of their fruit, using their ability, wins."

"You're on," Luke said. He tossed another apple to Kate, a banana to Danny, and kept a pear for himself. He held up another pear. "Are you sure you don't want to join in, Nova?"

"I'm good," she replied, quickly.

"Nova can be the judge," Kate said.

Danny, Kate, and Luke each placed their fruit in front of them and took a few steps back.

"I'm going to try something new," Luke said. "I apologise in advance if I set any of you on fire."

Danny's eyes widened. "Great, thanks."

Luke laughed. "Will you count us down, Nova?"

"Three, two, one, go!"

It was amazing to watch. Luke shot a burst of fire from his hand, as if he was holding a flame thrower. It hit the ground next to his pear first, before setting the fruit alight. He continued to hold the burst, and the pear began to shrivel within the flames.

Kate had summoned a swarm of crawling insects, who set upon her apple, tearing chunks off at incredible speed.

Danny waited a few seconds, then turned invisible. Because his clothes remained, Nova could see him walk towards the banana. He reached out, taking hold of it with an invisible hand. He held it up in the air for around five seconds, before the whole thing vanished.

"I did it!" he yelled.

The other two stopped. Luke's pear was no more than a shrivelled husk, and only the core remained from Kate's apple.

"Where did it go?" she asked.

"I made it invisible! I've never made anything else disappear before; I've been trying for weeks!" Danny reappeared, and so did the banana in his hand. "This is huge!"

"That's great man," said Luke. "Maybe you'll eventually be able to keep your underwear on when you use your ability."

"That'd be nice for all of us," Kate added.

Everyone laughed, and then Luke turned to Nova, grabbing another apple from his bag. "Why don't you give it a try?"

Nova swallowed. "I...I don't think so."

"Come on, Nova," Danny said, softly. "We're all the way out here, no one will see."

"I'm not worried about getting caught. I'm worried about hurting someone."

Luke cocked his head to one side. "Have you ever used your ability because you wanted to? Not because you were triggered?"

"No."

"What about in mastery Class?"

"I *never* use it," she insisted.

He gave a kind smile. "Let us help you."

Nova's stomach was churning, yet for some reason she found herself agreeing. Maybe it was peer pressure. Maybe she wanted to impress the others. Or maybe part of her – a teeny tiny part – wanted to use her power again. Just once. Just to see if she could do it on her own.

Luke put the apple on the ground in front of her.

"First step," Kate said. "Stop being nervous."

"I don't think that's possible," Nova muttered.

"Abilities are easier to control if your mind is clear. Take a few deep breaths."

Nova did as she asked, and though her stomach was still turning over, her heart rate slowed a little. "Now what?"

Luke pointed to the apple. "You need to focus on the thing you want to use your abilities on. Clear your mind of everything else, and keep repeating in your head what you want to do. You can even say it aloud if you want."

"Hold out your hand," Kate added. "It's not where your power comes from, but having it there can help to funnel the energy in the direction you want it to go."

Nova's mind was starting to feel clogged up.

"It's not always like this," Kate continued. "When you get used to using it, it'll feel as easy as breathing, I promise."

"I don't know if I want to ever get used to it." Nova took another breath. "I'll try. Can you guys take, like, 100 steps back?"

The three of them moved behind her, and all the way back to the tree line. Nova's heart was racing again. She closed her eyes, and tried to steady her breathing.

You can do this. You can do this.

When she felt ready, she opened her eyes again, and focused on the apple. She fought to clear her mind of everything else, held out her hand, and pointed it at the fruit.

Blow the apple up.

Nothing happened.

She sighed. "I can't do it," she yelled to the others.

"Keep trying!" Kate called back.

Nova took another breath.

Blow the apple up.

Again, nothing happened.

"This is stupid," she muttered.

"Don't think," Danny yelled. "*Feel*."

"Great advice, thanks."

Nova brought her attention back to the stupid fruit. She was getting mad now. Her friends were asking too much. How could they expect her to suddenly perform for them, when she'd never used her powers like this before? It was ridiculous. Besides, they didn't understand what she was afraid of. None of them had killed anyone before. Did they have any idea how dangerous this whole thing was? And they wanted her to do it, just for their entertainment? Maybe she should tell them exactly what she thought-

Something surged, and there was a loud crack from the space in front of her. Dirt flew into the air, spattering mud and moss into her hair, and knocking her back onto the ground.

Nova coughed, sitting up. The apple was gone, and there was a crater the size of a football where it had been.

There were whoops and cheers from the tree line, and seconds later she was pulled to her feet.

"That was so cool!" Danny said.

"Amazing!" Luke agreed.

"I've never seen anything like that," Kate said. "How do you feel?"

Nova opened her mouth, but couldn't find the words.

Kate smiled. "Don't worry, the first time you use your ability through choice is a big thing. Maybe we should call it a night for now?"

The group headed back up to the dorm building, both guys still talking about how awesome Nova's ability was. Once they reached the back door, they all silently snuck back inside, and split to go to their rooms.

"You did really well," Kate said when they arrived outside their own dorm. "You should be proud."

"Thanks," Nova murmured.

"The more you practice, the more you'll realise you control your ability. It doesn't control you."

Kate headed inside, and Nova followed behind. She was grateful for the darkness; it meant her friend couldn't see the worry etched across her face. Nova was still no closer to controlling this thing. It had only worked because she got mad.

She was pretty sure she would always fall victim to it.

CHAPTER
TWENTY-SEVEN

A Better Time To Visit

Nova, Kate, Danny, and Luke were finishing dinner the next evening, when Angela appeared at their table.

"Hello," she said. Her eyes lacked their usual dreamy gaze, and right now were fixed on Nova's. This was something new; she and Angela rarely interacted with each other outside of mastery class.

"Hi," Nova replied.

"You need to come with me."

Nova blinked. "Why?"

"Come on." Angela didn't wait for a response, turning and heading towards the doors.

"What was that all about?" Danny asked. He and the others looked as confused as Nova was.

"I have no idea." She watched Angela leave the cafeteria without as much as a backward glance. "I guess I should go with her."

Kate shook her head as Nova got to her feet. "You're not serious?"

"That girl's crazy," Luke muttered.

Nova felt oddly defensive of Angela. "She's not crazy. Anyway, I want to know what she wants."

"To see what your insides look like, probably," Luke suggested.

"Then I hope she can do it quickly, I've got homework." Nova picked up her tray. "I'll see you guys later."

"Do you want me to come with you?" Danny asked. "I can go invisible-"

"No. Please keep your trousers on." Nova didn't wait for any more offers of help, and headed to the doors. Once she had dumped her tray, she headed outside, where Angela was already walking away at a brisk pace. Nova had to hurry to catch up with her. The sun was setting, and the air was cool and damp.

"Where are we going?" Nova asked.

Angela didn't slow down at all. "You'll see."

There was something different about her tone, but Nova couldn't put her finger on it. Whatever it was, it kept her from asking any more questions, and she simply followed Angela down a path off from the courtyard. They walked for a while, past the lake, and away from the main school buildings. Several minutes later, the Tombs came into view. Nova had never come from this direction before, always approaching from the woods, and it was strange to see the place from the front.

It didn't look any more inviting.

"Angela," Nova began.

Angela didn't turn back, striding confidently in a way Nova had never seen her walk before.

Nova reached out, grabbing her arm, and stopping her in her tracks. "Hey."

When Angela finally looked at her, her eyes were so different, so intense. Almost like it wasn't her at all.

Nova dropped her arm. "Why are we here? What's going on?"

Angela smiled. "This is a better night to come down here."

"Huh? What do you..."

Then it all came back to her. *"You picked a bad night to come down here, Nova."* She'd heard those words when she spent the night in Max.

"*Kit*?" Nova asked, taking a step back.

Angela turned, heading around the side of the building. All Nova could do was follow, and they headed to the door she had entered through during the storm. There was a guard waiting. He was short, probably in his late 30's or early 40's, and had the kind of handlebar moustache usually reserved for villains in old movies. He glanced at Nova uneasily.

"See you soon," Angela said, walking away. She took a few steps, and then stood still. For a second or two she didn't move, then glanced around slowly, as if only now realising where she was.

What's happening to her?

Nova's thoughts were interrupted by the guard's impatient voice. "You're late."

She turned to face him, as Angela slowly walked back along the path, lacking her previously confident stride.

"Sorry," Nova muttered. "I didn't know I was supposed-"

He cut her off. "Come with me, and put these on." He

held out a pair of cuffs, the same kind she'd seen Kit wearing when he was walked through the facility.

Nova swallowed. "Why do-"

Before she could even finish speaking, he had snapped them over her wrists, and pulled her firmly through the door. He led her through the building, and with each step Nova's chest tightened. What was happening? Was she in trouble? For once, she hadn't been trying to sneak down there. She hadn't been trying to break the rules. Why was she in cuffs?

They reached the double doors to Maximum Security, and Nova's feet stopped moving. The guard tried to push her on.

"Why am I here?" she stuttered. "I don't understand."

"Shh," he hissed, glancing around. "Do you want us to get caught? I'm risking my neck here."

He's breaking the rules; this isn't official.

Is Kit responsible for all of this?

Mildly reassured she wasn't about to be locked away, Nova forced herself to move, and the guard took her into Max. The desk was empty; there were no other guards. Nova and the moustached man passed the other cells quickly, though she saw William glance up at her curiously from behind his book, and soon they reached the end of the corridor. The guard unlocked the wrist restraints, and left her alone without another word.

There was a plastic chair in front of the glass wall of Kit's cell. The cell opposite was still empty, as were the others leading up to his end of the corridor. He was alone down there.

"Hello Nova." His voice came from the darkness. Even

though the lights in the corridor and in the other cells were working, the ones in his cell were off. Nova wondered if they were broken, or if it was a choice the guards had made. How long had he been left in the dark?

She swallowed. "Hi."

"There's a chair, if you'd like to sit," he offered.

"Thank you."

It squeaked when she sat down, the only sound in the suffocating silence that surrounded them. Kit, still in the shadows, had yet to say anything else.

Why isn't he talking?

Nova fought the urge to tap her feet, though her heart was racing and sitting still felt like the hardest thing she'd ever done. Why wasn't he speaking to her? If he had orchestrated this whole thing to get her down there, what did he want? If it was to make her feel anxious, weirded-out, and self-conscious, then mission accomplished.

He finally spoke: "I enjoyed reading your note."

Oh crap.

Heat rose to Nova's cheeks. She could tell from his voice that he was smirking.

"That was a mistake," she gabbled. "I screwed it up because I was going to toss it away. The stupid ants picked up the wrong one."

"I see."

Silence again. Did he believe her?

"How did you get me here?" she asked, hastily changing the subject. "Why did the guard help you? And what did you do to Angela? Were you-"

He cut her off. "Can I answer one question at a time?"

She dropped her gaze, embarrassed. "Yes."

"The guard, Frank, owes me some favours. He'll be the one to bring you here whenever you visit."

"Whenever I-"

Kit stepped closer to the glass, into what little light there was, and the action ended Nova's sentence abruptly. She couldn't believe how someone stuck in a place like this, sitting in a damp, dark cell, could manage to look so *normal*. There she was, with her hair rapidly escaping her ponytail, a ladder in her stockings, and a ketchup stain on her shirt, while Kit remained...beautiful. There was no other word for it. The other kids Nova had passed – with the exception, perhaps, of William – had a sad, beat-down energy. Not Kit though. His eyes, though ringed with dark circles, remained a bright and piercing grey. His sharp features were so perfectly sculpted he would've been at home on the cover of any high fashion magazine. Though he was dressed in the same prison-style uniform as everyone else in the Tombs, he somehow made it look made to measure, with the shirt accentuating the muscles in his arms, and the trousers sitting low on his hips. It was almost unfair that someone who looked like he did was locked away in the dark.

"We both know you can't help but come back to this place," he said. "It would make sense to have a guard escorting you when you visit. I'm not sure what the conse-quences would be if you got caught down here." There was a smile playing on his lips. "Would you like to play a game?"

That caught her off-guard. "A game? What kind of game?"

"How about catch, or twister?"

"Very funny," Nova drawled.

"You have questions. So do I. We take it in turns to ask."

"It's not much of a game," she said.

"Humour me, my options are limited."

Nova chewed her lip. She couldn't deny that she was curious about Kit, and if he was willing to answer some questions, then she supposed she could offer him the same. "Okay. You start."

He thought for a moment. "How are you feeling? I haven't seen you since the storm."

Of all the things he could've asked, she was surprised that was his first question. "I'm fine, thanks." She paused, then added: "I mean, really, thanks. You saved my life that night."

"Try not to spread that around," he whispered. "I wouldn't want people thinking I've gone soft."

"It's my turn now, right?" she asked.

He nodded.

"What did you do to Angela? Is that your ability? You can control people?"

"Yes and no."

"Then what-"

He shook his head slowly. "My turn."

Nova fought the urge to stick out her tongue like a petulant child. "Fine."

"Do you like it at Tidemarsh?" he asked.

"I don't know."

He frowned. "That's not much of an answer."

"Neither was yours." She felt colour rise to her cheeks again; she wasn't usually so feisty, and should probably be a little more careful how she spoke to him. If she wanted him to continue the game, she'd have to give more. "There are days when I feel like I'm trapped," she added. "Like this whole place is just a fancy prison."

"Oh yes, very fancy," Kit said, eyes wandering around his bleak cell.

"Then there are other days when I know this is where I should be. When I'm here, I have less chance of hurting anyone, I have friends, and..." she trailed off. "It's my turn now."

"I'm all ears."

"What's your ability? Explain it to me, properly."

He took a breath. "I don't control people, like that nasty little creature from your dorm. Her power makes people victims; trapped in their own bodies, forced to watch and feel as they do things they hate. The people I enthral have no idea what they're doing, and have no memory of it afterwards. It's like they leave, and I take over."

"Enthral?" Nova repeated.

"Bewitch, possess, take control of."

"And you, like, *drive* their bodies?"

He smiled. "My turn."

Nova scowled. She was starting to get bored of this game.

"What did you do with Madeline's hair?" His eyes were fixed on her, as though she was a meal he was waiting to devour. Nova was in equal parts terrified of that look, and intrigued by it. It was like he was hanging on her every word, genuinely interested in what she had to say.

She took a glance down the hallway. They were still alone. Someone far away was screaming, but it may as well have been on the other side of the world. No one was listening to their conversation.

"I burned it," she said. "Out in the woods."

Kit grinned. "Very sacrificial."

"I couldn't risk it being found!" she hissed. "That was stupid, by the way, leaving it in my nightstand with the scissors. Why did you do that?"

He shrugged. "I'm a fan of the theatrical. I thought you'd enjoy it."

"And what would've happened if she'd found it?"

He pondered this. "I don't know. Probably something ghastly."

"To me," Nova finished for him.

"Yes, I imagine so."

"Thanks for that, then."

His eyes glittered. "And now I believe it's my turn again."

Nova cursed herself for walking right into that. "Fine."

He thought for a moment. "If you were able to get rid of your power, to never be able to use it again, would you?"

"Yes," Nova answered, immediately.

Kit's expression darkened.

"What? What did I say?" she asked.

"You don't understand the gift you have. You should appreciate it."

He didn't say anything else, and after a few seconds Nova cleared her throat. "I think I accidentally asked you another question, so I guess it's your turn."

"I think we're done for today."

Nova felt a pang of something. She wasn't ready for their conversation to be over. "Really?"

"Frank will be waiting at the doors. He will take you back to the storage room, and tell you the code to get in and out. He'll also show you where to find a phone that he's hidden in there. It has his number in it. The next time you visit, go back in that way, and use the phone to send him a message to say where you are. He'll come and collect you."

He's really thought this through.

"I don't know if I'll be coming back," Nova said, though her words sounded unconvincing.

"Whatever you say."

She got up and began to walk down the corridor, when she heard his voice drifting out from his cell.

"You can't change what you are, Nova. You need to embrace it, or you'll be as trapped as I am."

Unscheduled Stop

On Saturday, the sun was high and blazing, and the blue sky stretched on forever. In an attempt to escape the heat, Nova and Kate joined most of the other kids down at the lake. Nova had barely paid attention to it before now, and was only today realizing how large it was. As she stood at the shoreline with the woods behind her, the water seemed to stretch on in front for miles.

"It's all within the grounds," Kate said, as they dumped their towels and waded in. "At the other side there are more trees, and then the fence. No chance of escape by swimming," she joked.

Nova laughed. With the cool water at her waist and the sunshine on her skin, she couldn't think of many places she'd rather be.

It seemed like the other kids shared her view. Everyone was having a good time, and the air was filled with the sounds of laughter and splashing. Several students were laying on towels on the sand, and the rest were in the water.

A shark fin broke through the surface a few feet away,

followed by a dolphin and the huge shaggy dog Nova had seen at the pool. Angela was wading through the shallows, fully dressed and muttering to herself. Not far from her, several girls were laughing as they were whipped around in their own miniature whirlpool, that Harvey was controlling. A pair of trunks were floating in the air near the shore, which had to belong to an invisible Danny. Jason from mastery class was laying on the sand with his gloves off. Nova supposed that with his hands in the sand, there wasn't much damage he could do, and she was happy to see him smiling for a change.

Not everyone was having a good time, though. A few meters away, sitting on one of the large rocks jutting out of the water, was Madeline. She wore a foul expression, glaring at anyone who dared swim close enough to accidentally splash her. With her hair already at her ankles, and sprinkled with pink flowers, she looked like a miserable mermaid.

"What's wrong with her?" Nova asked Kate.

"I heard she got dumped."

"Really?" Whenever Nova had seen Madeline making out with the guard – which was more often than she would've liked – he hardly seemed reluctant to be kissing her. She wondered if the fact they'd been seen by her so many times had scared him off. After all, she doubted Tidemarsh encouraged the guards to date students.

Mental note: keep even further away from Madeline than usual.

Kate continued. "Yeah, she's not exactly got the best luck with guys. I don't know anything about this one, but the one before was a few years older. He graduated, and promised he'd call, write, come visit, whatever. Of course, he didn't."

"Why?"

"It's what happens." Kate said, simply.

"What do you mean?" Nova asked.

"After the kids graduate, they pretty much get as far away from this place as possible. Except the few who become teachers I mean. The rest don't keep in touch."

"They don't even write? Surely some would still have friends here?"

Kate shook her head. "I guess they want to move on."

They were interrupted by Luke, who popped out of the water just long enough to grab Kate and dunk her under. She spluttered to the surface a few seconds later, eyes blazing.

"Luke?! What the hell?!"

"Come on, Katie, it's only water."

"Don't you have any other moves? You've already done this, like, six times."

The two of them continued to argue – mostly playfully – and Nova tried to laugh along with it. But though it *was* pretty funny when Luke pulled his arm out of the water to find it covered in leeches, she couldn't get her mind off what Kate had said. Was it true that no one ever heard from the students who left Tidemarsh?

"This place isn't what you think."

Kit's words rang through her head. Maybe he really did know something about the school that the others didn't?

There was only one way to find out.

Nova made her excuses and left the lake early. She got changed, and then hurried through the woods towards the

Tombs. Even within the shade of the trees, the air was stiflingly hot, and she couldn't keep up the brisk pace for long. Within minutes her back, head, and everywhere else were slick with sweat. Trying not to think about the cool water of the lake, she pushed on.

There was a big part of her that wasn't thrilled with the idea of Kit seeing her sweaty, tired, and generally kind of disgusting. Then she reminded herself that it wasn't like he had many visitors. There was hardly a high standard to live up to. Besides, even if he thought she was repulsive, it didn't matter. She didn't need to impress a guy who killed a bunch of people. His thoughts on her appearance were irrelevant.

A figure came into view up ahead; it was the guard Madeline had been dating. Nova's stomach dropped at the sight of him.

Luckily, this time he was alone. That was one benefit of the breakup, she supposed, she wouldn't have to constantly worry about running into the pair of them again.

It was too late to turn around or try and hide, he'd already seen her, and raised his eyebrows in surprise.

"Hi," Nova said, coming to a stop. She wasn't sure what else to say. Was she even allowed to be this far into the woods on her own? She didn't *think* it was against the rules, but wasn't certain.

"Hello," he said, eyeing her curiously. "Nova, right?"

She was surprised he had to ask, seeing as his ex-girlfriend had made her eat dirt in front of him only a few days ago. Perhaps Madeline did it to so many girls that Nova was lost in a sea of soil-eating faces?

"Yeah, that's me," she replied.

He glanced around. "What are you doing out here?"

"I'm...taking a walk."

"In this heat?"

"Yeah. I...uh...like it."

What a thorough and totally non-suspicious answer.
Bravo.

Sure enough, he had a follow-up. "Really? I think it's kind of unbearable."

"Oh well...you know..." Nova internally cursed herself for that show of linguistic mastery. Why was she so catastrophically useless under pressure?

Luckily, this time the guard didn't ask any more questions. "Right. My shift is over now, so I'm going to get some lunch. You might want to change direction, there's nothing nice that way."

"Okay."

She waited until he disappeared, then continued towards the Tombs. Following Kit's previous instructions, she went into the storage room and sent the moustached-guard, Frank, a message on the hidden phone. Five minutes later he appeared and led her from the room. He didn't put her in cuffs this time, which she was grateful for.

When they arrived at the glass wall of Kit's cell, Frank left her alone. There was no chair today, but that was fine; she wasn't planning to stay long.

Kit had been sitting on the edge of his bed, staring at the wall, when she arrived. "Nova?" he sounded surprised. "I didn't expect to see you so soon."

"Do you have a minute to talk?"

He glanced back at the wall. "I don't know, I'm rather snowed under here."

"Funny."

Kit stood up. "You look-"

"Sweaty, I know."

He smiled.

"I need to ask you something," she said.

"Alright."

Nova took a breath. "You told me this place wasn't what I thought. What did you mean by that?"

"That there are things about Tidemarsh that you don't know." Kit seemed to choose his words carefully.

"Like what?"

He took a few slow steps around the cell. Eventually, as Nova was beginning to think he wasn't going to speak at all, he did.

"What we have here, is a rather tricky situation. If I tell you what I know, you'll want to believe what everyone else thinks about me: that I'm crazy. Or a liar. Or both. Either way, you won't come down here anymore, and once again I won't have anyone interesting to talk to."

"You think I'm interesting?" she half-joked.

"It's all relative. I'm in a box most of the day."

"Charming."

Kit wasn't wrong. He might've saved her on the night of the storm, but Nova had seen enough at Tidemarsh to understand that things weren't always what they seemed. He was locked away for a reason, and it would be stupid to take the things he said on faith. If she was realistic, she barely knew him. What reason did she have to trust he was telling her the truth? Even Kate thought he was lying about knowing things to get Nova down there.

"You're right," she began, an idea forming. "I don't

know you. You don't know me. Maybe I wouldn't believe you. So, let's change it."

Kit said nothing, though an inquisitive expression softened some of his sharp lines.

Nova continued. "Help me to trust you. Let's talk. No more questions about Tidemarsh, let's just get to know each other."

He leaned back against the wall of his cell. After a moment he simply said: "Alright."

"Why don't we start with the basics?" Nova began. "How old are you?"

It was as though he was unsure whether it was a trick question, as if he thought she was trying to trip him up somehow. Slowly, cautiously, he answered: "17. You?"

"16. How long have you been here?"

"On and off for 11 years."

Nova did the math. "You've been here since you were *six*?"

"Yes."

"What you did must've been..." she trailed off. She wasn't sure she wanted to know what a six-year-old had to do to get locked away in the dark for 11 years, and from the way his jaw was set, it was clear he had no desire to share it with her.

She jumped to a new question. "What do you mean *on and off*?"

He grinned, and once again it transformed his face. Nova didn't know how he could flit so easily between looking totally closed-off and intimidating, to playful and approachable, within mere seconds.

"Sometimes I like to escape," he said.

Then it *was* possible. Nova wasn't sure if that was reassuring or not. "When did you realise you were an Alternate?"

"The day I was brought here."

"You didn't know before that?"

Kit shook his head. "I only knew I was different. I didn't understand it. My ability has developed a lot over the years."

"What do you mean?"

He moved away from the wall, coming to sit with his legs crossed in front of the glass. This close, his storm-coloured eyes were impossible to look away from. His voice, too, had her hooked. It was like a balm; smooth and soothing. Even if what he was saying wasn't interesting, Nova was pretty sure she would probably be enthralled listening to him talk about anything at all.

"When Alternates start to notice and use their abilities, they are at a far more basic level. Someone who can read minds, for example, isn't necessarily able to do that right away. They might start by hearing the occasional stray thought. This moves on to sentences, and then to being able to hear the entire train of thought in someone's head. This can develop further, in some cases. A child who began as a telepath, might end up being able to plant their own thoughts in someone else's mind. The powers we initially become aware of, are often only a fraction of what we have the potential to be able to do."

"Wow." Nova's head was spinning. "So...my ability-"

"May not be exactly what you think it is," he finished. "Correct." His eyes sparkled, almost playfully. "How do you feel about that?"

"I don't know," she replied.

"Your power frightens you?"

"Yes," she admitted.

"Why?"

"Because I can't control it."

"You *are* it. Everything you can do comes from you; it draws energy from within your body."

Nova shook her head. "It's too powerful."

"Maybe you're not afraid of what *it* can do, but of what *you* can do."

CHAPTER TWENTY-NINE

More Questions

"Wait, what are you asking, exactly?" Luke asked.

It was late afternoon. Nova, Luke, Kate, and Danny were spending the last few hours of sunlight at the edge of the woods, facing out towards the lake.

Nova twisted a blade of grass between her fingers. "I don't know. Kit said Tidemarsh isn't what we think it is-"

Luke cut her off. "Why would you trust anything *he* says? I still can't get my head around the fact that you have a friend in the Tombs."

"He's not a friend," Nova corrected. "I mean...we're friendly, but I don't think we're *friends*. Not like I'm friends with you guys."

"He saved you from getting killed the night of the storm," Danny reminded her.

Kate nodded. "Exactly. You can bet your life that if I was trapped down there with either of you two guys – and those crazies – I'd 100% be sacrificing you to save myself. No offence."

Danny and Luke stared her down.

"None taken," Danny eventually said.

"*Anyway*," Luke continued, bringing them back on topic. "What makes you think you can trust this guy?"

Nova sighed. "I don't know if I do, but it's not only him. Kate said something about how the kids who leave here are never heard from again."

Kate held up her hands as Luke gave her a withering look. "I definitely didn't make it sound that dark."

"I just think," Nova said, before the two of them could start arguing, "That maybe there's something weird going on here."

Luke didn't seem convinced. "What are you expecting to find? That there's some big conspiracy? That the kids who leave are getting bumped off the second they walk out of the gates?"

"Of course not." Nova's face flushed.

"I don't think it's that weird for people to leave school and not visit," Luke continued. "Why would you want to?"

Danny interjected. "Tidemarsh isn't really like other schools though, right? It's one of the only places kids like us can be ourselves and not have to hide anything. We make friends and learn how to do things other people can't even imagine. Isn't it kind of weird that not even one of those kids would call or write once in a while after they graduate?"

Nova could've kissed him. "Exactly."

Luke shrugged. "We can't be sure they haven't. You've only got that guy Carver's word for it. Oh, and Kate's gossip."

Kate glared, and Nova interjected before she had a chance to say anything too cutting. "You're right. So why don't we find out?" She glanced at Kate and Danny for support.

Kate sighed. "I guess it couldn't hurt to do some digging?"

"What do you want us to do?" Luke asked, voice thick with exasperation. "Go and ask Ms. Juniper if she's secretly killing all the kids who graduate?"

"No," Nova replied, painfully aware she hadn't thought it through this far. "To be honest, I don't even know how-"

Kate came to her rescue. "Let's ask around. Carefully. We all know people who had friends who graduated. Let's ask them if they're still in touch. There has to be at least one, right?" She smiled at Nova. "Then you can stop worrying about this, and go back to worrying about accidentally blowing stuff up."

Luke gave in. "Fine. If it'll make you forget about this whole thing, we'll do it." He got up, wiped the dried grass off his legs, and headed off.

"What's his problem?" Kate asked once he was out of earshot. "He was so weird about it."

"His brother graduated a couple of years ago," Danny said, quietly. "He hasn't spoken to him since."

Kate's eyes widened. "Why didn't he say anything?"

"They had a fight before he left; they aren't on good terms. I guess he thinks that's why he hasn't heard from him. If Nova's right, and something bad is going on here, then what the hell happened to his brother?"

The three of them watched Luke head back to the dorms. Nova's chest felt tight. Finding answers was what they needed to do, but what if they didn't like what they found?

On Monday morning, during another mastery class where she refused to do more than watch the others, Nova decided to ask Angela more about Kit.

"When you were in the Tombs," she began tentatively. "Where did you live?"

Angela's voice was as dreamy as ever, as if she was reading a poem. "D block. Cell 3. I shared with Tina."

"What could she do?" Nova asked.

"She stabbed a guard."

"Oh, I meant her ability."

"I don't know," Angela replied. "We wore the collars, they stop you using your ability." She paused, then added, thoughtfully: "They don't stop you from stabbing though."

Nova blew past that pretty grim statement. "Did you see Carver much?"

Angela's shoulders stiffened. Her voice became flatter. "Sometimes. He wasn't allowed to eat with us, but sometimes I passed him in the halls when they were taking him to sessions."

"Sessions?"

"In the Tombs you get sessions with one of their counsellors. It's mandatory. It's how they figure out if you're ready to move back to the main school."

"But Carver's in Max. I thought those kids weren't allowed to leave?"

"I think they still go to session. I don't know why."

Nova braced for her next question. "When you saw him, what was he like?"

Angela thought this over for a minute. "He frightened me."

"Really? There are so many others down there."

Angela's eyes were fixed on the table. "He gets into your head; makes you do things. The others can't do that. The collars stop them from using their abilities to hurt you. Mostly. They don't stop Carver." Her voice lowered to little more than a whisper. "Nothing stops Carver."

Nova didn't ask Angela if she knew that Kit had been controlling her a few days ago. Hopefully she didn't. He'd used her to get to Nova, and that wasn't a good feeling. She vowed that the next time she saw him, she'd make him promise to stay out of Angela's head. Whether he'd listen would be another story, but hopefully now that she was visiting on her own, he wouldn't need to use anyone for that purpose anymore. Nova watched as Angela pushed her hand through the surface of the table as though it was made of smoke, muttering to herself as she did so.

This girl didn't need any more stress in her life.

Later, Nova visited Elizabeth. As she knocked on the door to her office, she fought against the butterflies in her stomach.

This is fine, she told me to come back whenever I wanted.

Elizabeth opened the door, beaming. "Nova, how are you doing?" She gestured for her to come inside and take a seat in front of her desk. "I was wondering when you'd come by again."

"Do you have a minute?" Nova asked.

"Of course." Elizabeth sat down and ran her hand quickly over her cup of coffee so that it disappeared. "I never remember to drink it before it gets cold," she said, when she noticed Nova watching.

"You don't keep the mug?"

"It's a terrible habit of mine," Elizabeth admitted with a smile. "I vanish stuff before I think about it. Anyway, what did you want to talk about today?"

Nova had come to ask about the kids who left Tide-marsh, but where the hell was she supposed to start with something like that? Every opening line in her head sounded so accusatory. While she gave herself time to come up with something better, she asked: "I was wondering; what were my parents like at school?"

Elizabeth leaned back in her chair. "Your mum was so smart. Top of all her classes, despite *my* best efforts." She smiled conspiratorially. "She was never smug about it, though. She was kind, tutored those who asked for help, gave other kids the chance to answer questions that everyone knew she knew the answer to. And she was funny too, she used to have those of us in her dorm practically rolling around on the floor with her impressions of the teachers. We were in your room, you know? I'm so happy you're up there now."

Nova felt warmth spread through her body, as it always did when she was able to talk about her mum. "And my dad?"

Elizabeth gave a gentle laugh. "A rebel. Always breaking the rules, sneaking out, and disrupting his classes. Of course, everyone loved him – even the teachers – because he was charming and made them laugh. He and I became friends first, and I introduced him to your mum. They fit together perfectly." She sighed, wistfully. "Liara and Rick brought out the best in each other."

"What happened after they left Tidemarsh?" Nova asked.

"They moved into a small house together. Your mum got a job as an accountant, your dad worked at a lumber yard. They got married, your mum got pregnant with you, and then..." Elizabeth trailed off.

Nova swallowed. "He was killed?"

"Yes." A tear slid down Elizabeth's cheek. "I'm sorry," she said, immediately wiping it away. "Even now, it's hard. We were so close, and for him to disappear from our lives so suddenly..."

Nova knew she should probably leave. Seeing anyone cry always made her uncomfortable, and seeing a teacher cry was that x1000. But she was aware that they had arrived at the exact topic she had come to ask Elizabeth about. This was her chance.

"Is that what most kids do when they graduate?" she blurted out. "Get normal jobs, I mean."

Elizabeth seemed slightly taken aback by the change in direction. "Yes. Students can do whatever they want after they finish their education. You're still a human being, Nova. If you want to be a writer, a scientist, or even a doctor, you can do any of those things. You can go to college, you can be an artist-"

"Are there any past students I could talk to?" Nova interrupted. "You know, to get advice? And find out what it's like after you leave Tidemarsh?"

"I could probably find an address or two, though most of them don't keep in contact."

"Why?"

Elizabeth considered this. "I suppose for the same reason regular people don't keep in touch with their old schools when they leave."

Nova kept going, mildly aware she might be pushing her luck. "This isn't exactly a 'normal' school, though, is it? You say it's like a family here...you'd think a few of them would come and visit or something."

Elizabeth's smile cracked, just for a fraction of a second, and then it was back in place. "That's true. I'll see what I can find for you, though you might find it faster to talk to some of the teachers. Like Miss Garrett, perhaps. And I'm always here, of course." She glanced at her watch. "I'm sorry, Nova, I have an English lesson to teach, we'll have to talk another time."

Nova got up and headed out of the office. On the way back to her dorm she reflected on the conversation. It had gone okay, she supposed. Nothing totally abnormal or suspicious. Elizabeth hadn't yelled, or even seemed annoyed that she was asking questions. Other than the brief flicker in her smile, the whole thing had been rather uneventful.

So why did she feel like Kit might be onto something?

CHAPTER THIRTY

Do You Have Any Friends?

The following day, while having lunch in the courtyard, Nova told Kate and the others about her chat with Elizabeth. Her friends reported that, despite asking around, they hadn't been able to find a single student who was still in touch with anyone who had graduated Tidemarsh.

"This is weird," Kate muttered, absentmindedly stroking Colin. "How can all of them have disappeared?"

Luke was pale, and his voice sounded far away. "I don't know." He was holding a small wildflower in his hands, twirling it between his fingers.

After a few seconds of silence, Danny, perched on the low brick wall beside the bench, spoke up. "Maybe Carver *does* know something. What else did he say?"

"Not much," Nova replied. "That we shouldn't trust Elizabeth, and that this place isn't what we think it is."

"What does he mean by that?" Danny asked.

Nova held out her hands. "I don't know, he's not exactly the easiest person to talk to."

"Maybe you should go back," Kate said. "Find out more information."

"You told me he was probably lying to me."

"That was before all of this," Kate murmured. "I'm starting to think maybe he might be right. You should go back tonight."

"Great, I'm sure he'll love answering even more of my questions." Nova sighed. Though she was getting used to sneaking through the woods at night now, and even going down to the Tombs, she still felt nervous at the thought of questioning Kit. She had no idea how much of what he said was genuine, and how much was him messing with her for something to do. Every time she went down there, she risked getting in serious trouble. What if it was for nothing?

Although she could get inside the Tombs any time she wanted, thanks to the phone and Frank, Nova decided to wait until she knew Kit would be out in the yard. Talking to him outside felt safer. He may have had Frank on side, but going into Max meant she was at risk of being seen by other guards, and Kit couldn't possibly take control of all of them at once. Plus, the other kids saw Frank leading her along to Kit's cell, and she had no idea how long it would take for one of them to rat her out. She was surprised they hadn't already. Were they so afraid of Kit that they kept quiet? Regardless, Nova decided that – if she could possibly manage it – she would try to talk to him when he was outside. She could speak to him without anyone else needing to know she was there.

She got there first, and was waiting by the tree when he came outside. He began to walk to his usual spot by the light, but caught sight of her sitting in front of the tree at their old meeting place.

"We're meeting out here again?" he asked, as he approached the fence.

"It feels safer," Nova explained. "Less chance of me getting caught and ending up..." she trailed off.

"Ending up locked away like me?" Kit finished for her.

"I didn't mean-"

"I know what you meant."

What a great start.

Nova cleared her throat. "Why haven't the other kids in Max told anyone about me?"

Kit let out a short bleat of laughter. "Who would they tell?"

"The guards? Ms. Juniper? Elizabeth?"

"The guards aren't exactly here to listen to our woes. They deal with us only when they remove us from our cells. If you stand still too long when they try to do that, they shock you or beat you. Not a lot of time for chit-chat there." His tone was cold. "As for Ms. Juniper? She likes to pretend this place doesn't exist."

"And Elizabeth?" Nova broached.

"They all know better than to attract her attention." Kit briefly surveyed the kids in the yard, before turning back to her. "Don't worry, your secret's safe."

"It's not *my* secret," Nova said, feeling defensive. "You could get in a lot of trouble too if they knew I was sneaking down to talk to you. Or that you and Frank were working together."

"I can't possibly imagine what more they could do to me. If you remember, I don't even have a toilet seat."

Nova bit her lip. Kit's life really sucked.

"You're always alone out here," she said, attempting to change the subject.

"You'd prefer I bring someone next time?" he asked.

"No. I mean I never see you talking to anyone; you're always on your own."

He quirked an eyebrow. "How do you know? You're not here every night. Maybe I'm making friendship bracelets and braiding hair when you're not around."

Nova laughed, relieved that he was making jokes again. "I'd like to see that." She cocked her head to one side. "Do you have any friends here?"

"I'm usually locked in my cell for 23 hours a day. That doesn't leave a lot of time to work on secret handshakes."

"Your idea of what friendship entails is really weird." Nova glanced around. "There are quite a few kids out here. You don't like any of them?"

"They're all from Max," he answered, simply.

"Are you forgetting you're from Max too?"

He grinned. "Fair. Okay, let's weigh up my options, and you can help me choose my new best friend. Someone to... play hopscotch with?"

"Seriously, when did you time travel from?"

He glanced over his shoulder. "Well, there's William, of course."

Nova grimaced, and Kit chuckled. "Yes, I'm not sure I'd enjoy spending my yard time reliving my darkest and most horrifying memories."

"I don't blame you there." Nova looked around, pointing to a boy sitting alone on one of the benches.

"What about him? He's about your age, and has that whole 'brooding loner' thing going too."

Kit looked offended. "I seriously doubt he's as good at that as I am."

"You work hard at it?"

"It's a challenge when you live such a free and cheerful life."

"So," she said, drawing them back to the topic. "Him?"

Kit followed her gaze. "He has razor claws."

"Really? That's the one?" Nova asked. "I saw him in the Tombs when the power went out!"

"Lucky you."

Nova considered this. "I mean, I guess it's only a problem if you plan to do a lot of hand holding."

"I don't see the point of a platonic male friendship without it."

She let out a snort-laugh, and Kit continued. "Besides which, he cut someone's throat when they disagreed about the best way to make a cheese sandwich. I'm not sure he's my best bet for friendship."

"You could never talk about food?" Nova suggested.

"Alright, well why don't we put him on the 'maybe' pile?"

Nova smiled again. Though the deadpan way Kit spoke could make him seem cold at times – most of the time, actually – as she started to get to know him, she realised it was just his sense of humour. He was dry, but would poke fun at himself as readily as he would anyone else. He didn't smile a lot, yet when he did his whole face softened, and gave him a sort of chiselled handsomeness that she knew Kate would really be into.

But Kate isn't here. Because she doesn't make friends with boys who kill a bunch of people.

Nova ignored the errant thought, scanning the yard for her next suggestion. Her eyes settled on a girl with short black hair. "What about her?"

"Hillary." Kit answered. "16. Killed a guard by turning his lungs to concrete."

"Maybe not. How about that one?"

"Thomas. 14. Turns into a giant snake. Likes to bite."

"Are you scared of snakes?" Nova asked, playfully.

"Ones big enough to eat me? Yes." His eyes glittered.

She pointed to someone else. "Her?"

"Deanna. 17. Enjoys boiling liquids, including other people's blood."

"Like...in test tubes or jars?"

"Unfortunately not."

"Fair enough." She scanned the yard. "What about him?"

"Ali. 16. The power of persuasion, like your friend Madeline. Unlike Madeline, Ali convinced a few teachers at his old school to jump out of the windows." Kit paused. "Nice singing voice though."

"Is that part of his ability?" Nova asked, curiously.

"No, but it's worth mentioning."

"Okay...what about him?"

"Kodie. 12. Frog tongue."

Nova waited. "That doesn't sound as bad as the others?"

"Sometimes he licks his eyes. It's rather off-putting."

"Sure, I get that...but in the grand scheme of things, it could be worse, right?"

"I suppose." Kit considered this. "And he only strangled two guards with his tongue, so I mean-"

Nova cut him off. "Why didn't you lead with that instead of the eye licking?"

"I don't know, that part always repulsed me the most. I mean...*eyes*." He shuddered.

Nova sighed. "You're right. You're not exactly overwhelmed with choices here."

"Perhaps not." He held her gaze. "But maybe we're friends?"

Nova smiled. "Maybe."

He didn't speak for a few seconds, then said: "We've talked a few times now, and you still haven't asked what I did."

"I know."

"Seeing all the other people down here...Aren't you curious about how I ended up in this place?"

Are you kidding? Try: "it's driving me insane!"

"Not really," Nova lied.

Kit saw right through that. "Are you worried I'll be offended if you ask?"

"Would you?"

"No. I don't feel ashamed of the choices I made. Whether they're ones I would repeat again now is another story, but I live my life without regrets."

"I'm not scared you'd be offended," Nova explained. "I'm scared it will be bad."

He smiled. "Based on where I live, I'd say that's a given."

"I know. I'm not an idiot, I know you're not locked up for forgetting to return library books-"

"Oh damn, those will be really overdue by now..."

"But," Nova continued. "If it's horrible – really horrible – I'll feel like I shouldn't come and talk to you anymore, and I don't want that." It wasn't something she'd admitted before, but it was true. She *liked* talking to Kit. He was scary and cold, and kind of a dick at times, yet he fascinated her. He made her laugh, and seemed genuinely interested in what she had to say. If she found out about what he did, about what was sure to be the kind of horrific crime that would curl her toes, it would all be over.

"Isn't that rather a risky decision?" he asked. "To blindly hope I'm a good person without knowing the facts?"

"I was in your cell for hours and you didn't hurt me," she countered. "That means something."

"I'm never going to live that down, am I?"

"I like talking to you," Nova said. "I'm going to trust my gut – which, to be honest, is probably a really big mistake because it's *always* wrong – and say that whatever led you here was either some kind of accident, or that it wasn't, and you're a different person now. Right?"

Kit was quiet for a moment, keeping his eyes fixed on hers. "Right."

She took a breath. "Then yes. We're friends. And I don't need to know anything more. Not yet."

CHAPTER THIRTY-ONE

Foot In Mouth

"What do you mean you forgot to ask him about the missing kids?"

Nova squirmed under Kate's scrutiny. She had been so caught up in her conversation with Kit, in the discovery that they had somehow become friends, that she completely forgot to ask him anything to do with their little investigation. Kate had not been thrilled when she asked her how it went the following morning.

Nova groped around for the right words. "I...I guess I forgot."

"You *forgot*? Weren't you the one who started this whole thing?"

"I know."

Kate folded her arms, though her expression softened. "You *do* like him, don't you?"

"We're friends."

"No, you and I are friends, and you sure as hell don't get as excited to talk to me as you do when you know you're heading down to that awful place to see him." She grinned. "He must be gorgeous, right?"

"He's..." Nova couldn't lie. "Okay, yes, he's gorgeous. He might actually be the most beautiful person I've ever seen, but honestly, we're just friends. I like talking to him. He makes me laugh, he's honest, and let's not forget, he saved my life."

"Uh-huh. This all kind of sounds like something you'd say if you were into him."

Nova groaned. "Can we please move on? Kit and I are friends. That's it. I'm sorry I forgot to ask him about the missing kids. I'll go down there today and do it, alright?"

"Perfect." Kate winked. "Sorry you have to drag yourself down there again."

Nova couldn't make Kate wait until tomorrow to pass on any information she gleaned, which meant tossing aside her previous plan of going to the fence that night, and instead going directly to Kit's cell. After dinner felt as good a time as any.

Unfortunately, she didn't get as far as the Tombs. As Nova was leaving the woods and heading over to the storeroom door, a guard rounded the corner. It was the same one who had been dating Madeline.

Why do I keep running into this guy?

He cocked his head curiously. He had a cigarette between his fingers, and blew out a cloud of white smoke. "Nova? What are you doing here?"

I'm visiting my friend. He's a dangerous killer with a psychic ability to control people by climbing into their brains and twiddling with things. Don't worry about letting me in, he's bribed a guard to do it.

"I'm here to see you." The words came out of her mouth before she had a chance to decide whether they were a good idea.

His eyes widened a fraction. "Me?"

"Yes."

"Okay...why?"

Nova should've anticipated that question, and was already kicking herself for jumping in feet first with her lie. It was too late to go back now, the only option was to commit. "I wanted to apologise. For all the times I accidentally...you know."

The guard glanced around, then quirked his head towards the woods. "Why don't we take a walk?"

"Great." It wasn't like she had a choice.

He dropped his cigarette and stamped it out, and they walked together past the tree line and into the woods. Nova's mind raced, desperately trying to think of something to say to get her out of this situation as soon as possible.

The guard started speaking. "Sorry to rush you away like that. What Maddie and I...well...it's not exactly something I want to shout from the rooftops. I'm sure you understand?"

I understand that it's against the rules and creepy.

Nova nodded. "Of course."

"It's over now, anyway," he said, moving a branch aside so they could continue. "She's a nice girl, but it was never going to last."

Of all the words anyone could use to describe Madeline, Nova was pretty sure 'nice' was low down the list, but she didn't say anything.

The guard must've read her expression though, because he smiled. "I know she comes across a little-"

Awful? Vindictive? Like one of the worst people in the world?

"A little cold. Trust me, once you get to know her you start to see another side. She's smart, beautiful obviously, and she has a good heart. She tries to hide it, but it's there." He paused. "I don't know why I'm telling you all of this. Sorry, I talk too much sometimes. All the time, come to think of it."

Nova gave a small smile. "I do too."

"I'm James, anyway," he said. "I'm not sure I ever introduced myself."

Nova bit back the urge to say what she really thought; that they'd hardly had the opportunity for introductions while his ex-girlfriend forced her to eat dirt.

"Are you enjoying it at Tidemarsh?" James asked. "You've not been here long, and this place can feel..." he searched for the word.

"It's different."

He laughed. "You can say that again. It was weird for me too."

"I guess it's a bit of a shock getting a job at a place full of kids who can fly and make stuff explode." Nova immediately bit her tongue. She had accidentally mentioned her own power. Did he know what she could do? Was a picture handed around to all the guards, with a warning not to make her mad? Did they know about Gary? Her stomach sank at the thought.

If James knew what her ability was, though, he didn't

mention it. "I knew about this place long before I became a guard."

"I thought Tidemarsh was supposed to be a secret?"

"Not if you grew up here."

That gave Nova pause. "Wait, you're an Alternate?"

"That's right."

"I had no idea!"

How could he be an Alternate? He seemed so normal. Sure, dating a student might've tipped him into 'ick' territory, but other than that, there appeared to be nothing unusual about him. Unlike most of the Alternates she'd met, who demonstrated what they could do within a few minutes – either on purpose or because they couldn't control it – James hadn't done anything to make her think he was more than a regular guy.

Nova wanted to ask what he could do, but something stopped her. He hadn't said what it was. Maybe he was like her, and didn't want to talk about it? Maybe he hated his power too? Maybe she wasn't so alone in that.

"I better get back," he said. "It was great talking to you, Nova." He gave her another smile, then headed back towards the Tombs.

She had no other choice but to go back to her dorm. It looked like she wouldn't be talking to Kit tonight after all.

Nova went to bed feeling restless. There was part of her, a big part, that wanted to try for the Tombs once more. But if she accidentally ran into James again, it would look less like a coincidence and more like she was up to something.

However, not going meant not getting to talk to Kit, and that made her chest feel weird and tight. It wasn't only the questions she wanted answered; Kate had been right about the fact that Nova looked forward to seeing him. Conversation with Kit was both easy, and like a really intense rollercoaster, all at the same time. She never knew what was coming next.

Laying on her side, watching through the window as the trees swayed in the moonlight, she wondered what he was doing now. She pictured him pacing impatiently in the yard, or laying on his cold, metal bed staring up at the ceiling. What was it like to have nothing to look forward to except an hour of fresh air late at night? She tried to imagine never feeling the sunshine on her skin. No one deserved to live like that.

Kit had killed.

So had she.

Why was he punished when she wasn't? She supposed his crimes hadn't been accidents. He must've wanted to kill. He was dangerous – everyone said so – yet the more time she spent with him, the more sure Nova became that he wouldn't hurt her. Maybe she was delusional. People at Tidemarsh had watched Kit for years; they had to know more about him than she ever could. Maybe his last victims thought they were safe too? Maybe he would turn on her, given the chance? She couldn't let her confusion around this boy land her in trouble.

She rolled over again. Everyone else was asleep, it had to be late. There was a creak of a bedframe as Laura got out of bed at the other side of the room. Nova assumed at first that she was going to the bathroom, but instead Laura walked closer and closer, stopping directly in front of Nova's bed.

"Hello," she whispered.

Nova sat up. "Uh...hi?" She glanced around the silent dorm. "Can I help you with something?"

"I was half expecting you to come and see me today."

Nova's chest felt like it was in a vice. "Kit?"

Laura's face stretched into a grin. "Don't look so worried."

Nova lowered her voice to barely more than a hiss. "You're possessing someone, to talk to me, in the middle of the night. I'd be crazy if I wasn't a teeny bit weirded out by that." Instinctively she pulled her blanket up higher. "What are you doing?"

"Right now? Talking to you and sitting in my cell."

Nova's curiosity got the better of her. "Does it hurt? Doing that while wearing the collar, I mean."

"It's not exactly the most comfortable experience, no. If we could continue this conversation in person, I'd appreciate it."

It was so weird hearing these words – typical formal-Kit speech – in Laura's voice.

"Is it safe?" Nova asked.

"Frank will be waiting outside for you."

"That didn't exactly answer my question."

Another smile. "It's safe."

Nova swung her legs out of bed and stood up, before remembering she was wearing her nightgown.

"Do you mind?" she said, cheeks blazing as she tugged it down self-consciously.

Laura – or Kit – gave a final smirk, before heading back across the room. "Spoilsport."

"And put her back where you found her," Nova hissed after him.

She didn't run into anyone else on her way down to the Tombs, and Frank escorted her to Kit's cell without any additional drama or excitement. That was good, Nova had had enough surprises for the day.

She sat in front of the glass, barely able to make Kit out in the shadows at the back of his cell. Once Frank had left, he stepped into the dim light. His eyes were bruised with tiredness.

"Do you ever sleep?" Nova asked, as he sat down in front of her.

"On occasion."

"I tried to come down today," she said. "I ran into one of the guards, so I had to turn around. It would've been too suspicious if he caught me coming down again."

"Which guard?"

"He said his name was James."

A shadow crossed Kit's face. "Stay away from him."

Nova quirked an eyebrow playfully. "Why? Are you jealous?" She'd only meant to tease him, but something in the stiff way Kit sat, and the way his unblinking eyes locked with hers, made her wonder if she might be right.

Finally, he spoke. "He's dangerous."

Nova rolled her eyes. "Yeah, yeah. So is everyone else in this place. You know it'd actually be nice to meet someone who *wasn't*." She changed the subject. "Anyway, I didn't want to come down here to talk about him."

"What did you want?"

"To ask you more about Tidemarsh." She took a breath, steadying herself for the next part.

"My friends and I asked around. None of us can find anyone who's still in touch with the kids who graduate. I even asked Elizabeth and she blew me off with some excuses."

"Of course," he said, flatly.

"You obviously have a theory about where they're going?"

"I do."

"What is it?"

His eyes twinkled in the way Nova had noticed they did when he was about to talk about something that interested him. "Do you remember what I told you about the ways in which powers develop?"

Nova moved closer to the glass. "Yes. We start with something weird, and then it gets bigger and weirder."

His lips twitched. "Correct. The purpose of Tidemarsh is to get the students into a state where they are in complete control of the most powerful form of their ability."

"That makes sense. They wouldn't want to send us out into the world if we couldn't control ourselves."

"Exactly."

She was lost. "I don't understand. What's so bad about that?"

"What if we're looking at it backwards? What if Tidemarsh isn't training students so it can let them go and live their lives in peace? What if those who run this place don't want to let them go at all?"

Nova tried to keep up. "What, like, they're still here?"

"No."

She groaned. "Do you ever *explain* things? You know you're impossible to get answers from, right?"

Another twitch of his lips, almost a smile this time. "Maybe that's the point."

"My friends think you're deliberately vague to make me come back. Or that you're making stuff up so that I have a reason to visit you."

"Would that be so terrible?"

Nova rolled her eyes, exasperated. "I don't like wasting my time."

Kit's voice turned cold. "Speaking to me is a waste of time?"

Oh no.

"I didn't mean that-" she gabbled. It was too late; the damage was done.

Kit stood up, turning away. "I'd hate to take up any more of your evening, Nova. In fact, perhaps you shouldn't come down here anymore." He disappeared back into the shadows of his cell.

"Kit-"

"This was a mistake."

Nova got to her feet. She was blinking a lot, which was ridiculous, because she never cried, and this boy absolutely wasn't about to make her start.

Before she walked away, she glanced back into his cell one more time. "You, and everyone else here are turning my head to mush. One minute I'm being told Tidemarsh is like a family; that I'm safe and should feel like this is home. Then here you are, telling me it's all a scam. That the staff are liars, who never want us to leave. I'm sick of being confused about it all. I feel so..."

"Trapped?" His voice came from the shadows, a whispering silhouette.

The Plan

It had been five days, and despite trying as hard as she could, Nova couldn't get Kit out of her head. It had taken everything she'd had to do what he said and stay away from the Tombs. There had been a couple of times where the only thing that kept her away was the thought of sneaking back into Max, only to be told to get lost.

This meant that her little investigation into what happened to the kids who'd left Tidemarsh had come to a standstill. Unfortunately, now that she was trying to forget the whole thing, Kate, Luke, and Danny had suddenly become very interested in Kit and the conspiracy. Every time Nova saw Luke, he peppered her with questions; getting her to repeat *exactly* what Kit had said over and over. For someone who had scoffed at the whole thing a week ago, he sure wanted to hear about it a lot.

Then there was Kate, who was just as bad, but in a different way. She kept asking what she clearly thought were casual sounding questions about Nova and Kit. Nova couldn't bring herself to admit aloud that she'd upset him, and so Kate was left confused about why the late-night visits to the Tombs had stopped.

Then there was Nova's real problem. She wasn't stupid, and it was getting impossible to ignore the fact that not being able to talk to Kit didn't sting just because she wanted answers to her questions about Tidemarsh. It stung because she missed him. It was like he knew her, the *real* her, the scary her. It was different for Kate and the others. To her friends, Nova's power was something cool; she could blow up fruit and knock a few things over. They didn't see her as a threat. Even Kate, who knew what she'd done to Gary, assumed it was a terrible accident. She had no idea that, though Nova had never consciously planned to kill her stepfather, it was far more complicated than a simple accident.

Kit *saw* her. She couldn't put the feeling into words, it was merely a whisper at the back of her mind. She'd told him nothing about what had happened to her before she arrived at Tidemarsh, yet somehow, he seemed to know exactly what she was. It was comforting. And kind of terrifying.

None of these realizations changed anything, however. She couldn't go back to Max. Not until Kit invited her. And clearly, he wasn't in any hurry to do that. Five days wasn't that long, not *really*, yet every evening, when she tossed and turned and desperately chased down sleep, she found her eyes roaming the dorm. She looked for anyone acting differently, wondering if one of them might be Kit. Of course, they never were. Nova was beginning to realise that he might be as stubborn as she was. They were at a stalemate.

That afternoon, while Kate, Luke, and Danny went down to the lake, Nova headed to the library alone. She didn't have the energy to deal with a conversation that would inevitably lead back to Kit and the Tombs, so had told her friends she had homework to finish.

The library was relatively deserted, with most of the other kids taking advantage of the gorgeous weather by spending the day outside. Nova plonked herself down into an armchair in the corner, in between two towering bookcases, and buried her head in a dog-eared science book.

An hour passed, and she had yet to write a single word in her notebook. The assignment wasn't even that hard, she just couldn't seem to focus. Eventually, Nova admitted defeat, closing the book heavily and leaning back in the chair.

"Tricky question?" A young girl with blonde hair and thick, red-rimmed glasses asked, from where she was standing at the far end of the bookcase to Nova's left.

"Something like that," Nova replied.

"You have a test coming up?"

"No, just homework."

The girl glanced at the window. "On a day like this? Surely, you've got better things to do?"

Nova sighed. "I guess not."

"That's kind of sad."

Nova wasn't exactly sure how to respond to that. "Okay?"

The girl came closer, and suddenly Nova recognised the confident saunter.

"Kit?" she asked, eyes wide.

The girl smiled in response.

"You need to stop doing this," Nova said, looking around to make sure no one was listening. "One of these days I'm going to start talking to a stranger, and it won't actually be you."

"That would be rather amusing."

"I bet it would," she said, snarkily, getting up from the chair and depositing the book back on the shelf. "You've forgiven me then?"

"Excuse me?"

"The last time we spoke you went all moody and said-" Nova turned back. The girl was watching her now with a mixture of confusion and annoyance. Kit had gone. Nova bit her lip. "Sorry, I was thinking out loud."

The girl didn't look convinced. She took her book and headed around to a different section of the library. Presumably one where she wasn't insulted by strangers.

A dark-haired boy walked over from the nearest bookshelf, eyes twinkling. "I was right, that *was* funny."

Nova prodded him angrily in the stomach. "I can't believe you did that."

"It's hard to hold them for too long."

Nova scowled. "You've gone longer than that before."

He let out a little laugh. "I'm sorry. I couldn't resist."

"Yeah, yeah. *Hilarious.*" Nova put her hands on her hips. "You're ready to talk to me again, I take it?"

"I may have been somewhat...sensitive when we last spoke."

"Sensitive, sure. You could also say cold and rude, but we can go with sensitive."

The boy's eyes, though brown, somehow managed to burn with the same intensity as Kit's own. "Cut me some slack; I'm not used to apologising. In fact, this might be my first time."

Nova wrinkled her nose. "That's not something to brag about."

"It means I'm rarely wrong."

"It *means* you're a stubborn arsehole."

He grinned. "Perhaps it's both. You look nice today," he said, changing the direction of the conversation so quickly that Nova only just caught herself before she smiled.

"Thank you."

"Will you come and see me later?"

"Maybe I have plans." She wasn't going to let him off the hook *too* easily for embarrassing her.

"Like a date?" His grin widened.

Nova blinked. "Would that be so strange?"

"Unlike Madeline, and your friend Kate, who goes through boys like they're about to become extinct, you don't date."

Nova crossed her arms, bristling at his words. "Oh really? And where did you get that idea?"

"Don't get upset."

"I'm not upset!" The words might've been more convincing if she hadn't practically shrieked them for the whole library to hear. Scuttling to the nearest bookcase, Nova pretended to be fascinated by the first dusty old book she got hold of.

"I'm sorry if I offended you." Kit was in someone else now: the 90-year-old, kaftan-wearing librarian.

"For your information," Nova said, coldly. "I'm busy tonight, meeting a very nice guy, who doesn't make me so mad I want to blow things up. Maybe I'll see you another time."

She didn't wait for his reply, slamming the book back onto the shelf and storming off. She was furious. Just when she thought maybe she and Kit were becoming friends, he practically laughed in her face at the notion of a guy being interested in her. She wasn't going to stand for that. She was going to show him that she wasn't some completely unlovable troll, and that all kinds of boys liked her.

There was just one problem. If her past experiences were anything to go by, there was a good chance she *was* some completely unlovable troll, and *no* boys liked her.

Maybe that didn't matter. Before she even reached her dorm, Nova had already formulated a plan. She'd show Kit how wrong he was by going on a date and rubbing it in his face. All she had to do was find a guy, take a romantic night-time stroll down to the Tombs when Kit *happened* to be in the yard, and *bang* – she would be a bridge troll no longer. She couldn't wait to see his face when he realised how wrong he'd been about her.

There were, however, a couple of small problems. The idea of finding some guy that she could convince to come down to the Tombs with her in the middle of the night, felt impossible. There was no point asking Luke or Danny. They'd want to know what was going on, and then they'd learn about her weird, confusing feelings for the body-snatching murderer. She wanted to ignore those for as long as possible.

She couldn't ask some random boy from school. It turned out that weird mutant boys were just as uninterested in her as the normal ones. As it stood, none of those at the Alternate Academy were currently jumping to take a night-time stroll *anywhere* with her, and the ones who might be willing to wander off with some girl they'd never spoken to, would probably be expecting to do more than hold hands.

Then it hit her. There was someone else! Someone she'd already spoken to a few times. Someone who she knew would stand a pretty good chance of already being down by the Tombs when Kit was outside. Someone who Kit would not be happy to see her flirting with. Someone who had already proven he had low low standards when it came to romantic partners. It was the perfect plan!

Or, alternatively, it was a hot dumpster fire waiting to happen. There was only one way to find out.

Not long after midnight, Nova took her usual route through the woods. She'd borrowed (without asking) a black sweater of Kate's, and once she'd brushed a couple of beetles off the sleeves, it was pretty nice. It hugged her figure more than the kind of thing she'd usually wear, though, and made her hyper-aware of her body.

She had also borrowed/stolen some of Kate's make-up, and had managed a relatively okay looking smoky eye. If no one looked too closely, at least. Her curls were their usual misbehaving selves, so she'd swept them up into a messy bun at the top of her head. Nova was happy with how she looked. In fact, she was feeling confident in her appearance for the first time in a long time.

As she got closer to the Tombs, however, that confidence began to wane. She took a few deep breaths to slow her racing heart, and almost turned back at least three times. The memory of how Kit had laughed at the very idea of her being on a date, however, kept her moving. He didn't get to laugh at her.

Nova reached the tree line and scanned the yard. After a minute she spotted Kit. He was down by one of the benches; standing alone, as usual. The first part had gone to plan: he was there. Now it was on to phase two.

As usual, there were no guards outside the perimeter of the fence. There were a couple inside, both waiting by the doors into the building. Neither of them was James. She wondered if he was even on duty at this time of night. If he wasn't, her coming down there was completely pointless.

It was pointless anyway. Do you have any idea what kind of trouble you could get into?

Though Nova hated to admit it, her stupid inner-voice was right. What made her so sure that James wouldn't immediately march her back to her dorm, and report her for being out of bed and lurking around a restricted building in the middle of the night? And even if he didn't, there was nothing to stop any of the other guards doing exactly that if they caught sight of her. Without Frank to walk her through the building, she was just a kid breaking the rules.

She sighed, accepting that she'd have to chalk this up to a bad idea, and preparing to head back to bed, when she saw him. James was heading out of the front doors, lighting up a cigarette. This was too perfect; if she got the angle right, she would be shielded from sight from the other guards, while giving Kit the perfect view of her conversation with James.

It was now or never. Nova took a breath and hurried down the slope towards the doors. She had no idea if Kit was watching. James' eyes widened when he caught sight of her.

"Nova? What are you doing here?" he asked.

"I couldn't sleep."

"And you thought you'd take a walk through the woods in the dark, and hang out at the most dangerous place in the whole of Tidemarsh?"

Nova wasn't sure how to answer that. James didn't sound mad, not really, just confused.

He glanced around, lowering his voice. "You're not supposed to be down here. Especially not at night, when these kids are out. We could both get into trouble if anyone catches us talking."

Nova was at risk of blowing the plan before it had even started. She had to act fast.

"I'm sorry," she said, reaching out to briefly touch his arm. "It was stupid, I know. I guess I felt like I needed to talk to someone. You were really nice the last time we spoke, so I thought..." She trailed off purposefully, the way she'd seen girls do in movies. It always worked for them, at least. "I'll go back to the dorm."

She turned, briefly catching sight of Kit watching her, before James' voice brought her back.

"Don't be sorry, we can talk. Why don't I find you tomorrow? We can have lunch?"

Nova was barely listening, silently trilling at the fact that Kit had seen her super-hot arm touch. "Great."

"I'll talk to you tomorrow."

She nodded. "You bet." Nova headed back into the woods, purposefully denying herself one last glance at Kit. She knew the rules – never look back.

CHAPTER THIRTY-THREE

New Friends

"Angela, can I ask you something?" Nova said.

Angela glanced up from the book she had been reading. Mastery class was running late – Miss Garret had been called away to undo something that had happened at the pool – so her students were killing time until she got back.

"Yes," Angela answered.

Nova steadied herself. "Why were you in the Tombs?"

The book Angela had been holding suddenly fell through her hands as if they weren't there. She looked down, concentration setting her face, as she reached to pick it up.

"Why do you want to know?" she asked.

"I want to understand why some kids get put in there, and others don't. You don't seem..." Nova trailed off, searching for the right word, and coming up short. "You don't seem like the kind of person who belongs down there."

"I *don't* belong down there," Angela snapped.

"No. Of course. That's not what I meant." As usual, Nova had said the wrong thing.

Angela put the book down on the table. When she spoke, her voice had lost its usual dreamy tone.

"I learned about my power when I was six years old. My dad thought I was weird. Broken. My mum thought I was special. Dad left. Mum and I were fine on our own." Her expression clouded. "Then she got sick. I looked after her for as long as I could, but she needed to go into a hospice. I wasn't allowed to come, so they sent me to live with my dad. He wasn't a good person." She paused, her eyes landing on the table. Her hands weren't solid anymore, passing through the wood every time she tried to place them on top.

"Couldn't your mum ask for you to go somewhere else?" Nova asked.

"She didn't remember me."

Nova reached out to take her hand. It was like vapor; she couldn't get a hold. Angela didn't seem to notice.

"I didn't mind," Angela continued. "She was still my mum. Before they took her to the home I looked after her, and we still laughed and hugged. It was different to how it used to be, but still good. When they took her, they said it wasn't safe for me to stay in the house on my own." She scowled. "It was safer than being with him."

"You don't have to tell me if you don't want to," Nova said, sympathetically.

Angela barely paused for breath. "The last time he tried to do it, I punched him. My hand went right through. He laughed." A slow smile drew across her face. "He didn't know I'd been practicing. I knew how to make it solid again. I did it. I grabbed his heart and squeezed it as hard as I could." She cocked her head to one side. "It didn't feel like you'd expect."

"He...died?" Nova didn't know why she asked. She couldn't imagine many people surviving someone putting their hand into their chest and using their heart like a squeeze toy.

Angela continued. "I couldn't get my hand out; my power stopped working. The neighbour found us a few days later. She called the ambulance, and we went to the hospital. Everyone kept asking how it happened. They cut him open to get my hand out. Then they didn't know what to do with me after. Elizabeth came with Madeline, and they brought me here."

Nova swallowed, trying not to picture what it must've been like for Angela to spend several days with her hand in the chest of her dead father.

"Why did she bring Madeline?" she eventually asked.

"She can make people do things. That's why they let me go."

"They put you in the Tombs because of what happened?" Nova asked. That seemed pretty unfair based on the circumstances.

"And because I fought the guards," Angela explained. "When I got here, I wouldn't speak. I wouldn't move. When the guards tried to take me to meet Ms. Juniper, I hurt them. One died. Seeing him lying there, it all became real – my father was dead too. Really dead. He could never hurt me again. I started laughing, and I couldn't stop. They put kids in the Tombs who can't control themselves, or don't care. They thought both of those things were true about me."

"Why did they let you out again?" Nova asked. "They realised you weren't going to hurt anyone else?"

Angela nodded. "After six months I started talking. I told them why I did what I did to my father, and that I didn't mean to kill the guard. I hadn't tried to hurt anyone since they locked me up, so Elizabeth said I was safe to come out." Angela met Nova's eye for the first time since beginning her story. "Elizabeth saved me."

Nova was more confused than ever. Angela said Elizabeth saved her. Kit said not to trust her. Who was right?

A couple of hours later, Nova and Kate were sitting out in the courtyard, when they were interrupted by a male voice.

"Elizabeth would like to speak with you."

Nova looked up from her maths homework – which she had been racing to finish before their afternoon class – and saw James. He didn't smile; as if they had never spoken before today. If he was pretending this hard not to have even had a conversation with Nova before, she couldn't help but wonder how much trouble he would get into for having been in a relationship with Madeline.

Nova's stomach churned at the thought of visiting Elizabeth. "Oh. Okay."

She got to her feet, shrugging at Kate's curious expression, and followed James. He had a small cut on his lip, and she briefly wondered what caused it.

Maybe Kit did it in a fit of jealousy?

She shook away the ridiculous thought as they headed

towards the main school. Instead of going inside, however, James led her down the path between that building and the dorm.

Nova was confused. "Aren't we going to see Elizabeth?"

"No," James said with a smile. "I said that because you were with your friend. We're not really supposed to hang out."

Suddenly she remembered; she'd agreed to meet him when trying to prove her point to Kit last night. She'd been so thrilled about not making a total fool of herself, that she'd already forgotten about their arrangement to meet today. A new wave of unease washed over her; she didn't want to give James the wrong impression. She didn't want to *actually* date him. He was much older than her for one thing, and besides which, she could only imagine the horrors Madeline would inflict on her if she found out.

Luckily, James didn't seem to be looking for anything like that. As they walked the grounds he kept a fair distance, talking cheerfully about his favourite foods, the weather, the fact that he had an unnatural fear of ducks, and other decidedly un-romantic things. After almost an hour, Nova was confident he wasn't interested in her romantically at all. Maybe he just wanted a friend?

"Sorry," he said, as they approached the lake. "I guess I haven't really stopped talking."

"That's okay. I really enjoyed hearing the duck story."

He laughed. "It's nice speaking to someone who actually listens." His smile faltered. "The other guards...most of them want to talk about women, or sports, or the last time they had to restrain an Alternate. It gets old fast."

"Is the Alternate thing hard to hear, because you're one of us?"

"I don't take it personally. Most of them think bragging about pinning down a guy who can turn things to ice makes them sound tough, but it's still a 14-year-old kid that they're knocking to the floor. I don't think that's something to be proud of." James gestured to his lip. "That happened last night when I told another guard he was being too heavy-handed with one of the kids."

"He *hit* you?"

"Thought I needed to be 'put in my place'. He's an ass. At least it got him away from the girl."

"That was really good of you," Nova said.

"I guess that's part of the reason I wanted to be a guard," James continued. "So that the kids who are like I was, have someone on their side, you know?"

Nova liked that. She couldn't imagine how terrifying it must be to be locked away in the Tombs; especially for people like Angela who were there because of a mistake. Having a guard who was sympathetic to Alternates – who truly *knew* how it felt – was so important.

"How long have you been working here?" she asked.

"This is my first year. I graduated last summer."

That meant he was 19. Nova supposed his relationship with Madeline was a *little* less weird in that case; she had probably known him when he was a student. Sure, it wasn't exactly healthy in terms of a power-dynamic, but Madeline was probably one of the only students at Tidemarsh who could manage a relationship like that. If he got out of line, she'd make him eat dirt.

"What made you want to stay?" Nova asked. "I heard most kids who graduate kind of go MIA."

James picked up a pebble and skimmed it across the surface of the lake. "To be honest, I didn't have many other choices. I was never close with my family, and the day I stepped in front of my mum to protect her from my dad's fists, was the day he told me never to come back."

Nova considered this. "A lot of the kids here seem to have...*not great* relationships with their parents." James, Kate, Angela – and of course – Nova herself, all had stuff going on at home that was far from idyllic.

Not that Gary was ever her dad.

"I've got a theory that stress helps our abilities to manifest. That's why so many kids here seem to have come from rough childhoods." He shrugged. "I don't know, it's just an idea. Anyway, Tidemarsh was the only place I ever felt like I belonged, like I had a family, you know?"

"I think so."

He smiled again. "I know it's hard to get used to. Trust me, it gets easier."

They sat down on the sand. The sun was warm, and there was a gentle breeze, heavy with the scent of the forest behind them. Nova realised she was enjoying herself. James was easier to talk to than she'd first thought. He wasn't like the other guards she had seen and heard about; he was an Alternate like her, and his home life sucked too. The two of them had things in common. She didn't want to date him, but he didn't seem to want to date her either, so maybe they could be friends?

"What's your ability?" she asked. "You don't have to tell me if you don't want to."

"I can show you if you want?"

"Okay."

James got to his feet. "Stand up."

She did as she was asked, brushing the sand off her legs.

James continued. "I want you to use your power on that rock over there."

Nova looked over to where he was pointing, at a rock the size of a football by the water's edge.

"I don't think so," she said.

"Trust me."

"You know what I can do?"

He grinned. "Of course. 'The exploding girl', right?"

Nova knew it was naïve to hope the guards didn't know about her ability, but it still stung to think of them talking about her.

"*I'm* not the one who does the exploding," she muttered.

"You have to admit, though, the name has a ring to it."

"If you know what I can do, you know you don't want me attempting it on that rock."

He laughed. "It'll be fine. Trust me."

She wasn't sure if she *did* trust him yet, but he was a guard: it was his job to keep her safe, right? Besides, she was curious about his own ability. They were alone; her chance of hurting anyone else was low.

"Fine," she said. "Don't come crying to me if you end up with bits of rock in your face."

He laughed again. "I'll keep that in mind."

Nova turned to the rock, focusing on it the way she had when she was with Kate and the others. The energy began to build inside her, growing stronger and stronger. Warmth spreading from deep inside, along her extremities, tingling her fingertips.

Nothing happened.

She frowned, then tried again, holding her hand out this time. The energy built, and built...and again nothing happened. She dropped her hand in frustration. "It's not working. I can't always control it."

"It's me."

Nova turned to face him. "What do you mean?"

"I can block other Alternates from using their powers."

"Wow, that's...I imagine that's pretty useful in the Tombs."

"It comes in handy," he agreed. "I think that was why Elizabeth was so keen to recruit me."

Nova marvelled at his gift. If she had someone like that blocking her abilities, she'd never have to worry about getting mad ever again. "All I need is for you to be around me every minute of the day," she joked.

He grinned, then glanced at his watch. "I should get going. This was nice. Kind of like something normal, you know?"

"Oh sure," she said, casually. "People blocking other people's superpowers. Totally normal."

"Okay, maybe not that part, but hanging out, talking about regular stuff."

"You didn't do that with Madeline?" Nova felt awkward mentioning her name. Madeline had been the elephant in the room throughout their conversation. Except this elephant was blonde, gorgeous, and prepared to make Nova lick a toilet seat if she so much as looked at her the wrong way.

James didn't seem to mind the mention of his ex. "Maddie...she was usually the one who did the talking. My job was to agree with whatever she said."

Nova smiled. "I think that's what most people do."

"Anyway, I better get back; my shift starts in 10 minutes." He smiled. "I'll see you soon."

CHAPTER THIRTY-FOUR

A Tiny Bit Jealous

When Nova got back to her dorm that evening, there was an air of panic. All heads snapped in her direction when she opened the door, and there was a collective sigh of relief when they saw it was her.

"What's going on?" Nova asked the sea of faces.

"We're having a...little trouble," Laura began.

"A little?" Orlaith interrupted. "Try a whole potato sack of crap, and then you'll be closer to it."

Nova looked over to Laura's bed, where Jasminder, Ria, Meredith, and Beth were all frantically using scissors to snip a potted plant. At first glance, this didn't exactly seem like a crisis.

"I don't understan-" Before Nova could finish her sentence, a tendril shot out of the plant at lightning speed. It was at least six feet long, and still growing as it snaked its way along the floor.

"Get it!" Beth yelled, as Jasminder charged after the escaping vine. Ria cut it off at the base, and Jasminder brought the rest back.

"It won't stop growing," Ria explained. "Laura can't stop it."

"How did it happen?"

"I was trying something new," Laura said, cheeks reddening to match her hair. "This has never happened before, normally I can control the growth easily."

"Except when it comes to Madeline's hair," Orlaith muttered.

Laura scowled. "That's *why* I was doing this. With the plants I can control the growth. With Madeline's hair it was different. I tried accelerating the growth on the plant to see if I could figure out how to reduce it again. *Obviously*, I haven't been able to do that."

"We have to get rid of this thing before Maddie comes back," Orlaith said. "She'll lose it if she sees this. She hates anything 'weird' in the dorm anyway, but a plant that does the same thing as her mad hair? She'll flip."

The door opened, and everyone spun around.

"Well, don't you all look creepy and suspicious?" Kate said, entering the room. "Why are you staring at me like that? What's going...what the hell is that?" She pointed to the plant, and when Nova turned back she saw it was already as tall as the ceiling.

Kate stormed over. "Laura, I thought you promised to keep your projects to the greenhouse. Remember the poison ivy incident?"

"Don't remind me," Orlaith muttered. "My bum itches just thinking about it. How did it even get in our beds?"

"Can we please focus?" Laura yelled, running her hands through her hair. "Madeline is going to be here any minute, and we have a plant threatening to take over the dorm!

What are we going to do?" She turned to Ria. "Can you get rid of it?"

Ria's eyes widened. "That's a bit bigger than a cigarette."

"Please!" Laura sounded desperate.

"Even if I could, you know my ability doesn't always stick. Besides, what if it keeps growing? I don't think we want a butterfly that gets as big as this dorm, do we?"

"Christ, that would be horrifying," Orlaith muttered.

"I'm not cutting off a butterfly's legs," Jasminder said, eyes wide.

Meredith winced. "You would if it tried to eat you."

"The only person who can stop this is you," Beth said to Laura. "I know you can do it."

In the time the girls had been speaking, the plant had already spread across half of the dorm, and was still growing. Things were being knocked off the walls and bedside tables, as the tendrils took over any available space.

"It's got my bed!" Ria yelled, as vines wrapped around over and over again until the blankets were completely obscured from view. As they stretched to the back of the room, over to Kate's bed, a sea of insects swarmed out from underneath, across the floor, and up the walls. A glass on Madeline's bedside table fell off and shattered onto the floor.

"It's tearing this place apart," Kate said, grabbing Colin from the floor and tucking him into her pocket. "Do it now, Laura."

Laura took a deep breath. "Okay." She moved over to the bed, placing her hands on the plant. The rest of the dorm went silent. All eyes were on Laura. She stayed absolutely still, hands fixed to the base of the plant. After a minute, she spoke: "I think I did it."

Nova scanned the room. The tendrils had stopped spreading, and were all still. Several of the girls cheered, and Jasminder hugged Laura. "I knew you could do it!"

"What the *hell* is this?" Madeline's voice came from the doorway, where she stood with wide eyes.

Laura hurried over, beaming. "Maddie! I've figured it out!"

"Figured what out?" Madeline seethed.

"How to fix your hair!" Laura gestured to the plant victoriously.

"You have five seconds to explain why our dorm looks like a rainforest, before I make you *eat* this whole plant."

While Laura and a couple of the other girls went to placate Madeline, and convince her to let Laura touch her hair again, Nova hung back with Kate and Ria.

"I guess that could've been worse," Kate said.

"I'm glad you didn't have to use your ability on it," Nova agreed. "I hate the thought of us having to cut bits off of a giant butterfly."

Ria shuddered. "That would be horrible. It's probably for the best anyway, I don't think my ability is sticking so well right now."

"What makes you think that?" Kate asked.

Ria held out her left arm and rolled up the sleeve of her shirt. There were six circular burns on her skin. Each looked raw and painful. "One of my butterflies must've started to turn back last night."

"It burned you?" Kate asked, eyes widening.

Ria shrugged. "Must have. I don't know why though.

Weird thing is, it happened when I was sleeping and I didn't even wake up. Probably for the best; they hurt like hell now. I bet it would've been way worse if I wasn't asleep."

"Did you find the tiny sadist?" Kate asked. "I could feed him to Colin."

"No, it was nowhere to be seen when I woke up. Lucky for him."

Eventually the other girls convinced Madeline to let Laura fix her hair, and after a tense few minutes while they all waited for some kind of horrific Rapunzel incident, there was peace in the dorm. The plant was chopped up and piled in the corner, ready for a stealthy disposal the following day, and everyone climbed into their beds.

Though Nova fell asleep quickly, she was once again woken up in the middle of the night by her dream. It was the same as before; long dark corridors, screaming, cold hands dragging her back. She wished she could get through a whole night without visiting that awful place.

Or seeing Gary's face.

Now that she was awake, though, she realised wasn't alone. She could feel the weight of someone else, sitting at the end of her bed. There was a shape in the shadows. As she reached for her lamp, a whispered voice in the darkness stopped her.

"Don't."

Nova sighed. "I'm really not in the mood for the switching faces of Kit Carver." Then the realisation hit; whenever Kit possessed someone, he took their voice too. This was *his* voice.

The clouds shifted outside the window, and in the few seconds of moonlight she saw it was him. Not Kit in someone else's body, but Kit himself, sitting on the edge of her bed. She sat up straighter.

"What the hell are you doing? How did you-"

"I told you, Frank owes me some favours. And please don't talk too loudly, I'm not exactly supposed to be here."

"What did you do for Frank that he's willing to risk letting you out of your cell?" she whispered. "No, wait, scratch that, I don't want to know."

A flash of his grin. "That's probably wise."

"How long have you been sitting there?"

"What's the least-creepy answer?" he asked.

"I'm not sure there is one."

"I haven't been here long. I wasn't sure whether to wake you, it looked like you were dreaming."

"A bad dream," she said with a shudder. "You can wake me from that one any time."

She could hear the smile in his voice. "Good to know."

"No, I don't mean...don't come here in the night!" Nova gabbled.

Kit glanced toward the door. "I can't stay long."

"Okay. Then what do you want?"

"I wanted to ask about your walk with the guard yesterday."

Nova swallowed. "How do you know about that?"

"I know everything."

"Then surely you don't need to ask what happened?"

His voice was sharp. "*Did* something happen?"

Nova groaned. "You're really frustrating, you know?"

"You frustrate me too."

"I doubt that."

His tone changed. "Oh, you have no idea."

There was something in the air between them. A tension, a crackle that Nova hadn't felt before. It made her stomach tighten. She was aware that, other than the evening she spent in his enchanting cell, this was the closest they had ever been without a wall of glass or a fence between them. If she wanted, she could reach out and touch his hand. What would that feel like?

For God's sake Nova, you've touched someone's hand before.

Not his.

"So?" he asked.

Nova shook away the errant thoughts about touching him. "No, Kit, nothing happened. We're just friends."

He sounded doubtful. "He's not the kind of person you can be friends with."

"You don't get to decide who I-"

Kit cut her off. "He's not the person *anyone* can be friends with."

"Because of his ability?" she asked.

Kit nodded.

"It seems pretty perfect to me," she said. "At least when he's around I can't accidentally hurt anyone."

"You can't purposefully hurt anyone either."

Nova scowled. "Unlike you, I don't *want* to hurt anyone."

"Not yet."

She brushed past that. "Anyway, like I said, *you* don't get to control who I'm friends with. It's your fault I started talking to him in the first place, after everything you said about me not possibly being able to find a boyfriend."

"I wouldn't dream of trying to control you, and that's

not what I said." Then he smiled again. "Were you trying to make me jealous?"

"No!" Nova insisted, quickly.

"I have to say, I'm flattered-"

"I didn't say that!" she hissed. Kate stirred in the bed opposite. Nova and Kit waited. She didn't wake up. After a few seconds, Nova continued, her voice less than a whisper. "I did it to prove to you that I *could* get a guy if I wanted. That I'm not totally repulsive to everyone."

"I see." He seemed to be considering that, and then unexpectedly got to his feet.

"You're going?" Nova asked, unable to hide the disappointment in her voice.

"I should get back before I'm missed."

"That was all you came over here for? To ask about James?"

"Yes."

Nova swallowed. "Oh. Well, goodnight. I guess."

"Goodnight, Nova."

Then he did something she never could've predicted. He reached down, took her hand, and brought it briefly to his lips. A white-hot electric current passed between them, painful and wonderful, all at once. As his lips pressed softly against her hand, Nova found she had forgotten how to breathe.

He let go, eyes meeting her own. "I *was* jealous."

Before she could reply, Kit turned and disappeared into the darkness.

I'm in trouble.

CHAPTER THIRTY-FIVE

Time To Let Go

Nova didn't think it was possible to suck more at mastery class, bearing in mind that for the first few weeks she hadn't even used her power. Now that she was finally trying it out, she was somehow worse than ever.

Miss Garrett had moved the other students to the back of the room, and placed a balloon in front of Nova. All she needed to do was make it burst. It was simple enough in theory, yet every time she tried to focus, her thoughts drifted back to Kit's visit. What had he meant? Was he being serious when he said he was jealous? Why had he kissed her hand?

"Take your time, Nova," Miss Garrett said encouragingly, bringing her focus back to the room.

Nova took a breath, holding out her hand, and trying to start the energy surge inside her. She shouldn't be thinking about Kit. Most likely he was messing with her; doing some kind of weird emotional manipulation for kicks. What else did he have to entertain himself with these days? She shouldn't think about it anymore, or she'd drive herself crazy trying to puzzle out the mind of someone who everyone else already knew was one of the most dangerous people in Tidemarsh.

The kiss felt nice though.

"Maybe we should take a break." Miss Garrett's voice cut through Nova's wandering thoughts again. Nova put her hand down, cheeks reddening.

At least there's no one in this class who can read minds.

Later, at lunch, Kate pounced. "What's going on with you?"

"What?" Nova asked, fork halfway to her mouth.

"You know what," Kate replied. "You've had a weird look on your face all day."

"That's just my face."

Kate snorted. "Don't try to fob me off. You're thinking about *him*, aren't you?"

Nova quickly stuffed her food in her mouth, so that it would be harder to talk. "No. What? Who?"

Kate made a buzzer sound. "Wrong answer. Come on, don't keep secrets from your best friend."

Nova couldn't fight the smile that crept across her face. "Are we best friends?"

"You've got someone better?" Kate asked.

"No, it's...I've never actually had a-"

"Don't go soft on me, Nova. Part of the reason I like you is because you're not into the touchy-feely stuff." Kate raised an eyebrow. "And don't avoid the question. Are you daydreaming about Carver?"

There was no use keeping secrets, Nova knew Kate

would drag it out of her eventually, and part of her really wanted to talk about the whole thing. She told her friend about Kit sneaking into the dorm, and the things he had said.

"He got out of Max on his own?" Kate asked, eyes widening.

"I'm pretty sure the guard, Frank, helped him."

"That's not exactly reassuring," Kate said. "*No one* is supposed to be able to get out of the Tombs. Especially Maximum security. The fact that a guard helped him...how much power does your boyfriend have?"

"He's not my boyfriend," Nova said, quickly.

Kate wasn't listening. "I thought it was bad enough that he could, like, mind-control others. The fact that he can get out of that place and take a stroll right into our dorm makes me uneasy."

"He wouldn't hurt anyone," Nova insisted.

"You can't be sure of that. You know he's done it before." Kate paused, then softened her tone. "Maybe he wouldn't hurt you. Clearly, he likes you, but that doesn't mean it's safe for everyone else. Who knows what else he did on his little walk?"

Nova felt like she needed to defend Kit. "I'm pretty sure he just wanted to talk to me. He wanted to know what I was talking about with James, so he came to ask me about it."

"And that was it?"

"Yeah. Well, he kissed my hand too."

Kate's eyes lit up. "He kissed you?"

"My hand," Nova repeated.

"That's kind of sweet."

"I guess," Nova said, as if she hadn't been thinking about it non-stop since he'd left.

Kate sat back in her chair, exhaling. "Wow. I mean, I've never seen the guy; only heard the other kids talk about him. I never got the impression he was that type."

"What do you mean?" Nova asked.

"The stuff I've heard…it's not exactly *sweet*."

Nova leaned forward, forcing herself to fight against the part of her that wanted to shut her ears to the whole thing. "Tell me."

"He killed a lot of people before he got here, and then when he arrived, he killed more. Everyone says he's unstable; that he laughed after he did it, and the whole time they were locking him up too. They said even Elizabeth is scared of him."

Nova shuddered at the thought of that much violence; of Kit not feeling even an ounce of regret. That wasn't the boy she knew.

But if she was honest with herself, she didn't really know him at all. They had been talking for a few weeks, and that was nothing in the grand scheme of things. In all the times they had spoken, had she ever even learned something real about him? It wasn't entirely his fault – she'd actively avoided asking about his crimes up until now – but wilful ignorance was still ignorance. How could she allow herself to develop any kind of feelings for someone she barely knew anything about?

Kate must've sensed Nova's unease, because she added: "He was a kid when he came here, though, right? People change. Sometimes."

Can anyone change that much?

Can someone who has killed ever be safe? Can they ever be good?

That evening, when Nova once again found herself sitting cross-legged in front of the glass wall of Kit's cell, he asked her a question.

"Why do you come down here?"

"I like talking to you," she replied. "And, of course, for the atmosphere."

On cue a kid several cells over started screaming. Others yelled at him to shut up, while a girl somewhere further down began to laugh hysterically.

"Yes, it's a real treat," Kit mused. "But you started coming to the Tombs before we ever spoke."

Nova had guessed this conversation might happen at some point, though she had hoped to avoid it for as long as possible.

"You already told me your theory about that," she said, stalling for time.

"That you did something terrible, and feel like you belong in this place?"

Nova nodded.

"Was I right?" he asked.

"I get the feeling you *always* think you're right."

He grinned. "That might be true." He clearly wasn't ready to let this drop, and waited expectantly.

Nova sighed. "You don't have a theory about what I did?"

"I do."

"And?" she asked.

He paused, holding her gaze. "You killed someone."

Nova didn't want to blink, to look away. She held Kit's

gaze steadily, despite the tears that bit at the corners of her eyes. She fought them back. For some reason, she couldn't stand the idea of him seeing her cry, of him thinking she was weak.

"Yes," she said, finally.

"Tell me about it."

If it had been said by anyone else, Nova would've said no. She didn't want people examining the events of that afternoon like she was part of some gruesome true crime documentary; pouring over the facts, lapping up every horrible part because it excited them. That would've made her feel used and dirty.

Kit was different. He wasn't asking because he was curious about the gory details. He was asking because, she was beginning to realise, he was as interested in learning about her as she was about him. If she wanted to know more about his past, she would have to share her own story.

"It was my stepdad," she began. "Gary. We had a fight and I lost control."

"What did you fight about?"

Though it was harder to say it out loud than she had expected, she wanted to say it. She *needed* to say it. She had kept it bottled up inside for too long now.

"He took my mum's locket," she said, eyes on the floor now. "It was the only thing of hers I had left, and he was trying to sell it." She took a breath, speaking slowly. "It was like something in me snapped, I couldn't do it anymore."

"Do what?"

"Lie down and accept it, be quiet and take it like I always had. Since my mum died, I never once yelled or even argued with him. He and his new wife either treated me like their own personal slave, or like I didn't exist, and I never fought back. It was like I was watching it all happen." She shook her head. That wasn't right. "No, it was more like I was asleep, only half-aware that this was my life. When he tried to take that last piece of my mum away, I finally woke up. I finally fought back. I told him how I felt, and he didn't like it. He hit me."

Kit's face hardened. "He hit you?"

Nova's voice was thoughtful. "That wasn't even what did it, though. He said some stuff about my mum, and it was like everything changed. I wasn't just awake, I was *alive*, and I was angrier than I'd ever felt. Everything he'd done over all those years, it was like a poison in my body, and I needed to get it out."

Nova had been staring at the floor for the longest time, and finally met Kit's eyes. His expression was unreadable.

"Did you want to kill him?" he asked.

"I didn't even know about my ability before that day."

"Did you want him dead?" Kit persisted. "Did you fantasise about it at night? Picturing him falling down the stairs, or getting hit by a car?"

Nova thought about it. "No. I wanted him gone; not dead. I wouldn't wish that on anyone."

"Were you happy after it happened?"

"I was *relieved*," she admitted. "Relieved that he couldn't hurt me anymore. That I wouldn't have to be afraid of the weird way he'd started looking at me. I wasn't happy. I would've been *happy* if Elizabeth had arrived five minutes earlier, and taken me away before it could happen. It was an accident."

"Then you should stop feeling guilty."

Nova gave a small smile. "Right, because it's that easy."

"Alright, then look at it this way; you're nothing like the others down here. All of them either planned to kill and hurt, or did it by accident and feel no regret."

Even you?

She didn't ask. Instead, she said: "Fine, maybe I don't belong down here. That doesn't mean I can't feel guilty for what I did."

Kit shrugged. "If you want, though guilt is a wasted emotion."

"I thought that was regret?"

"Either way, you should stop punishing yourself over a mistake, because that's all it was, a mistake."

Nova exhaled. "A pretty big one."

"And still a mistake. In all honestly, it sounds like the man got what was coming to him. He was an idiot trying to light a cigarette on the forecourt of a petrol station."

"I'm the petrol station in this analogy?"

He smiled. "Next time I'll think of something prettier. Anyway, every time Gary treated you badly, stole your belongings, made you feel unsafe...that was another strike of a match. Eventually, his luck was going to run out. You can't control what you are – your biology – but he could control how he treated you. Yet he kept on striking those matches." Kit softened his tone. "You're not a bad person, Nova. Anyone who talks to you for more than 30 seconds can see that."

That did it. A couple of tears slid down her cheeks before she could turn away.

"Thanks," she said, wiping her face. She took a deep breath, and with it, felt some of the heaviness that had been weighing down on her for so long, drift away. "You're good at this."

He smiled. "I know."

"It really sucks that you're stuck down here."

"I know."

CHAPTER
THIRTY-SIX

The Note

Nova spent the next day feeling like she was balancing on a seesaw. One minute she was soaring – her guilt over Gary was finally starting to fade, and she was actually enjoying her time at Tidemarsh – and the next she felt herself crashing down to the ground. Her friendship with Kit was more confusing than ever, and she was being pulled in all directions. One second so sure that he was a good person who was misunderstood, and the next that Elizabeth and the other teachers couldn't *all* be wrong: he had to be locked up for a reason. And in between all of that was the question that still whispered in the back of her mind: what was happening to the kids who graduated?

Nova felt like she hadn't spoken to Elizabeth in a long time, but even if she arranged another meeting, what else was there to say? If she asked any more questions, or spoke about her worries, Elizabeth would want to know where her concerns came from. Eventually, Nova would put her foot in her mouth and mention Kit, and that wouldn't lead to anything good. At best, Elizabeth would put a stop to their night-time visits, at worst, Nova might end up in the Tombs herself, for breaking so many rules.

When Nova got back to her dorm that evening, there was a folded note on her pillow. She opened it, keeping her back to the rest of the room.

I need to talk to you about something, and I think you know what it is. Meet me outside the Tombs at midnight.

Nova was back at the top of the seesaw again. What did Kit want to talk to her about? It sounded serious, though that didn't necessarily mean anything. She reminded herself that, with Kit, nothing was ever as simple as it seemed on the surface. He could have something important to talk about, or he could be inviting her down to make cryptic jokes about the weather. He was impossible to read. She shouldn't get excited over this.

I need to find something perfect to wear!

If they were meeting outside the Tombs, did that mean he would be out of his cell again? The thought of being close enough to touch him, to maybe even feel his lips brush the skin of her hand again, sent goosebumps rippling through Nova's skin.

The handwriting was different from the note he'd left with Madeline's hair. Nova marvelled again at his ability; that he could take on someone's body, voice, and even their handwriting. She glanced around the dorm, wondering who he had possessed to write this one. Was it possible he was still there? Everyone was busy getting ready for bed. No one appeared to be acting any differently than usual. She was pretty sure he wasn't in the room right now.

She got into her nightgown and slipped under the blanket. The others began to get into bed, and one by one the lights went off. After a while, the talk and laughter died down. Nova watched the clock on the wall tick closer to midnight.

At 11.30 PM, she got dressed. She couldn't risk waking anyone by turning on her lamp, so had to choose her clothes by moonlight. She grabbed a pair of jeans and a black shirt that Kate had given her, and clumsily applied a little make-up, praying she didn't look too much like a clown who'd been dragged through a bush.

15 minutes later, Nova was in the woods, hurrying along her well-trodden path towards the Tombs. She could see a figure waiting down by the main doors, and her heart began to race. As she got closer, she saw it was James.

Very funny, Kit.

Nova wondered if he'd chosen to take James' body because it was the closest, or because he was teasing her for hanging out with the guy.

"This is a weird choice," she said, as she headed over.

He grinned when he saw her. "I wasn't sure if you would come; I know my note was kind of..." he trailed off.

"Confusing? Vague?"

"Definitely. I couldn't find the words, I'm not good with stuff like that. Come on, this way." He turned, heading in through the door behind him.

Nova paused for a second. She'd never heard Kit admit to not being good at anything.

"Are you coming?" he asked from inside.

"Yeah, okay." She walked through the open door, and he closed it behind her.

"You probably know what I wanted to talk to you about, right?" he asked, as they headed down the corridor.

"With you, I try not to guess. I'm usually wrong."

He laughed. "Maybe I'm more mysterious than I thought. That's cool."

This doesn't sound like Kit at all.

Nova had never heard him use the word 'cool' before; it was decidedly un-Kit. The gnawing feeling at the back of her mind intensified, and she was struck by a horrible thought: what if this wasn't Kit in James' skin? What if it was James? If it was, what did he want? She was going to have to tread carefully to try and figure out who it was, without accidentally revealing her friendship with Kit.

"Why did you send me a note, rather than inviting me in person?" she asked.

"Well, it's not like I could go into your dorm in the middle of the day."

Crap, that works for either guy.

"How are you doing?" she asked, flailing for a question that would give more away and coming up empty.

"Honestly? Sick and tired of looking at the same walls."

Ugh, that doesn't help either.

Nova tried something else. "What made you choose this place?"

"It may be the most secure building in the school, but it's also the best place to go if you don't want to be seen. There are lots of places that are always empty. It means we can talk without being disturbed."

She was pretty sure this was James, his way of speaking was too different to Kit's, as was the way he walked.

Was she 100% sure?

No. She kept following him through the maze of corridors, hoping for inspiration to strike.

"Maddie keeps trying to talk to me," he said.

"Oh really?" Nova couldn't keep the disappointment out of her voice. It was James. Just James. "What does she want?" she asked.

"Says she wants me back. It isn't going to happen. Things were good at the start, but they went sour fast."

"Mmm," was all Nova could say. Her mind was racing; she had to try and think of a way to get out of there without it being suspicious. James inviting her down here in the middle of the night suggested that maybe he was looking for something more than friendship, and by coming down, she might've accidentally given him the impression she was interested. If she kept the conversation as platonic as possible – and maybe even mentioned having a recent bout of diarrhoea or something – James might think she only came down because she saw him as a friend. If she got really graphic with the details, he might even cut this whole evening short.

"Phew," she began. "My stomach's been feeling really weird today-"

James wasn't listening, he was still talking about Madeline. "I mean, don't get me wrong, she's gorgeous. And fun, really fun, but...you know how she is."

Nova felt a ball in the pit of her stomach. "Yeah, I do." While they were on the topic of her dorm-mate, she decided to pause her plan of grossing him out to ask: "Why didn't you stop her?"

"What do you mean?" James asked.

"That night in the woods when she made me eat dirt. Why didn't you stop her?"

He stopped walking, and ran his hand through his hair.

"You know, I keep asking myself the same thing. I guess I was kind of in shock? I was so terrified of you telling someone about Maddie and me that I just froze. I really need this job."

And I really needed not to eat dirt.

James continued. "It was crappy of me not to help you, and I'm sorry. Maybe tonight will go towards making it up to you." He didn't elaborate, and started walking again. Nova had no choice but to follow. She couldn't help but think that whatever he had planned would have to be pretty damn spectacular to make up for that. As in fireworks, rollercoasters, or at the very least, some kind of amazing sandwich.

After a few more minutes, they ended up in an area of the Tombs she had never been in before. This hallway was somehow even more depressing than the rest of the place. The walls were a dark, dingy green, and several of the lights on the ceiling flickered. One of the small windows was boarded up.

"Where are we going?" Nova asked.

"We're nearly there," James said. He pointed to a door up ahead, marked 'Showers'.

She paused when they reached the entrance. "In there?"

James glanced at the sign, then laughed. "Trust me, it's not as depressing as the rest of this place. Come on."

He went inside first. Nova wasn't sure whether to follow. What could be in there that could possibly be of interest? Unfortunately, she didn't know her way out without him, and if any of the guards spotted her, she'd be in serious trouble. She found comfort in the fact that this was an unlikely place to choose for a first date. Maybe it wasn't anything romantic at all? Besides, she and James were kind-of friends. She didn't have a reason not to trust him.

The first thing that struck her when she entered the room was that James had lied: it was exactly as depressing as the rest of the building. It was like the bathroom in her dorm in terms of layout, but darker and decidedly less clean. The tiled walls were cracked and hadn't been white in a long time, and the showers along the back wall gave off a nasty smell that spread across the whole room. There were patches of black mould in the corners of the stalls, and puddles of dark liquid stagnating over the drains. The middle of the room had the same row of sinks as in the dorm bathrooms; though they were grimy and yellow, as if they'd not been scrubbed for years. Several had taps that were taped up and unusable.

"This is...nice," Nova joked.

James laughed again. "I know, it's not exactly the Ritz. At least it's private. We can talk here without having to worry about anyone walking in or overhearing us."

Nova kept her tone light. "What did you want to talk about?"

James grinned, and then kissed her.

CHAPTER THIRTY-SEVEN

You Should See The Other Guy

Nova froze, so taken aback by James' kiss that she didn't know what to do. After a couple of seconds, she regained control over her limbs, and pushed him away. "No. I don't want to."

He grinned. "Let's stop playing games." He leaned in again, but this time she pushed him away before he could kiss her.

"No." Her heart was racing, palms cold and sweaty at the same time. "I'm sorry, I don't want to."

He cocked his head, confused. "You read my note? You came down here to meet me in the middle of the night?"

"I didn't realise that's what you...I don't see you like that," Nova insisted. "I just want to be friends."

James snorted. "We both know you weren't looking for a *friend* every time you followed me and Madeline, or every time you sought me out after."

"It's not like that."

He wasn't listening, not really. His smile wasn't like a regular smile. It was cruel and frightening, so different from the one she'd gotten used to seeing. He leaned in a little closer. "We both know why you're here. You're all the same."

Nova swallowed, trying to hide the fear prickling across her skin. "James, I think you're a nice person-"

"You think I'm *nice*? *Nice*? Well, that's great for you, but I didn't invite you here to be *nice*." He took another step closer.

Nova backed up. "James..."

Another step. "You have two options. You can choose to have *nice* James, like Madeline did, or you can choose the other version." He lowered his voice. "A few of your friends have had the other version. They didn't enjoy it."

Nova's blood ran cold. "I don't-"

His grin widened. "Without their powers they can't do much. Then I get my buddy Karl to wipe their memory. Easy, saves the hassle after. You don't want that, do you? I bet you want to remember it. Girls like you, the ones who act like virgins, they always want it really."

What was happening? Where had this come from? Why was he being so horrible? Nova thought for a moment it was some awful joke he was playing, but when she looked into James' eyes she knew; this had been beneath the surface all along. He wasn't joking. He was showing her who he truly was.

She took a breath. "Don't do this. I don't want to hurt you."

He laughed. "I kind of want you to try."

"I mean it, my power-"

"Doesn't work on me, remember?" Another step, he was practically standing on her toes. His breath smelt like stale cigarettes. It made her want to gag. "If you planned to blow me to pieces, I'm afraid you're out of luck. So, what's it to be? Your way, or mine?"

Nova's heart hammered, and she tried to swallow back the fear crawling up the back of her throat. James was a liar. He had never wanted to be her friend. She had been an idiot and now she was in danger.

She shoved him away and made a break for the door. She'd barely made it six feet when he grabbed her, pulling her back, and throwing her against the wall. Nova cried out as she hit the tiles; white-hot pain shooting through the back of her head. James grabbed her hands, forcing them above her head as he brought his lips to her neck, slurping hungrily against her skin. Her heart was beating so hard against her chest she was sure he could feel it. Her eyes darted around for a way out. She wanted to scream, but they'd walked for so long and not seen a single person. No one would hear her.

That's why he chose this place.

No one is coming to help.

If she was on her own, then she wasn't going to make it easy for him. She wasn't giving up without a fight. If she couldn't use her ability, she'd use what she had. Nova brought her knee up, hard, between his legs. James screamed out in pain, loosening his grip. She made another break for the door. She was there, tasting freedom for less than a second before he yanked her back into the room.

"You shouldn't have done that." He dragged her back across the room, flinging her into one of the shower cubicles. She stumbled, lost her footing, and crumpled into the corner, hitting her face on the floor. Pain shot through her nose like a hot needle. Slowly, she pulled herself up so that she was sitting on her knees. The cold, stagnant water from the shower floor soaked into the legs of her trousers.

James stood in the entrance, blocking her exit, and breathing heavily. The colour had drained from his face, thanks to her kick. Still, his smile had returned, and he chuckled as he leaned one arm against the wall of the shower. He knew he had won.

"Wow, I wasn't expecting you to put up such a fight."

"Let me go, James," she insisted. She felt blood trickle from her nose down to her lips, and wiped it away on her sleeve.

"You remind me of someone," James said.

"I said let me go."

He ignored her. "One of the girls from your dorm... Rita? Ria? Something like that. The black one."

Nova stared him down.

"It wasn't meant to be her," James continued. "I'd been waiting around the back door of your dorm to see if you snuck out again after I told you to go back. She was the one who came outside instead. Apparently, she gets her cigarettes from one of the guards, and when she saw me she thought he'd sent me to do the trade instead. Made it easy to get her down here." He smirked. "She fought back at first. A lot. She split my lip! I got her back for that, though."

Nova's stomach churned. The cigarette burns on Ria's arm flashed before her eyes.

"Not that she has any clue about it," James continued. "Karl wiped her memory clean. After his turn, of course."

Ria's words came flooding back. *It's so weird though, it*

happened last night when I was sleeping, and I didn't even wake up.

Clearly a fan of the sound of his own voice, James was still talking. "It was nice having Madeline there whenever I wanted her, but there's something about seeing the spirit of a girl who fights it, and then seeing that spirit die...it's kind of intoxicating, you know?"

Crack.

A tile to the left of his hand had split, right down the middle. James glanced at it, instinctively moving his hand as if he had caused it to break. He hadn't. Nova knew right away that she had done it. Her ability had broken through, just a tiny bit.

His eyes met hers, and she saw that he knew too. He took another step closer. "You're stronger than I thought. I guess I let my guard down." He took a deep breath, closing his eyes for a few seconds. When he opened them again, he smiled. "There. That should do it. We don't want any accidents, I'd hate to end up like your stepdad." He chuckled. "Poor bastard never saw that coming, I bet." He held out his hand. "Are you sure you don't want it the easy way?"

Nova heard voices; faint at first. Getting closer. Someone was coming. She got up, but before she could even try to yell out, James had already pulled the curtain across the cubicle and clapped a hand across her mouth. He stood behind her, and she felt the cold metal of his electronic baton against the skin of her back. A warning. If she tried to make a noise, he would turn it on.

There were footsteps, and through the thin curtain, Nova saw the outline of two people come into the room.

"10 minutes," a male voice said.

The other didn't respond. They moved closer to the stall Nova and James were in, then walked past. There was silence for a few seconds, before a shower turned on a few cubicles down.

Nova had no idea how long she was trapped there, with James' hand across her mouth. The blood from her nose was sliding down his fingers. She could taste it now.

The baton was still pressed against her back. Was James' adrenaline wearing off? Had he realised yet how insane this whole thing was?

She watched as a cockroach climbed out of the shower drain, and wondered with a kind of pitiful hope if Kate had sent it. That was beyond doubtful. She was asleep when Nova had left, and had no idea about the note. Kate had no reason to send any bugs after her.

The shower turned off. Whoever was inside had finished and would soon be leaving. Nova's heart raced even faster. She had to make a choice right now. If she screamed, she would be heard by the kid and their guard, but she risked James hurting her. There was also a good chance that the other guard could be one of his friends, and she shuddered at how much worse this thing would be if there were two of them. Of course, there was also a chance that the other guard wasn't a psycho rapist, and that he would rescue her from this whole horrible mess.

Her other option was to do nothing, and hope that James would simply have a change of heart and let her go once the kid had gone.

She didn't see that happening.

Nova made her choice, and bit down on James' finger as

hard as she could. He screamed in pain, pulling his hand away.

"Help me!" she yelled.

James pushed her to the side, and she hit her head again on the wall. A sharp pain shot through her skull, and Nova fell to her knees. James made to wrench open the shower curtain, but someone on the other side beat him to it.

He was tall, broad shouldered and shirtless, in only his baggy orange trousers. Though Nova's head was fuzzy, and her vision blurred, she saw that his hands were cuffed in front of him. He was wearing a shock collar, and his black hair was damp at his shoulders. His arms and chest were covered in tattoos, though she couldn't focus on what they were.

Kit.

Kit looked at James, then at Nova, and then back to James. A deep, angry, guttural sound escaped his throat, and he grabbed James by the collar. The fact he was handcuffed didn't seem to make a difference. He threw the guard down onto the floor so roughly Nova was sure he cracked the tiles. The electric baton slid across the floor towards the toilet stalls.

The other guard from outside rushed in. Kit moved quickly, slamming him against the wall, head-butting him, and knocking him to the ground.

James got back up. Kit was fast, kicking him in the stomach, knocking him back repeatedly, until he was on the floor again. The other guard got up, shakily, and Kit turned to him, fire in his eyes.

"Don't," Nova whimpered, with as much energy as she

could muster. That guard hadn't hurt her, he didn't deserve whatever Kit could do to him.

Kit paused, a muscle in his jaw twitched, and then his fist collided with the guard. The guy fell to the floor. He was unconscious, but – Nova hoped – still alive.

"What about him?" Kit asked, glaring down at James. Nova had never seen so much fury on one person's face.

She glanced at James. How many other girls had he brought here? How many of them had no idea of all the things he'd done to them? How many hadn't had someone come to their rescue?

She wanted him dead. She wanted it more than anything.

But she wouldn't have any more blood on her hands. She would go to Elizabeth, and it would be up to her what happened to him. No one else had to die because of her.

"Don't kill him," she said. "We need him alive."

Kit held her gaze for the longest time, his jaw set. He looked as though he was holding something back, something he wanted to say. His eyes flicked back to James, who was now barely moving on the floor.

"No," Kit said. He reached down, pulling James by the collar and throwing him across the room with a strength Nova had never seen before. James hit the wall and crumpled to the floor. Kit stalked over and aimed a kick at his face. Then another. Blood spattered Kit's chest.

"Kit!" Nova yelled. "Stop!"

He ignored her. He bent down now, slamming James' head against the floor with his handcuffed hands again and again. Then he started punching him, over and over until there was nothing but a bloody mess left. James was dead.

Kit stayed leaning over the body. He wasn't even out of breath. He reached into James' pocket and pulled out a key. He used it to unlock his handcuffs, and they clattered to the floor. Kit tossed the key into the nearest drain.

He leaned frighteningly close to what was left of James' face. "Thanks."

Nova's heart was racing. She shuffled back, as far as she could go until her back hit the cold tiled wall. Kit had killed someone right in front of her. Beaten him to death with a ferocity and ease that she'd never seen before; never even *imagined* before. Who was this person? Not the one she felt safe with. Not the one she thought was probably filled with regret over the things he had done.

No. He enjoyed killing.

Kit stood up now, and scanned the room. He caught sight of Nova by the wall, and strode over, cocking his head curiously when he saw her expression.

"What?" he asked, with a tone that implied she couldn't possibly be looking like that because she had seen him beat someone into a bloody pulp moments before.

Nova shook her head, lost for words.

Kit glanced back to James' corpse. "He deserved it."

"I asked you not to," she whispered.

Kit looked as though he was about to speak, when they heard more voices. People were coming.

Kit held out his hand. It was slick with blood. "Come on."

A guard was dead. Kit had killed him. If she took his hand, what was she signing up for? If she didn't, what would happen then?

The blood from Kit's hand dripped onto the floor. He

was watching her with anticipation, just waiting for her to take his hand. She had to make a choice, right now.

Drip, drip, drip.

* * *

***Nova's story continues in Alternate Academy:
Shadowed Truths coming June 2024***

 OTHER BOOKS

The Alive Series

Alive? Book 1

Still Alive? Book 2

Barely Alive Book 3

ACKNOWLEDGEMENTS

I want to extend my heartfelt gratitude to the wonderful people who have supported me throughout the journey of bringing Alternate Academy to life. First and foremost, I want to thank my husband, David, for being my unwavering rock, and never tiring of listening to me go on and on about characters he had yet to even read about. Your love and support mean the world to me.

To Susan Harris, I owe a massive debt of gratitude. Thank you for being my sounding board, sharing your wisdom, and for always encouraging me to embrace the darkness! Your guidance has been absolutely invaluable.

I also want to thank Melanie Newton, for her tireless efforts and the clear, constructive feedback that has helped shape this book into what it has become.

A special shoutout to Helena, who came to my rescue during a moment of complete blankness, to help me think of the most important name in the series!

Last but not least, my boys, Clark and Oliver. Thank you for reminding me every day why books and imagination are some of the most important things in the world. Your curiosity, enthusiasm, and laughter fuel my creativity!

Thank you all for being part of this journey. I can't wait to see where we go next!

ABOUT THE
AUTHOR

Melissa grew up in a small town in the U.K. and has been an avid bookworm since childhood. She began writing short stories at the age of seven and - despite the fact that no one seemed interested in publishing a story about a rabbit who made ice skates out of kitchen utensils - her love of writing grew from there. Melissa wrote the first draft of her debut novel, 'Alive?,' at 16.

Melissa is a mum to two boys, and when not writing or playing trains with her sons, she works as a teacher. Melissa also regularly attempts crochet projects that may or may not resemble the intended creations, and enjoys reading, and playing video games.

melissawoodsauthor.com